Defiant, She Advanced

Legends of Future Resistance

George Donnelly, Editor

ISBN–10: 1941939023
ISBN–13: 978–1–941939–02–4

Cover design by Alchemy Book Covers.
Formatting by Polgarus Studio.

To the Free Library of Philadelphia,
Welsh Road Branch —
where I discovered science fiction in 1981.

Contents

The Slow Suicide of Living Again

by Wendy McElroy

A restitution agency employee's reality begins to crumble after a close call.

I am the skin of darkness on walls. A cat in silent dance, I glide from shadow toward the staircase draped in night. I freeze.

"She came in here," a hoarse male voice calls out from the sidewalk in front of the crumbling apartment complex. There must be two of them in the darkness.

I am trapped in the courtyard. The U-shaped building is two-stories with a staircase in the center leading upward. I need to crash for the night, in safety, and this place is as good as any — or was. Now it's a cage. *Shit.* This didn't need to happen. I stayed too long in the no-go zone and home won't be 'til tomorrow.

The courtyard is dead still as the speaker and whoever's with him listen. I can't make it to the steps without risking detection. Cold sweat drenches my armpits despite the hot California night.

"Are you sure?" a baritone whispers from no more than six feet away.

"Yeah. And she's a looker. I saw her in the headlights of that last car. Twenty something. She'll bring a nice price."

The baritone laughs. "And only slightly used when we're through." The chuckle breaks off. "No way out of here?"

"Only through an apartment and out the back."

"Then I'll cover the back." Footsteps retreat to the sidewalk and fade quickly.

One down. One left. I chance a step toward the staircase.

He slams my back into the wall with teeth rattling force. "You're not going anywhere," the words float to my nose on the odor of cigars and tequila. "What's this?" He feels the strap of an overstuffed canvas bag that's slung over my right shoulder and the fingers of one hand fumble to take it off. I grab the distraction.

My left knee shoots into his groin, and he drops like wet sand, gasping to the ground. *Why do men forget they have testicles?*

I leap over his crumbled body, leather boots clicking on the stone stairs as I race upward.

"Bobby!" the grabber manages to scream and footsteps race into the courtyard in response.

A flashlight flicks on as Bobby kneels by the groaning man and demands, "What happened?"

I do not wait to listen. On the second floor, I kick open an apartment door and slam it shut but I stay standing on the outside. I move quietly down the outside hallway to where it blind-ends into a brick wall. Climbing onto the cast iron rail, I reach up to the ledge of the building's flat rooftop and hoist my weight up and over just as the men make it to the slammed door.

"In here," the kneed man speaks like a strangling chicken.

On the roof, I lie trembling from exertion and fear, trying to silence my heartbeat, to stop my breath. They are in the apartment below, tearing through the rooms, smashing items in frustration.

"She made it out the back," Bobby declares as he steps back into the outside hallway. "She's gone," he accuses the man who still breathes in a soft moan.

They leave without another word. Soon there are no footsteps but the men are likely better at stealth than me. I need to wait until it is safe, until it is morning. I won't move before dawn when traffic wakes the street and sunlight fills people's eyes so that acts aren't veiled by darkness. The no-go zone will be safe enough then to run as fast as I can to the nearest transit.

Meanwhile, the rooftop is chilly beneath my T-shirt in sharp contrast with the hot August air. A shiver of pleasure trips down my spine and, for a moment, it is enough to enjoy the sensation of safety, to soak in the cool and the warm, the fresh air and a rustling tree. My mind wanders.

The men are traffickers. They scoop up 'recruits' for the sex rings that are booming business in the no-go zone. And I am just their type because no one would notice — let alone report — a hole where my body used to be. Except, maybe, M. Blumenthal Restitution — the company for which I work. Murray takes a strangely personal interest in me. *Strange* because he doesn't look down my blouse to check out its ample assets. How ample? Men talk to my chest, directing conversation to "the girls" rather than looking me in the eyes. I once pulled a gun on a man for doing that and made him talk to my eyes. They are hazel and piercing beneath cropped brown hair. I think they're my best feature. But I'm in the minority.

Ah, well, maybe it's a fatherly thing with Murray. *He is going to be so pissed at me.* I sigh.

Today was a routine run to pick up paperwork in what used to be downtown Los Angeles. An easy job. Starting from the Free Zone that used to be Santa Monica, it is a straight shot east on Interstate 10 from the ocean to my destination — 7th Street in Old Town. My papers and permits were in order, and I had a round-trip ticket for the street trans. It slides right past the no-go areas between Free Z and Old Town, the areas where I get into trouble, and where I cause it. I lived in one of them before the city civil wars. Today, I watched familiar buildings flick by and I thought I saw…

Doesn't matter. The image flashes in my mind. Graffiti on a wall: **If you meet John Galt on the road, kill him.** Even now the words draw me, disturb me, and I don't know why. I push them away.

Murray is going to be so pissed that I got off and missed the last tran. At least I got the paperwork first.

The stars above me glisten as though wet, so wet they hurt my eyes, which I close. But it isn't the stars causing pain. *I hurt.* As shock and adrenaline recede, I feel the impact of being slammed into the wall and my neck screams. I reach for the shoulder bag now lying to one side and scratch through the bottom for the hypo I keep loaded with pain killers. *There it is!* I let it drop from my fingers. *I may need to be alert. Or, at least, able to come to in a flash.*

I settle back down. Despite the pain, sleep begins to creep and I surrender.

* * *

7 a.m., when the first trans pauses at the pick-up point, I am waiting.

"Bad neighborhood," the armed guard inside comments as I hand him the return ticket. "Especially for a little lady like you."

The tone is friendly so I ignore the remark and sit down.

An hour later, Murray Blumenthal's tone is far less friendly. "What the hell are you thinking?" Murray squawks at me from over the bright green bow tie that wraps his oversized neck. "Wait!" He raises a pudgy hand to cut off a protest that isn't coming. "Don't tell me... you *aren't* thinking at all these days! Right? Am I right!" A deep breath heaves his chest. His restless fingertips tap the thick brown envelope I'd slipped immediately in front of him ten minutes ago when I entered the office. It sits unopened in the center of a massive wooden desk that fills the otherwise stark room. He taps the envelope throughout my short verbal report.

"Mac, what am I going to do with you?" he appeals to thin air.

The name is MacKenzie Jones but he likes to call me Mac... and I like it too, though I'd never tell him so. I stare down at my hands, mimicking contrition.

"Why did you get off in Westwood?" he demanded.

"Just an impulse, Boss. You know me, I'm wild and crazy."

He grimaces. "It was the 'If you meet John Galt on the road, kill him' thing, right?"

"What?!" *What the hell...* "How do you know about the graffiti? Am I being followed?"

"Getting off the trans is not wild and crazy, Mac. It's stupid. And if you wanna get yourself killed, make sure you drop off my paperwork first. We're a team here at the agency."

I bite back an angry response. *Right now, Murray, this team player wouldn't piss in your ear if your brains were on fire!* "It is my life," I protest instead.

"Ah, just get out," he shakes his head in disgust. "And don't think you're leaving the Free Zone any time soon. You're riding a desk until I say you're not."

"I'm the best field agent you've got."

"You're reckless and I don't need the stress. So take some pity on an old man, and shut up and listen!" His hand slaps down on the envelope. "You're grounded until I decide you're not. And I want your report in writing by the end of the day." This time the pudgy hand prevents my snap back. "Verbal isn't good enough this time, sweet cheeks. In writing."

I shove my chair away hard with a satisfying scrape. As I reach the door, his words stop me cold. "How did you know about the rail?" he asks.

"What?"

"The rooftop. You said it was pitch black and you'd never been to the building before. How'd you know there was a rail that'd get you to the roof?"

I shrug. "Hallways have rails. What's the big deal?"

I open the door. Murray's secretary Sophia looks up expectantly at me from her desk in the small outer chamber. "How did you know about the John Galt thing?" I throw the question to him over my shoulder.

"The same way you knew about the rail. Now get out of here. Write up the report and go home."

If you're lying to me, Murray, I'll come back to chew your ass. I shudder at the sudden gruesome image.

* * *

Home is warm and welcoming like the shower I'll take in a few minutes. I throw my shoulder bag into a corner by the front door and a flare of pain lances my neck. I bolt-lock the door behind me. No need to be alert any more. I retrieve the purse, find the hypo and plunge away the pain. *A few bites of food, a splash of hot water, a few hours sleep, and I'll be shiny.* That's all I need from life. That and a door to shut behind me.

Home is a modest tenth-floor walk-in that's plenty big enough for a single gal who is AWOL half the time. I bought it for the tiny balcony that perches over the strip of park called the Palisades, with a clear view of the roiling ocean and the mind-stopping sunsets every night. When my brain gets too busy, I sit and let the thoughts clean out.

Like most people, I've a lot to forget. The SoCal wars left us all scarred and staggering. Widows, orphans, the maimed, the raped, the homeless, the heartless… Hard to believe the two years of blood started on a corner of Wilshire Boulevard in front of a post office. Started with a modest but persistent protest after the cops shot and killed another black teen in the back. Night after night, the crowd swelled and became raw with violence. Police retaliated like soldiers in combat against a foreign enemy. Looters blended in with those who called for justice or revenge. And, then, the racial tension boiled over and just kept coming, kept spreading. Blacks against whites, whites against Hispanics, the gangs against everyone, Asians on rooftops guarding their homes and businesses with guns.

Nowhere was safe. I was a graphic artist in Westwood when violence arrived on the welcome mat of my loft apartment. A gun I didn't know how to use was all that stood between me and…

No! No memories tonight. The past can't change. And the Free Z is as safe as any place can be. The price of moving to the privately owned community is to buy insurance from a private defense agency and learn to use a gun. There aren't many rules here for those who stay peaceful but everyone provides their own defense. That way, an attack on the community has to conquer each street, one person at a time.

I grab the remnants of Chinese take-out from the fridge along with a fork and settle down at the table with one chair that I call "kitchen." A newspaper from a few days ago is open at the obituaries. I flip through the rest of it slowly, skimming items without much interest, until I hit the last page.

A photo. A man in a lab coat stands in front of a white board covered with second-order differential equations. Beneath him is the caption,

"Pacific U. Celebrates Physics Breakthrough by Fast-Track Prof." I stare at the photo for a long time without moving. The room darkens around me.

I wake up face down on the kitchen table with dawn streaming over me. I wake up fast, jerking my head with neck-stabbing agony. *Holy shit!* Overslept. A shower starts my sprint to Blumenthal's.

I will not admit it but I'm glad to ride an agency desk today because crunching numbers is the sort of challenge my brain can handle right now. I navigate a tower of file folders, being careful with data and calculations because each file is a person's life. Each is a restitution case that's arbitrated and needs a dollar value or some other payback Blumenthal's can collect. Murray's reputation and profits rest on the payback being fair. Some cases are easy. A vandalized car gets repaired and the vandal pays for the garage, the inconvenience, the cost of crime solving and collection. The sticky stuff comes with crimes like assault. What's the price of a broken arm or a shattered hand? Is it worth more to a pianist than a housewife? Math and precedent establish the answer — but it's never a satisfying one. It's only the best we can do. That's why the Free Z's emphasis is first and foremost on preventing the crime from occurring.

Number crunching is no-glamor work but as necessary to the justice biz as guns. Old Towners never get it but they never fail to ask me about it, usually over a drink or meal invite. *What the hell, it's free food and booze.* I explain from rote how private police operate and defense is a business. The slice of justice that's restitution takes place after a case is settled and payment is due. Over the inevitable next round of drinks, I give Olders a "see Spot run" version of private justice.

Smith is burglarized. Two detectives from Acme Defense Agency arrive. Their fee comes from the perp, just as a good lawyer's fee comes from a defendant. They solve the crime to get paid and they want to avoid lawsuits for "bad" behavior because those destroy profits *fast*. Strong incentives to be quick and efficient. And, so, the detectives knock on Jones' door with the damning evidence they've collected against him and hand him a bill. If he's guilty, he usually pays up rather than face an expensive process, including arbitration. If he's innocent, he usually arbitrates because the cost is likely to fall on the detective agency.

After arbitration. That's where I come in. I'm a Restitution gumshoe. Smith comes to me. For a healthy fee paid by Jones, we assess and collect. If Smith doesn't like the risk or delay, he sells us his arbitration judgment and we collect it all.

"So how ya doin' today, sweetie?"

The throaty cackle that passes for Murray's voice raises my focus from the paperwork. "Only half here," I admit.

"Well, it's a fast-moving world. Maybe the rest of you'll arrive by lunch." He peers into my eyes. "Didn't sleep well or are you planning to pack those bags?"

"No, no, I slept fine. I'm just..." my tongue doesn't wrap around the right word, "...preoccupied."

Murray perches his massive posterior on the corner of my desk and asks softly, even though we are alone, "I thought you'd be madder than a wet cat at desk duty. Not quiet. Quiet has me worried. What's bothering you, kid?"

Why not? I retrieve the newspaper that I'd stuffed in my purse, still folded open to the last page. I throw it on the desk.

Murray picks it up. He examines the photo for a long moment then shifts his stare to me. "This upsets you? Why? Do you know him?"

I shake my head.

"Then what is it about the photo?"

"I don't know," I lie.

Murray's scrutiny returns to the photo. "Can I take the paper with me?"

I nod then ask, "Why?"

"I want to check out who he is. Or, maybe, I don't want you staring at it all day and getting even quieter. Who knows? I'm a complicated man with a multiplicity of motives." At the doorway, he pauses. "You really don't know why you're upset?"

"No."

Disbelief is palpable in his squinting eyes and the assessing once-over they give me. After Murray leaves, I whisper aloud, "If you lie, I lie. I'm upset because I understand the goddamn math on the board. I even see where a negative sign has been dropped. So tell me, Murray, how does a graphic artist understand second-order differential equations better than a physics prof?"

I don't need the photo. I grab a scrap of paper and duplicate the equation but with the negative sign where it should be. I tuck the paper into my purse because I don't want it lying around where someone can find it. I don't know why.

* * *

In the lunchroom, Sophia plops down in the chair across from me and starts to chat about nothing with a vigor I admire. As usual, she has an extra sandwich and pushes the cellophaned square across the table toward me. Tuna fish today. My favorite.

Sophia sits alone in Murray's outer office, day after day, which gives her a case of logorrhea whenever there's a spare ear. Little wonder. It must be dead boring in there because I never see her do anything in the office other than eat lunch. And, then, when she goes home, there's no family or friends. Not many people pay attention to a middle-aged, plump matron. The fact that I don't get up and leave seems to be attention enough for her to be happy.

I unwrap the cellophane. *What the hell, free food.* Only I'm not hungry today and the sandwich suffers neglect.

"No appetite?" she finally asks, interrupting a monologue on how I'd be so much prettier if I put on a few pounds. Them's fighting words but her blue eyes twinkle kindly enough behind thick glasses, and I can bear a bit of mothering today.

I nibble the sandwich and toss back onto the cellophane. "Actually, I feel like having tomato soup."

Sophia is surprised. "I don't think we have any, dear," she says, scanning the closed cupboards on the lunchroom's far wall as though she has x-ray vision.

I resume nibbling. "Doesn't matter. I don't like soup."

"But you just said…"

I shrug. "I'm a complicated woman with a multiplicity of motives."

She removes her glasses and cleans them with a tissue retrieved from the cuff of her sweater. She waits.

"I've been thinking about the wars," I tell her and wonder why. She and I never speak of the war or of anything unconnected to work. "Sophia, what happened to you during the war years. I mean, did you always live in the Free Z — in Santa Monica?"

Again, surprise. She swallows a slug of coffee. "No, I moved here about a year ago to work with Murray."

"Did you have…" I cut the question short.

"You can ask me anything, dear, I do so enjoy our lunches."

"Did you have a family?"

"Yes, a daughter," Sophia answered softly, "but she killed herself. My daughter's name was MaryAnn. The thing I miss most is the laughter. She laughed all the time, even in her sleep. I would give anything to hear it one more time."

"Why did she…?" I bite into the sandwich in order to avoid finishing the question.

"Why did MaryAnn kill herself?" Sophia finishes my sentence.

I nod.

"Awful things happened and she couldn't live with them." A tear slides down Sophia's cheek and into the corner of her mouth.

I'm sorry I asked. I know better. Everyone has a story about the wars and too many of them end with a death. The old woman is as close to a friend as I have in this office but feeling compassion is painful. "So, why did you want to work with Murray?" I shift into another gear.

Sophia fumbles at the sweater cuff and pulls out a crumpled but clean tissue to dab her eyes. She clears her throat to recover a voice before stating, "His work is more important than you know. I need to be part of it."

I laugh derisively then add quickly, "That's not directed at you, Sophia. I just… I'm not sure I trust Murray any more. I don't think he always tells me the truth, and maybe he's not telling it to you either."

Sophia leans in and whispers, "Why don't you trust him?" She reaches out and touches the back of my hand even though she knows I hate being touched. "Is it happening again?" she asks.

"Is *what* happening?"

A long, hard stare from behind the glasses holds nothing of the former kindness in it. "Then I guess not," she leans back. "But you need to take the rest of the day off. I'll clear it with the Big Guy." She shifts the gears herself with a smile. "So how are you going to spend the afternoon, dear?"

"Well, I have a new book of puzzles I bought that looks challenging enough to lose myself in for a few hours."

The smile deepens. "Good. I know how fond you are of word games, riddles and clues."

* * *

I go directly home after lunch. *Maybe I should buy a cat.* I wonder as my purse hits the corner wall by the front door and slides to the floor. *Something alive to greet me...* Then I realize, *What an odd thought.*

I cross over to the shelf on which I stack canned goods and take out a lonely can of tomato soup. *When in the name of God did I buy that? And why?* I hate tomato soup. The pop-lid opens with a rip that sounds too loud in the silent apartment. I eat the cold red gel with a spoon and viscerally remember how much I truly, truly do not like tomato soup. I put the can down in disgust on the kitchen table, then pick it up, then put it down again.

Without thinking, I carefully peel the label off the can. I read the ingredients listed on the print side and then flip the label over to the white inside that hugs the can's surface. What I see hits like a rock to the forehead. There is writing. Sentences in my own handwriting. They say, "Our name is MaryAnn Weslez. Our husband is Kenneth. Our son is Carl. Don't let them go. Fight."

I remember little of the afternoon that follows. Moments of it flash through me. A truck rumbles under the balcony. The phone rings. An urge to urinate goes away though I don't remember how. The phone rings. A neighbor comes home from work and turns on the television. A cramp hits my fist and I realize I have been clenching the crumpled label.

A knock on the door. *How long was I sitting?* The sun is sinking. Spectacular oranges and reds spread across the sky and reflect in the ocean like a ribbon of fire. A knock at the door again.

"Mac? Mac, it's Murray and I'm not going away. That's what happens when you don't answer the phone."

I unclench my fist, uncrumple the label and read, "Our husband is Kenneth. Our son is Carl. Don't let them go. Fight."

After scratching through my purse, I let Murray in. I close and lock the front door and point my gun directly at Murray's head. With the hand still holding the label, I motion him to the couch I call "the living room." He sits and mutters something incoherent. I hand him the soup label. He frowns in confusion, reads and blows out a long, shuddering breath.

"I thought we cleaned out the apartment, Mac. Two guys scoured every inch of it. But, this, this was written on the inside of a…" he checks the other side of the label, "of a tomato soup can? Sonofabitch. You're good."

"It's my handwriting."

"I shouldn't be surprised," Murray tells himself. "She's a bonafide genius at hiding messages and encrypting everything." He looks past the gun into my face, "The last time you used the ol' trick of writing with your finger on a windowpane — you know, like kids do — so steaming it with your breath makes the words pop out. I guess paying the window washers was a waste of money."

Another frustrated breath blows through his lips. "I gotta admit. I'm at my wit's end with you, Mac. You can't even be trusted with a straight-shot run into Old Town."

I interrupt, "If you see John Galt on the road, kill him."

"Yeah, that's what did it for you the last time, too. You painted the Galt thing on the window of a wrecked shop months ago, where you could see it every time the trans slid by. I thought 'bout sending someone to whitewash the damned stuff but, then, I thought, let it stay. Like a litmus test for how well everything's working."

I pull back the hammer on the gun. "Who am I?"

"MaryAnn Weslez. Mac, Mackenzie, was my daughter."

"Where are my husband and son?"

"Dead," he states simply. "Excuse my bluntness, sweetie, but going through all this for a third time kinda makes it feel routine."

"The third time?"

"The third and the last 'cuz we're not going through this again. Maybe it coulda worked, maybe, if you weren't so mule-headed contrary."

I tremble with coldness that could be anger or fear, or both. "What could have worked?" I pronounce the syllables carefully, "and be very, very careful about what you say. I'll shoot if anything isn't true."

Murray raises his hands, examines the palms and starts to talk into them. "It's a question that's dogged me since I got into the restitution biz. I know how to make someone whole if a bicycle's ripped off or a car's been dinged. But what about someone whose life is train-wrecked by violence, a person who's lost everything or everyone and nothing can be whole again?"

I repeat, "Be very, very careful."

"I always am, sweetie. 'Bout two years ago, as the wars sped toward the end — though nobody knew it was ending back then—" He looks abruptly up into my face. My grip on the gun handle tightens. "Do you remember how bad it was just before the Zone treaties? Had to get that bad, I guess, before the need to survive kicked people in the head hard enough to stop. Remember?"

"Yeah, I think I remember but, then, I recently discovered I don't even know my own name. So a lot of my memories are up for grabs right now."

Murray continues in the same dry manner, "You and your husband Ken worked in a lab together in Free Z, synthesizing chemicals for weapons. That wasn't the job you trained for but the wars caused a lot of career detours. Near the end, when the streets got violent, you lived in the lab instead of trucking back and forth. Carl, too, because you thought he'd be safer there with you.

"Anyway, there was a break-in at the lab. The three guys were part of a gang and they wanted drugs. You didn't have what they wanted but they didn't believe it and tried to make you talk. First, they tortured Ken 'til it went too far and he died. In front of you. Then they threatened Carl to make you spill but you couldn't tell them where the drugs were because there weren't any. When they shot Carl through the head, they probably became believers. There was nothing in the lab, nothing you could give them. Then you were just a messy detail to clean up. You, they gang-raped and left naked for dead in the parking lot across town."

The gun had been sinking but I raise it again.

"You were in the hospital for weeks, kid. Then, after your body healed, you tried to knock yourself off twice — once with drugs, once by slashing your wrists."

My eyes jerk to my wrists. Two deep scars slice up my arms, each at least six inches long. *Why have I never seen those before?!* I must have spoken out loud.

"Because you didn't want to," he states simply. "But enough of you wants to see, wants to live that both suicides flopped. That's where I come in. Your mom brought you to me, she begged me to put you in a program we'd just launched. Sophia was willing to pay anything to get you back."

For the first time, it connects. If I am MaryAnn, Sophia is my mother. "She paid you? For what? I work for you, why would she…"

Murray shakes his head. "No. You never did any work. I sent you on errands to pick up worthless papers and I let you shuffle through dead files because we needed to watch you, to test you out."

He goes back to the thread of thought. "When Sophia pushed you through my door, I asked you one question. 'What does restitution look like, what would make you whole?' You said, 'I want to be new. I want a different life. Make me forget.'"

"And you were lucky 'cuz forgetting is what the program is all about. It makes people whole by tearing them down and putting them back together, but different — as somebody who hasn't been broken in half by life. So that's what I did. You were brainwashed, marinated in drugs. And then there was hypnotism for new memories, behavior modification… MaryAnn died so Mac could live."

"I don't believe you. A mother wouldn't give up her daughter."

"Oh yes she would, if the other choice was suicide. She knew you'd succeed at that sooner or later." Murray stands and removes his jacket, ignoring the gun pointed at him. "It's hot," he explains, draping the jacket beside him as he sits back down.

"You created Mac Jones?" My mind tries to wrap around the concept.

"No, you did. What I gave you was a name. The rest of Mac, well, you wanted to get as far away from MaryAnn as possible. No math, no science, no family, not even a mom who loves you. That's the closest to restitution you could get."

"And it's fallen apart three times? That's some program you've got." The words are hostile but the gun dangles at my side with the hammer no longer cocked.

Murray stares at the lowered weapon. "Yeah, it is some program. It worked like a charm on four other people. You're our only failure, Mac. It's like the suicides — as much as you wanna die, that's as much as you wanna live. Enough of MaryAnn remains to make you fight tooth and nail to remember."

He crosses the few steps separating us. "The apartment where you were attacked? With hundreds of thousands of buildings between Old Town and Free Z do you know why you chose that one?"

"You and Ken lived there as newlyweds. That's why you knew the rail was a fast path to a flat roof. Every time we 'wipe' MaryAnn, you search for clues to where she's gone, and you don't even know you're doing it. The other MaryAnns leave a trail of breadcrumbs that always bring you home because MaryAnn doesn't really want to die. That'd mean losing the only part of her family left — her memories."

Murray gently unfolds my fingers from the gun's grip and takes it from my hand. "You won't be needing this, sweetie." He slips it into an inner pocket of his jacket on the couch.

I crumble like a rag doll to the floor, beyond standing, beyond tears, with no words to describe the spreading deadness in my veins. "I want—" I began.

"No, this ain't happening again. It took under a month for you to come out of it this time. I'm not soaking you in more drugs, I'm not messing with your memory. It's over, and you either move on or kill yourself."

"I can't move on. Everything about Mac is a lie and I only get glimpses of MaryAnn. I'm no one."

Murray puts on his jacket. "You are both."

I glare up at him. "You've stuffed me into limbo. I'm no one unless I'm lucky enough to 'come to' and see my husband being tortured and my son being killed on the inside of my eyelids for the rest of my life."

"In a nutshell," he states bluntly.

"You are a lie… and cruel. You talk a good game about restitution but someone like me, who really needs it, me you dump like garbage."

His face flushes with anger. He reaches down, grabs my shoulders and shakes. "Snap out of it! I've knocked myself out over you. And, in case you care, a mother who loves you is waiting downstairs in my car, waiting to find out if she still has a daughter."

I blink.

"Only one thing left to do." From another pocket, Murray pulls out another gun. The grip is wrapped in a handkerchief to prevent fingerprints.

"You want me to kill myself?"

"Yeah, with your mom sitting outside, that's what I want you to do. Snap out of it! The gun's a gift."

"I already have one — unless you're a thief as well as a liar."

"This one's unmarked, untraceable, and you throw it away afterward."

"After what?"

"Like I said, there's only one thing left. I found one of the guys who killed everyone you love, including MaryAnn."

A shock of ice tightens my throat as I snatch the gun from his hand, keeping the handkerchief in place. "You're telling me to kill him."

"I'm not telling you anything 'cuz I know better. I'm saying you have a street gun in one hand, and a woman downstairs who'll give you any alibi you want. Here." He hands me a piece of paper.

I stare at the name and address. "How will killing him bring back

Kenneth or Carl?"

"It won't. Nothing will. But it might bring you back.

"Like you said, for people like you, restitution is garbage. The roughest thing about the game I'm in is just that. People who need it are the ones who can't get it. Someone will never be whole again."

I try to rise from the floor and fall backward on my ass.

He continues, "The only restitution left is Biblical: 'an eye for an eye'."

I make it to my feet this time and cross to the kitchen table on which I carefully lay the address and the new gun. I stand staring at the wall for a long moment before turning back to Murray. "It's an Old Town address. I'll need travel papers, bribe money…"

"Sophia'll get you fixed up and I'll be sure you're traveling to Old Town on real business so it'll be legit if anyone checks. But you'll need a lot more than paperwork, sweetie." He inclined his head toward the table and the scrap of paper. "The guy is a decorated cop and the bloodhounds of Old Town will hunt down his killer and tear her apart. You need a big shiny plan."

I have one. "I'm going to—"

"Don't tell me. I don't wanna know."

* * *

Night falls on Old Town. The city consumes itself, like a fan, in closing. Lights extinguish, noises soften, pedestrians enter the comparative safety of home. The pavement is quiet. Lights blaze only in bars and strip clubs, the only motion is from stray cars and alley dwellers — the drug dealers, sex-sellers and homeless.

I press against the wall of an alley that's across from the cop depot. I see him walk down the entrance stairs and onto street duty. He struts with an arrogant presumption of impunity. After checking again for the gun in my purse, I slink through the shadows after him.

I am the skin of darkness on walls. A cat in silent dance, I glide between shadows through the thick black night. Tonight a man's brain cells will leave his skull. The blood and grey matter will not bring back my husband or son. But I may meet MaryAnn.

The Slow Suicide of Living Again by Wendy McElroy © 2014 Wendy McElroy

About the Author

Wendy McElroy is an individualist anarchist and individualist feminist who has published twelve nonfiction books and anthologies as well as hundreds of articles in publications ranging from Penthouse to Penn State. Her e-home is WendyMcElroy.com. She has scripted and edited several dozen documentaries and written for a syndicated television show, as well as working as a contributor at FOX News for five years. An aspiring science fiction writer, McElroy is turning *The Slow Suicide of Living Again* into a full-length novel.

Thompson's Stand

by Jake Antares

Mr. Thompson is fighting a war with bricks in the business district. And he's losing.

Thompson threw his hands up a moment too late. A half-brick caught the right side of his face, shattering his glasses. He felt himself involuntarily drop to one knee. Rocks and sticks continue to fall in a hail around him. Despite his throbbing right eye and the sticky blood cooling on his cheek, this was the first moment of rest he'd had all day.

He took the glasses off and held them out at arm's length. He watched the mob approach hesitantly through a projected blue screen that read "No Connection." Thompson tossed the now useless frames to the dirt.

"You—" he started. His voice was cracked and dry but he resisted the urge to cough. "You can't scare me." He made a show of wiping his forehead and then flicking the blood from his fingers. "I am not afraid of you."

He'd been followed by the horde for blocks, at first trying to show composure, then walking more briskly. Now he found himself in this park with his back to the river and no way to run. The crowd should have been more afraid of him than he was of them. They had good reason to be, or would have just a few days ago.

Thompson looked up, squinting at the sun with naked eyes for the first time in years. Drones filled the sky making deliveries, analyzing traffic, filming, photographing, transmitting hundreds of petabytes of information to data centers that no longer even existed. It was only a small surprise to him that none of them carried the star-eyed eagle logo of the national security forces.

As if reading his mind, a man stepped out in front of the mob and spoke. "Nobody comes." The man had an accent and gestured toward the sky. "You look up there, but they don't come."

The man waited for Thompson to respond, frowning. "Give up," he added. He was short and stocky with a wide nose on a wide face. He looked almost kind except for the thick cudgel that swung loosely in his left hand.

Thompson rose to his feet again. The swelling around his eye throbbed as he brought his face up to meet the other man's. "I won't let you degrade me, if that's what you are thinking of. You can't bring me down to your level." Thompson paused, "You'll have to kill me first." Thompson wasn't sure he meant it, but just saying it made him feel as if he'd thrown a punch.

A new flurry of sticks, bricks, and shouts flew from behind the stocky man. Thompson turned his back to them, a few hit him, but most bounced on the grass or crumbled on the cement path beside him. The attack ended suddenly, and Thompson turned back around to see the stocky man holding up a hand, quieting the crowd behind him.

"My name is Len. What is your name?" The man said calmly as if they were meeting in a bar, a job interview, or a car charging station.

"It's Thompson." He held his chin up and glared as he said it. He thought he saw some recognition in the man's eyes.

"Nice to meet you, Thompson."

"Mr. Thompson," he asserted, feeling bolder and determined not to be.

"OK, Mr. Thompson," Len continued, "you do what we say now, OK? No drones, no police is coming."

Thompson would not let himself be threatened. When someone came up behind Len and spoke into his ear, Thompson took a chance and pulled out the comm-stick he had in his pocket. He held it low and projected in the silent only-me mode.

Len must have noticed his eyes glaze as they focused on the comm-stick's holographic projection. He stepped toward Thompson slowly. Len was holding his hands up as if Thompson were the one holding a weapon. Len was showing an empty right hand and a thick piece of wood in the other. Thompson thought of the stunner he'd left in a drawer in his office, never imagining he'd need a greater weapon than his name and ID card.

"Please see news if comm-stick working." After a beat he added, "Mr. Thompson."

Thompson switched the comm-stick to the news feed and the words of the synthesized voice hit him like no brick or bullet could have.

"...tional Security Corporation CEO and CFO Brandt have agreed to what is being called Second Abolition. All citizen indentureship contracts have been suspended in the wake of the violence. All so-called slaver contracts, leases, debts, and bills of sale are declared null and v..."

"You are not slaves," Thompson shouted first at Len and then at the others with him. "You should be thankful you have food to eat. What are you going to do now? You signed the contracts and now you want out. This won't stand, no way. You're fucked. You're homeless."

"We are free," Len said quietly, and not without a bit of sadness.

"...looting and fires reported at locations in several cities including the offices of human resources megacorp, Thompson People and Energy. Several executives of TPE have been found dead of apparent suicide, all others have been asked to report to th..."

"So fuck you then." Thompson was looking around as he spoke, searching for an escape route. "You're free now, kill me, I don't care, fuck you. Be poor. Let your kids get sick and die. I'll go get a pardon, get some money. I'll be on the beach and you'll be picking up my trash."

Len took another step toward him. Thompson threw the comm-stick, and it bounced off Len's chest and fell to the ground. Len picked it up and continued to approach. Thompson backed away. His shoe slipped on the broken, discarded glasses, and he fell backward. He found himself looking up at Len. Len held the comm-stick out to him.

Thompson slapped the hand away and scrambled to his feet.

"Unlock, please." Len pushed the small black cylinder into Thompson's hand.

Thompson eyed the cudgel Len was holding and threw the comm-stick as far away as he could.

A few seconds later, a boy came running to Len's side carrying Thompson's comm-stick.

"Unlock, please," Len said offering it to Thompson again.

"There's no one you can call," said Thompson. "If you think you can steal my money with this, you're out of your mind. I'll be fine. I've got friends, even if I turn myself in. You're just a piece of shit, and I won't let you degrade me." He made a show of holding his thumbprint to one end of the cylinder while scanning his retina with the other side to unlock it. "All yours chief, amigo, comrade, a lot of good it'll do you. We still own you no matter what the news says. It's just a matter of time."

Len looked weary as he took the now unlocked comm-stick, held it up to the side of his neck and waved it in a tight circle. The lock on the metallic collar around his neck snapped open and dropped to the ground.

Len rubbed the pale skin on his neck where the collar had been before turning his back on Thompson and leaning down to unlock the collar of a small boy. When the boy's collar dropped he raised to fists in the air and smiled up at Len. Len passed the comm-stick to the next person in line.

He turned again, pointing his thick bludgeon in Thompson's direction. "You free, Thompson," he said. "You free and…" he pointed the stick at Thompson again, then at the boy, then at himself. "Now, three free men." Len put a heavy arm around his son's shoulders, looked back one last time at Thompson, and started walking home.

Thompson's Stand by Jake Antares © 2014 Jake Antares

About the Author

Jake Antares is a writer and translator who grew up in Philadelphia and lived most of his adult life in Japan. He is currently completing his first novel. Connect with him at JakeAntares.com

Under the Heel of the Aether Imperium

by J.P. Medved

Arla Lightrider is caught in a galactic conspiracy when she agrees to transport a strange alien on her aethership.

"I thought human brood mothers were confined to raise offspring, not given aetherships."

Arla wriggled her fingers underneath her nose, a gesture that, on the alien's home world, would have been interpreted as rude surprise and contempt.

"Maybe *Hasani* brood mothers." She spat the word out. "But I am not Hasani."

"Yet this world is controlled by their Imperium. And you are human, like they, are you not? What are you, then, if not Hasani?"

"I am a daughter of the Merchant's Compact, a free woman. And I wasn't *given* my ship, I earned it, like every other honest trader." She'd paid more for her tradeship than this alien would ever know.

"You are bold to admit such a relationship openly. There aren't many merchants left who would, after the crackdown."

"The alleged crackdown. Free trading's not outlawed yet. And even the Imperium can't be everywhere at once." She brushed a stray lock of shoulder-length brown hair from her face.

The alien's nose tentacles wriggled in a way that could have been either pitying condescension, or polite worry. Arla couldn't tell.

It continued, in that rolling voice peculiar to the Carth, its words of accented tradespeak sounding like the clatter of pebbles swirling around the bottom of a stream, "And what if I were an Imperium agent, sent to spy out and report on Compact members?"

Arla's eyes narrowed. She didn't know if the Carth could read human facial expressions, but if it couldn't understand her scowl, the two slow pats on the butt of her revolver, riding comfortably down in a holster at her thigh, were unmistakable.

"That's what my Ellis is for."

"And against a squadron of Imperium dragoons?"

Arla glanced around the large, crowded room. Other than a diminutive Weeg at the bar looking at her just a little too intently with its wide, watery eyes, and a pair of Malicks arguing by the door, everything at Manrac's Spice and Intoxicant Tavern was as it should be. As it had been the other times she'd visited looking for work after a run to Eutheri. *The other times we visited*, she reminded herself with a pang.

The low light of paraffin lamps cast much of the room and its maze of squat tables, booths, and sunken acid baths in shadow. It was the kind of lighting most of the patrons preferred for the type of business that occurred at Manrac's. Her father hadn't liked it, and only started coming here after more legitimate work became hard to find for Compact traders. After the arrests.

Seeing no immediate threats in her quick survey, she fixed her eyes back on the Carth, "You got a point to all these hypotheticals, or you simply wasting my time?"

The tentacles wriggled slight amusement, "I knew you were Compact before I even sought you out."

Arla shifted her weight.

"The signs were obvious, for one who knew where to look: ship docked at a very specific repair shop, to avoid export taxes, no record in the planetary trade papers of the arrival of such a ship, but discreet inquiries, through certain middlemen, into local cargo or transport needs. And the ship itself, heavily armed, a modern design of brass and steel, hardly any wood, with aetherium wings larger than many luxury aether yachts. Not something private individuals on most worlds are even allowed to own."

Arla's trigger finger twitched. The Carth had described the *Profit and Luck* perfectly.

Perhaps sensing her agitation the alien rumbled on. "I prefer to do business with you precisely because you *are* of the Galactic Merchants' Compact. I value the honesty of a free trader over the convenience of a licensed one, and I have a desire, as you do, to keep my business to myself, and not see it recorded in Imperium ledger books."

"And what business is that?"

"Transport for me and various of my personal belongings to the city of Thu'tachc on New Aureliun."

Arla sucked in a breath, "That's too far."

"I can pay a fair price."

"Look uh—"

The alien seemed to draw itself up, "I am apellated Ry'th, Thousandth and Eleven of the Homemaker Brood."

"Look, Rahith—"

"Ry'th."

"Right, that's what I said. Look Rahith, even if I could find someone willing to share the berth with you, or someone looking to send any kind of cargo from here all the way to that rock, it still wouldn't be worth the time and trouble to me. That's almost a month's travel, not counting stop-offs for air and food. And there's precious little on New Aureliun to pay for the return journey."

"Two thousand capitals. And not in Imperium paper. Borean minted gold."

Arla had been trained by her father to be wary of deals that appeared too good to be true. "There's no such thing as a free lunch," he always said.

"You kill somebody?"

Ry'th's undernose twitched distress, "Nothing quite so pedestrian. I am a writer, and the things I write are not much loved by the Imperator and his government. Various of my colleagues have… disappeared."

So. A fugitive then. His high fee was to compensate for the high risk of taking on his business.

She crossed her arms, "Twenty-five hundred."

"Twenty-two hundred, and I'll restock your ship with food and air when we arrive."

A pause.

"Deal." Arla wriggled her fingers to indicate agreement. "You already seem to know where my ship is, when would you like to—"

"Immediately. This evening if possible."

She nodded. "You will, of course, sign the standard contract." The Imperium had recently declared Compact contracts unenforceable on the worlds it controlled. Planetary governments which had once happily competed for Compact arbitration customers now turned them away where they did not report or arrest them. Still, enforceable or not, a contract was a contract, and she made all her customers sign them, as had her father. The Compact's blacklist still held some power, even though printing it without a license was illegal, and obtaining a printing license these days was functionally impossible without being a vocal Imperium supporter.

The alien's nose tentacles waved assent, and Arla stood. "I'll see you at duskenhour then. Bring payment in full." She dropped a two-decame coin on the table before leaving. The Weeg at the bar, she noticed, was gone.

* * *

The *Profit and Luck* took off less than fifteen minutes after Ry'th's arrival that night, at the Carth's nervous insistence.

True to his word the alien brought only himself and a few personal effects, including a small but deceptively heavy valise, and two and a fifth gold cubes, bearing the stamp of the Borean Metal Conglomerate. These last he passed over to Arla, handling them as if they were worth no more than tharn meat. The young aethership captain bit into them, testing the soft give of the rare metal, before secreting them away in one of the many hidden compartments aboard the *Profit and Luck* and unrolling a contract for the alien to sign.

The owner of the repair shop where she'd docked the ship was Mar Tornald, an old retired Compact trader. A friend of her father's who didn't ask questions and didn't give a quald's shit for the new Imperium trading regulations and taxes. His spacious warehouse on the edge of one of the smaller towns on Eutheri played host at any time to a number of tradeships, mostly Compact, but some Guild, and even a few Unaffiliated. Arla knew most of them — veterans of the aetherlanes like her father — though there were fewer than ever nowadays.

One ship docked nearby had caught her eye. She didn't recognize it as either Compact or Guild, but it had a curious, oblong design and, more importantly, a particularly clean and shiny section near its nose, roughly in the shape of a Compact Affiliation Sigil. As the Imperator's fist closed on the Compact, more and more traders were abandoning it, it seemed.

With the alien safely ensconced in the passenger quarters, Arla turned the crank to open the aetherwings. She extended three segments, just enough for the *Profit and Luck* to lift slowly off the packed dirt of the warehouse floor but not enough to send her rocketing into the roof. With a practiced ease she pushed the yoke to angle the wings and the ship glided forward, passing several others before exiting neatly through the open warehouse doors.

Once under open sky she cranked the wings out another several segments and the aethership, reflecting gravity waves now like a mirror reflects light waves, rose past the warehouse roof and other buildings surrounding the large courtyard. Finally above the constricting walls she eased out another few segments of the wings and the *Profit and Luck* accelerated even faster skyward.

Careful not to go too quickly, lest the wind resistance tear the tradeship apart, Arla brought them out to the black of aetherspace in a little under an hour. She heard some movement but no yelps or howls of surprise from the passenger cabin as the aetherium coated wings did away with the gravity within the ship. An experienced traveller, then.

Arla pointed the ship west, orienting herself by the continents of the planet visible through the thick glass porthole at her feet. The biggest aetherlane out of Eutheri was located just over the rise of the planet, where Port Otero had been built, its orbital railroad bringing ships into aetherspace in a mere quarter of an hour. She'd foregone that convenience for the anonymity of her friend's repair shop.

She rolled the wings out to their full length and angled them to catch the slight planetary current, which sent the ship skidding around the globe. As the land and seas spun below, she concentrated on the curved horizon ahead. She'd done this dozens of times before and knew what she would see as the aether transit point and wheel of Port Otero came into view. She knew to expect the glittering wings of dozens of other ships, swirling in a carefully orchestrated dance as they took to the lane or, arriving off it, lined up to dock. She knew to expect the giant glass beacon orbs, fed with oxygen to keep their paraffin lamps aglow and ringed with mirrors to reflect and amplify their light and guide ships into the port and its orbital railway. She expected, but always enjoyed seeing, the giant circular port itself, spinning by means of carefully angled aetherium plates to provide gravity to those inside, its curved surface twinkling through portholes with the light of hundreds of gaslamps.

What she did not expect, was the entirety of the Imperium's Fifteenth Fleet, laying in wait between her and the aetherlane transit point.

Through her telescope she recognized the Fifteenth's flagship battle cruiser, *Authority's Fist,* floating darkly in the midst of a host of the smaller, but no less deadly corvettes and stingwhips that made up the bulk of the Imperium Aether Navy. Behind them she saw the station and the aether transit point, swarming with even more Imperium ships. Even as she watched, a stingwhip gunboat pulled alongside a medium cargo tug and shot out grappling hooks to draw the ships together for boarding.

What could the Imperium be doing here? This wasn't good. She had no local licenses, and after the crackdown… She made a snap decision, and was hastily turning the *Profit and Luck* even before the thought had finished forming. She'd take them through the transit point at Port Dranel, on the mining settlement of Eutheri's fourth moon. It would mean a longer journey overall, since that aetherlane took a roundabout way to the transfer at Cyther that would put them on the correct 'lane for New Aureliun, but it couldn't be helped. Better a longer journey than any issues with her passenger, and much better than letting tax-hungry Imperium officers aboard her ship.

But it was too late.

Even as she turned, the flash of a heliograph from an Imperium corvette ahead caught her eye. It spelled out:

"UNIDENTIFIED... YACHT... COME... ABOUT... AWAIT... INSPECTION."

More flashes not aimed at her went out from the corvette and two nearby stingwhips fanned open their aetherium wings and starting moving towards her.

"Tharn spitting zast drinkers!" she cursed.

She had no choice now. She couldn't outrun the entire fleet. With a grunt she heaved over the aetherwing yoke to slow the ship and turned the vessel to be side-on to the approaching stingwhips. As the ship's momentum ceased she retracted the 'wings and in a few short moments they were floating dead in the aether.

A rustling behind her announced the arrival of her passenger to the bridge.

"Is anything the matter?"

She couldn't tell if it was just the low gaslight playing tricks, but the Carth looked markedly smaller than before as he floated in the entryway, his nose tentacles quivering in distress.

She gazed out the viewport at the oncoming ships as she answered, "Looks like the Imperium is searching every ship near the transit point. But we should be fine, doubt they're after us with a whole fleet."

There was a sharp intake of breath, and a new voice, not the Carth's, said, "No, it's me they're after."

Arla whipped around at the sound and saw that the Carth floating in the doorway had been joined by someone else.

Her Ellis cleared leather in the space of a breath and the business end of the revolver pointed, unwavering, at the stranger.

"Who in the infinite hells are you and how did you—"

The stranger, a human, cut her off. "They'll kill you if you let them board."

"Someone's of a mind to be killing, and you're looking at her. Now answer me. Who are you and how did you get aboard my ship?"

"I stowed away inside my friend here," a nod towards the still floating Carth followed by a rueful smile, "Not the most pleasant method of travel."

"Inside—?"

Again the stranger, a young man, cut her off, "Perhaps we can get into the finer points of Carth biology and Brood rearing practices another time. Right now I feel it is my duty to warn you that you are in mortal danger if they search your ship and find either myself or my good friend Ry'th aboard."

Who was this louse? "No, *you* listen planetpounder, you're on my ship without permission or payment, and you're an insufferable posh bounder to boot. So we're going to stay here and I'm going to hand you over to the first Suppression Minister that crosses over from that Imperium boat." She would have spit if they'd been in gravity instead of weightless aether. "I don't like the Imperium, but I like freeloaders less."

His face was pained, "No you don't understand. They'll kill you for even knowing me."

"But I *don't* know you."

"That won't matter to them."

It wasn't what he said, but how he said it, that gave her pause. He was deadly serious, and for the first time she noticed the little signs of fear that her father said always betrayed men. A timor of the voice, a widening of the eyes, a tremble in the hand floating by his side.

"What are you, a notorious murderer or something? Did you steal the Imperator's wife?"

The man's expression was grim, "Worse, at least in their eyes. I am a traitor to the Imperium."

"Oh, are you a writer too?"

He shot her a quizzical glance. "No." He shook his head. "But we don't have time to detail my crimes. If you're going to turn me over you must decide now."

Sparing a quick look out the porthole she saw he was right. The first of the stingwhips was almost within Fetler gun range.

Arla's father, Jak Lightrider always used to chide her for her impetuousness. He explained that carefully thinking through one's choices and using reason to find the best course of action was preferable to relying on brute instinct. Arla trusted her gut more than he was comfortable with. That she was right more often than not hadn't seemed to faze him and those times when her gut did fail her, it failed spectacularly. Like with the farmer boy on Elenel or the investment of all her savings at the tender age of sixteen in that traveling Yorak's miracle tonic. Those times her father had let her make her own decisions, and she learned painful lessons. She hoped this would not be one of those times.

Her pistol disappeared as fast as it had filled her palm, and she spun back to the controls of the ship.

"Does this mean you'll help us?"

She ignored his question and gestured at the Carth.

"Rahith, if that is your real name—"

"It is not. I am Ry'—"

"Get to the topside turret. Do you know how to operate a Pathlian two-pounder?"

"I was actually an observer of the Pathlian navy when—"

"Good, get up there and load it but don't aim it anywhere unless I tell you."

The Carth floated back down the corridor.

"And you—"

There was the barest of hesitations, "Uh, Toren."

"Toren, how much do you know about aethership controls?"

He grinned as if she'd made a joke, then covered it up at her withering stare. "I have some passing familiarity."

"Can you handle the starboard Fetlers and heliograph shutter?" She gestured to the console on her right.

The man nodded and glided forward with a practiced ease to take his place beside her, the place she had occupied when her father was captain of this ship.

Arla shook her head to clear the memory. The Imperium craft were close now.

"What are you going to—"

She held up a hand for silence, her other poised over the quick-release lever.

The flashes of heliograph light from the oncoming gunboats were easy to translate, "REMAIN... POSITION... PREPARE... FOR... BOARDING."

There. They were too close now to turn around in time. She hit the quick-release lever hard, nerves making her use more force than she needed. The springs her father had installed still worked, and the aetherwings shot out to their full length in an instant.

Immediately the *Profit and Luck* surged forward as the wings caught the aether current.

"Do you know the heliographic code for a distress signal?" Her heart was pounding now.

He replied quickly, voice taut, "Yes, I'm familiar with the entire heliographic alphabet."

She spared his face a glance. Few planetpounders bothered to learn that method of communication beyond a few simple words.

"Send an emergency signal to those stingwhips, tell them our wings malfunctioned and are stuck."

"That won't work for long." He was already tapping out the message, manipulating the heliograph shutter with the speed of a practiced expert.

"It won't have to," she shot back, as she angled the ship to head straight at the oncoming Imperium vessels. *Louse.*

She could see the panicky bursts of light coming from the two stingwhips, and her brain translated them automatically.

"CHANGE... COURSE."

"RETRACT... WINGS... HALT... FOR... INSPECTION."

Toren's hand flitted back and forth as he continued to broadcast the distress signal at them.

The Imperium ships were reacting slowly to Arla's desperate maneuver and they began turning out of her path and attempting to change direction to match her new velocity. But they were too slow.

The *Profit and Luck* barreled past them. They'd never be able to reverse direction and catch up to her in time. Now Arla just had the entire rest of the Fifteenth Fleet to worry about.

She could already see Imperium ships changing course ahead as her tradeship shot into their midst.

"EMERGENCY... WINGS... STUCK... REQUEST... ASSISTANCE... EMERGENCY."

Responding heliograph flashes lanced out from the titanic bulk of the Imperium flagship, *Authority's Fist.*

"CHANGE... COURSE... AWAY... FROM... TRANSIT... POINT... HELP... DISPATCHED."

Indeed, three corvettes and at least five stingwhips were maneuvering on an intercept course.

"Tharn spit!" Arla's teeth clenched.

"I told you it wouldn't work for long. Should I tell them the yoke is stuck as well?"

She could have slapped him. "How about instead you—"

"Man the starboard Fetler gun and be quiet?"

"No, jump into the aether without a diving suit!" she bit back.

She only needed a bit of room to maneuver. If she could stay out of Fetler range for the next few minutes she might be able to throw them safely through the aether transit. If the Imperium battle cruiser and corvettes didn't open up with their big, long range guns, that is. Too many ifs.

She angled the ship slightly away from the transit point. She was still on a path that would bring her incrementally closer to the point, but *technically* she was obeying the orders from the battle cruiser. Maybe that would be enough to buy another few seconds.

The Imperium ships ahead of her altered their courses to match her new intercept.

"Uh—"

"I see them."

Another half dozen Imperium craft had peeled off from the main fleet and were also now moving to intercept her. If she could just get past that first beacon orb, she could jink hard to starboard and hopefully be through the transit point before the Navy vessels caught on to her intentions. Or, more likely, they'd blow her to smithereens.

"CHANGE… COURSE… TO… HEADING… 5, –2, 7."

Hells. An order that specific was hard to interpret broadly, and the heading was one that would bring her farther from the transit point, not closer.

"Let me fly. I've flown with Imperium ships. I know their limits. I can—"

"If I hear one more word out of you I pledge to thork I will put a bullet through that posh mouth of yours."

He shut up.

Arla leaned into the speaking tube, "Rahith, can you hear me?"

The voice that returned was metallic and tinny, "Yes brood mother, I can."

"Is the gun loaded and ready?"

"It is."

"Good, stand by for orders to fire, we may need it soon."

She wasn't past the beacon yet, but the heliograph signals from the Imperium ships were getting more insistent. If she didn't turn to the new heading they'd open fire.

It was now or never.

She made as if to turn and follow the course ordered by *Authority's Fist,* but at the last second she instead swung the tradeship around in a tight arc aiming to go behind the Imperium ships and then straight on to the transit point. Warning heliograph light flashed out, as the Navy craft scrambled to turn and meet her new heading.

A spray of Fetler fire erupted from one of the corvettes ahead of her, the incendiary rounds flashing across her path before being caught in the planet's gravity well and arcing into the atmosphere.

"ONLY… WARNING… ADJUST… HEADING… OR… BE… FIRED… UPON."

Arla waited another few seconds, then pulled the yoke hard, digging against the aether and putting the *Profit and Luck* into a steep ascent. More fire shot out from the corvette, and it was joined by several nearby stingwhips. The distance was still too great, however, and their bullets sunk to burn up harmlessly in the planet's atmosphere.

The tradeship rolled and turned, Arla's evasive maneuvers bringing them closer and closer to Port Otero and the transit point. The Imperium ships were getting closer now too, matching her turns and feints. A shell from a larger gun whipped past the viewport, its burning phosphorous leaving an afterimage across her eyes like a glowing trinidian gash.

"We can't keep this up, you should—"

"Rahith!" she bellowed into the speaking tube, "Return fire!"

Almost immediately the *Profit and Luck* shook with the dull thunder of the Pathlian two-pounder. The shell flew neatly between two stingwhips, missing both.

"Do you have a trill oil boiler?"

"What? I— yes, of course. How else would we keep the ship warm in the aether?"

"Good."

"Hey! Where are you going?"

"I'm going to save us."

"Get back here before I—"

But he was gone, already floating out of sight in the passageway behind the bridge. The bright corona of a nearby exploding shell brought her attention back to their angry pursuers. She couldn't take the time to track down Toren. As she spun the *Profit and Luck* around, she hoped that whatever he was up to wouldn't cause too much damage.

"Tharn sucking toff."

The enemy ships were closing in now, despite Arla's artful evasion. Every turn, roll, and jink was only delaying the inevitable. The net was closing. Her impetuousness was going to get her killed. A spray of Fetler fire from a corvette caught her port aetherwing, tearing out a chunk of aetherium panel in a burst of glittering shards and causing a noticeable drag on that side which Arla had to compensate for.

Ry'th in the turret above continued to pound away with the Pathlian gun, and continued to miss spectacularly. His efforts probably didn't even rise to the level of nuisance for their Navy adversaries. Arla managed to line up a lucky shot after a tight dive, firing the linked Fetlers to catch a stingwhip in the flank. She smiled with grim satisfaction as the *Profit and Luck* sailed past it and she saw the ragged holes in the cockpit.

The transit point was agonizingly close now, but in between it and her were two corvettes and at least four stingwhips, and even more behind her, slowly but surely gaining aether. The corvettes were turning to line up a broadside of their big guns. She peeled to starboard. Imperium gunners were conscripts, like most of their military, but given enough ammunition even conscripts could hit a moving target.

The shots from the first broadside all went wide, but the second volley came closer, and she yanked the *Profit and Luck* upwards. A shell from the next salvo cut her starboard aetherwing clean in half, and all of a sudden the ship was spinning.

Frantically she rolled the crank to retract the first half of the port 'wing, equalizing the aetherium force on both sides of the ship. The spinning stopped, but now the *Profit and Luck* was practically dead in the aether. Her maneuvers to stop the spinning had bled off much of their velocity, and the shorter 'wings meant she couldn't make turns or dives as quickly as before. And she was closer to the Imperium ships now than ever. One more good shot from them and they were finished. Arla fired off a burst from the Fetlers in frustration, even though they were aimed at nothing in particular.

"Are we pointed at the transit point?" The voice seemed to come from far away.

"Huh?"

"Point us at the transit point, and kindly prepare for rather substantial acceleration."

She'd forgotten Toren was even back there. But she complied, angling the nose of the *Profit and Luck* towards the aether transit point visible just past the Imperium vessels. Her ship responded sluggishly.

"Ok, we're—"

Her words were interrupted by a massive roar and she was pressed backwards into the leather of her seat as they shot forward. The entire ship was shaking with what sounded like one, long, sustained explosion.

The enemy corvettes were a blur as they passed by below, the *Profit and Luck* moving too fast for their gunners to even track. Arla fought with the yoke to keep them on course, and a glance out the starboard porthole showed her that the forces of the acceleration were bending what was left of the aetherwings backwards.

The brass-ringed transit point came up at her alarmingly fast. To her sides she saw a few desultory shells from Imperium ships fly past, but as she got closer to the transit they stopped completely. Even the Imperium wouldn't risk destroying a transit point just to stop a single tradeship.

She leaned hard on the yoke to set them on the right approach to the point, almost clipping an aetherwing against one brass edge in the progress. Another split second and they were through.

* * *

The ship was cold as they limped into orbit around Serratt Hold, and not just because of Arla's frosty mood, either. Toren had burned up practically all of the *Profit and Luck*'s trill oil with his makeshift rocket.

He'd poured it into the garbage lock, at the rear of the craft, before lighting it and opening the lock. With a spare rubber hose he'd emptied the tank into the lock, pumping it smoothly for a sustained burn and giving them the speed necessary to escape the Fifteenth Fleet.

That his presence had made it *necessary* to escape the Fifteenth Fleet in the first place was a matter of some contention with Arla.

"So you say you're a naturalist."

"Yes."

"So the Imperium government dispatched an entire aetherfleet for a single naturalist."

"It does seem that way, yes."

"I'm still not clear on the 'why' of that." Her arms were crossed, as much in anger as to keep warm. They'd burned everything they had to burn, extra clothes, papers, and some of the wood cabinets inside the ship that her father had carved, in the first few days on the aetherlane. But it was almost a week to Serratt Hold, and they'd finally had to resort to wearing aether diving suits without the helmets to keep from freezing to death. Even then Arla's teeth chattered constantly. The Carth, used to such conditions on his home world, simply slowed down his circulation and went into a light hibernation.

Arla and Toren had been over this same ground half a dozen times already during the flight. Each time he'd cagily avoided an outright answer, or plead ignorance, or simply refused to answer — her threats, anger, and cajoling notwithstanding.

This time was no different.

"It would seem we are in the same boat, then."

Her teeth ground together. "Fine. Then I'm under no obligation to take you to New Aurelian. The contract Rahith signed was for one passenger, and your name's not on the manifest."

"If that is your wish I certainly won't oppose you. We'll pay for your repairs when we reach Serratt Hold, and then book transport with some other trader."

His face made her want to punch him. The thick beard almost hid the calm line of his mouth, and his dark crimson eyes, a typical Hasani trait, betrayed no hint of anger or disappointment at her decision.

She could have forced it out of him at gun point, of course, or held him at bay with the Ellis while she searched the valise the Carth had lugged on board, but she couldn't violate a man's property or mind just to satisfy her own curiosity. He had already pledged to pay for the damage to her ship and several capitals more besides to make her whole for the violation of her contract terms. She had no right to expect more according to the Compact's own guidelines.

The rest of the journey was spent in peevish silence.

As the bright beacons that represented the Serratt Hold aetherlane exit approached, Arla unscrewed the bulky gloves of the diving suit and gripped the maneuvering controls. Experienced aethership pilots could pull out of a 'lane at almost anyplace they wanted, deftly playing the forces of aether and gravity against each other to avoid being pulled apart by either as they made the transition. Her father could do it, but only when he had to. For most pilots, nineteen-year-old Arla included, the only option for leaving a 'lane was at designated transit points, where the aether current slowed enough to allow a safe transition back to regular aetherspace.

They'd passed hundreds of such points in the week of travel they'd spent on the 'lane, and seen other ships pulling in and out of them. Arla was aiming for a very specific point. One that, she hoped, would shield them from the wrath of the Imperium long enough to ditch her troublesome passengers, fix up the *Profit and Luck*, and be on her way to some fringe world to lay low for a while.

Once they transitioned safely out of the aetherlane and through the transit point it was only a short few hours to their destination.

Serratt Hold was, technically, alive.

It was one of the last of the great carkoni and it made the vast spinning wheel of Port Otero look like a child's bicycle compared to its bulk. Ten battle cruisers as big as *Authority's Fist* could fit, lined up end-to-end, inside the immense breathing chamber which was the home to most of Serratt Hold's inhabitants. Aetherium deposits glittered all along the outside of the knobby, pocked carapace of the beast.

Hundreds of years ago creatures like this used to haunt the aetherlanes, swimming through the currents and preying on ship and crew alike with their powerful pincers and vicious teeth. They'd been hunted almost to extinction, or rendered mindless and tamed like Serratt Hold by determined parties of boarders and marines, who'd fought through the great monsters' natural defenses; parasites as big as a man that mindlessly attacked any intruders, much like the white blood cells in Arla's own blood attacked an invading virus. Every now and then, tales drifted from the galactic fringe of ships and convoys lost to dark, indescribable monsters, but here in the central worlds only lifeless husks, or half-dead zombies like Serratt Hold remained.

Serratt Hold had been a roving trading port for decades now, staffed by descendants of some of the first boarders to invade and lay claim to her. Arla's father had brought her here several times over the last few years. It had become a haven of sorts for Compact traders as, though its captain swore nominal fealty to the Imperium, and a garrison of dragoons was stationed to keep the peace, neither the captain nor the dragoons were very vigorous in enforcing Imperium taxes and laws. It helped that the commander of the dragoons happened to be the captain's nephew, and that a stream of anonymous gifts had persuaded even the most law-and-order of the rank-and-file dragoons to look the other way.

A low whistle sounded from the door behind Arla.

"I've read of beasts like this, and seen the woodcuttings, but I've never viewed one in person. The words and illustrations do not do it justice."

Arla ignored the man as he floated into the bridge with her. Her hands were already losing feeling in the frigid air, and the cold only served to remind her of how much she despised him.

She hailed the carkoni and a flurry of heliograph signals from one of the lidless eyes of the great aetherbeast directed her to steer into the vast maw and gave her a docking berth number in the breathing chamber as well. She aimed the ship outwards, tracing a lazy arc to bring them head-on into the razor-lined mouth.

"Incredible," Toren whispered.

As they passed the jawline of the creature and entered its gaping maw the scale of it became even more apparent. A virtual forest of pitted, ghost-white teeth, each twice as tall as a man, extended around them in all directions, growing steadily smaller as the *Profit and Luck* followed the line of paraffin beacon orbs deeper inside. They passed other ships leaving the port, none of which Arla recognized. There was so much space inside the mouth that she hardly had to adjust course to avoid any of them, and she never had to shorten her damaged 'wings.

They also passed several discrete Fetler emplacements, rotating barrels protruding from blockhouses built out of hollowed-out teeth. Arla didn't remember seeing quite so many the last time she was here. The Compact's weakness and the Imperium's negligence had contributed to a rise in pirate activity lately. There were even rumors that some of the bigger pirate fleets were actually *privateers*, secretly granted funding and letters of marque by the Imperium to target Compact traders and interests. It looked like the owners of the Hold weren't taking any chances.

As they entered the throat, the beacon orbs became fewer and fewer. Replacing them was a soft, diffuse light that seemed to come from the walls of the massive, circular passage.

"Is that the Carkoni Radiance?"

"No, it's the starglow of the gods. You're dead and this is Hell." The chattering of her teeth somewhat lessened the effectiveness of the sarcastic retort. Of course it was the tharn damned Carkoni Radiance. What else would it be?

The original men to board these monsters of the aetherlanes had been surprised to find that the interiors of the beasts were lit, sometimes brightly so. Many deep sea fish on watery planets exhibited the same type of luminescence and, of course, the mating glow of the Tal-Ruitha was well-known enough to be the subject of poetry. Some beings of science postulated that the light inside the aethermonsters was not for mating purposes, or even to attract prey, but had developed to aid the living parasites which fought off invaders, fixed breaches, and helped break down large food pieces for digestion.

Many even held that these parasites had once been shipwrecked traders, who had devolved over the centuries to mindless creatures that served the carkoni, as their symbiotic relationship grew. The parasites had been exterminated long ago on Serratt Hold, and the captain and other owners of the trading port now filled most of their roles. It was the subject of several jokes in the various pubs and taverns of Parnum's Town.

After a turn to avoid the toxic digestive chamber, the *Profit and Luck* emerged at last from the passage and into the breathing chamber. The light coming off the walls was brighter here, and several large mirrors, strategically placed, amplified it and cast the little city below them into something approaching true daylight. The massive chamber stretched out for miles. Along most of its surface a veritable jungle of algae and other, less recognizable, plant life sprawled, their effluvia providing oxygen to the creature and atmosphere to the chamber.

Spread out along roughly a tenth of the bottom half of the chamber was a sizable trading city. Buildings of polished bone and still-living cartilage, shaped and carefully cultivated into spindly towers and airy warehouses, jutted upwards in the low gravity. Tethered aetherships floated at the ends of docking minarets, and clockwork harvesters trundled along the algae farms at the outskirts of Parnum's Town.

Arla had requested, and been granted, a docking berth inside one of the cartilage hangars. In weighing the necessity to be discreet versus the desire to escape quickly, she thought the covered space of the hangar preferable to the open visibility of a docking minaret.

"Go wake your friend. As soon as we land I want you off my ship."

"Of course." And he was gone, floating through the hallway behind her.

As she lowered the aethership, retracting 'wing segments to let the low gravity of the monster pull them in, she angled for a wide landing pad of transplanted chitin. It was twice as wide as a tarryball pitch, and half again as long, and was surrounded on three sides by long hangars of smooth, off-white cartilage. She brought them down just outside the hangar bay marked '17' in tradespeak numerals, and then, with one segment still extended, she glided the ship forward under the arching roof. A few careful turns of the crank and the *Profit and Luck* settled softly on the chitin floor.

Gravity had gradually resumed in the ship during the descent, but it was weaker here than on a proper planet, and she had to remind herself not to push off from her seat too quickly lest she sail into the bulkhead above her. Checking her Ellis was in its holster, she made her way gingerly to the rear of the ship.

She needn't have worried. Inside the passenger cabin, both the Carth and the stowaway Hasani were gathering their things and making ready to depart. She watched them from the doorway for a moment before going to open the rear hatch, grunting as she spun the wheel to unlock it.

The hatch swung open with a clang, and warm, humid air rushed in. After dropping the wooden ramp she yelled behind her, "I want my payment and then I want you off my boat!"

The Carth shuffled down the ramp, carrying the heavy valise and still moving slowly after its recent hibernation. Toren followed him, and held out a leather package to Arla.

"I *am* terribly sorry, for what it's worth."

She scowled, but took the package and opened it.

"There's a little extra in there, for your troubles."

She had to hide her surprise; nearly four thousand capitals worth of gold in there, if it was real. A bite into a cube pulled at random confirmed it. She made herself choke back an involuntary 'thank you' directed at the Hasani man's retreating back.

As her pair of ex-passengers made their way out of the hangar a flash of silver caught her eye. Two berths down, reflecting the light from a new arrival, sat a curiously shaped, oblong aethership. An uneasy feeling bubbled up from the bottom of her stomach.

She hopped down the ramp, taking its whole length in two bounds with the low gravity, to get a better vantage point. The nose of the ship came into view and the sick feeling in her stomach intensified into full-blown alarm. On its nose was a shiny section, exactly the size of a Compact Affiliation Sigil.

Frantically she scanned the hangar, then the landing pad outside. She saw a small figure, darting along the edges of the pad, ducking in and out of hangar berths. As it came closer she could tell it was a Weeg, and it had a very familiar look.

She hop-ran to the door of the hangar. "Wait! Toren, Rahith, something's wro—" but as she reached the landing pad, and the two fugitives turned back to the sound of her voice, she saw she was already too late.

Overhead hurtled three Imperium stingwhips, and even as she dropped to one knee and drew the Ellis from its holster a squadron of dark crimson-clad dragoons spilled around the sides of the hangar, their Morely repeating rifles held at-the-ready underneath black spiked helmets.

They moved with precision, surrounding Toren and Ry'th while a squad advanced on Arla, kneeling exposed in the hangar bay door. For a brief second she considered running, but the eight rifles pointed at her didn't waver, and she'd never get past the hovering stingwhips in her already battered ship.

She lowered her revolver to the ground where it was retrieved by a sneering Imperium officer while two troopers wordlessly hoisted her to her feet and steered her towards Toren and Ry'th, the muzzle of a rifle digging painfully into her back. These dragoons were far too disciplined to be the local garrison, and she didn't recognize the patches on their shoulders, stylized ruby-red human skulls, as belonging to any known unit in the Imperium navy.

As she was corralled in with Toren and Ry'th her fear gave way to anger.

"You thrice-damned zast-drinkers. I'm not even part of this!"

The officer of the dragoons answered her, "Yours is the ship that blasted out of Eutheri a week ago, or would you like to try explaining that Fetler damage in some other way, free-trader cur?"

How had they gotten here so fast? She spared a glance at the mysterious oblong aethership in the hangar behind her. The Weeg was nowhere to be seen.

One of the hovering stingwhips dipped and landed lightly on the chitin in front of them. Almost immediately its main hatch opened and a ramp was run out to the ground. Down the ramp came two dragoons, wearing the same curious skull patch as the others. They took up positions on either side as behind them emerged a tall, sinewy Hasani woman from the stingwhip's depths. She moved down the ramp like a predatory felai, gracefully deliberate and visibly dangerous. Behind her marched two more dragoons.

The Hasani woman wore the impeccable dark crimson uniform of an Imperium Aether Admiral, and the red-gold star pinned to her breast marked her as a member of the Royal Family. Her auburn hair was done up in a severe bun. As she came closer, Arla started. She recognized the sharp lines of that grim face from lithographs and recruitment posters; this was no low-ranking cousin or third-rate family-by-marriage. Before them stood Tel Rani, Princess of the Imperium, and second in line to the throne.

The woman's blood-red eyes passed over Arla with scarcely a pause, and settled on Toren.

A thin lipped smile crept over the woman's face, and Toren spoke, his voice tight with anger.

"Hello, sister."

Her smile widened.

"Hello, *traitor*."

* * *

At least it was warm in here.

"My name's not Toren."

"So I gathered."

He looked almost sheepish or, at least, as sheepish as one could look while strapped to the side of a corvette holding cell, floating in the zero gravity of aetherspace.

She let the silence hang before continuing, "I knew you were a big lout, I didn't realize you were first in line to the throne of the whole tharn-damned Imperium big."

"I'm sorry—"

"Do you have any idea what kind of suffering I've had to endure because of your government? Your father?" she bit out.

"Look, I know, that's why—"

"No, you don't know! You have no idea what it's like to be persecuted and harassed for just wanting to trade freely, to live your life as you've always led it. You have no idea how it feels to be forced to take more and more dangerous jobs because Imperium pressure has scared planetary governments and commercial aggregates away from doing business with you. Until one day you're forced to head up a Compact aetherium mining expedition into the fringes, and you never come back, and the last thing your daughter receives from you is an official condolence letter from a Compact representative."

She stopped for a ragged breath, willing her eyes dry.

"I didn't—"

"You didn't care. Living fat off the stolen wealth of a thousand systems. Your father—"

"Is a monster."

She stopped short at the vehemence in his words, and he continued, his subdued voice conveying an intensity she hadn't seen before.

"I may not have endured your pain, but I still know right from wrong or, at least, I've recently come to. You'll notice the three of us are in the cell together." He nodded towards the still silent Carth next to him.

Arla remained quiet, but the bitter expression on her face softened a little. She *was* curious why the famous Cal Mor, golden boy of the aether racing circuits, Prince of the Imperium, and first son of the Imperator, was bound by his wrists and ankles to the wall of an Imperium aethership.

"I've always been the black quarg of our family. While my sister was close with our father, I took much more after our mother. When she died, my father was left with no moderating influence on his passions. Combined with the ambition of my sister I am convinced this led to his grand galactic unification project. I was by nature more interested in aether racing, science, and books than conquering star systems, but I went along with their plans. I even commanded the Second Fleet during the final push against the Forli Republic."

He paused at the memory, his eyebrows drawn down.

"I'm not sure why—"

"I hope you will pardon the necessity of a little background to understand why we find ourselves in this situation."

"I know why *I'm* here," she muttered. "Poor customer selection criteria."

He continued, a little faster now, "My father, worried by my disinterest in politics, especially as I was to succeed him, hired a new tutor, an acclaimed author and political naturalist from an alien world. His teachings finally captured my interest in the subject but not, I think, in the manner my father hoped. The new tutor introduced me to the banned and subversive section of the palace library. The thrill of reading and examining together something which was forbidden first captured my curiosity, for though it was my right as a member of the royal family, my father had always kept that part of the library under lock and key."

Cal Mor's eyes had a faraway look.

"But when the excitement and novelty wore off, the ideas began to take hold. I'd never read anything like this, certainly not in the dry textbooks of my previous Hasani tutors. Here were the thoughts of radicals, anti-religionists, anti-monarchists, freethinkers. Never before had my view of the galaxy and my place in it been so called into question. My tutor, also, had a hand in this, forcing me to think through assumptions and challenge, as he called them, my premises."

The Prince looked apologetic. "I say all this so you will understand my frame of mind in the events that were to follow."

"As I questioned my own beliefs, so too did I begin to question the policies of my father. So it will, perhaps, not be surprising that when I made my momentous discovery I did not, immediately, report it to my father the Imperator."

Arla twisted to look at him.

"It was all because of a mistake in an aether race. The Quinns Cup. I skirted too close to the boundary of a lane, hoping to catch a faster current and gain some advantage. Instead the tip of a 'wing pierced the lane. I was dragged out of lanespace back into normal aetherspace and it was all I could do to keep the ship together, as this was not a transit point. I lost most of the port 'wing in the process.

"I found myself in an uninhabited and still, to my knowledge, undiscovered star system. A search through my telescope found a good-sized planet on which I could land to fix my broken 'wing.

"As I flew across the face of the planet, seeking a suitable location to land, I felt a tug on my ship and it began sinking rapidly to the surface, much faster than even a broken aetherwing would explain. I fought with the craft and turned it from my previous course, and the downward force lessened, my fatal crash avoided, but I made a note of the location of that mysterious force.

"When I finally did land it took me several days to repair my ship, and in between bouts of work I undertook to examine the location of the mysterious force which had almost been my end. A few hours hiking brought me to the place, and I noticed immediately several large, open deposits of a curious type of mineral.

"I found as I approached that my body felt heavier, my movements more difficult. Passing my hand over the material I felt it drawn downward. Finding this curious I chipped off a small piece with my knife, and pocketed it before returning to my ship.

"Upon returning I examined it further but, other than a strange, crystalline sheen, could find nothing to explain its properties. I would study it properly back at the palace, with a real microscope. Absently I placed it on a discarded section of my damaged aetherwing and this was almost my end.

"Within moments I felt an intense heat at my back and as I turned, an explosion knocked me off my feet. A hole the size of a Torrd skull had been blown in the discarded wing section, right where I'd placed the strange material. Naturally, before I left that place I gathered an even larger sample to study, being rather more careful to encase it and keep it from touching aetherium.

"My experiments with the sample over the next few weeks occupied the whole of my passion and soon became known to my sister. Upon her inquiries I excitedly confessed all I had learned about what I now dubbed 'anti-aetherium' for its gravitonic nature and explosive interactions with its twin."

Here the Prince grew silent, and Arla guessed at his thoughts.

"She wanted to turn it into a weapon."

"Worse. She wanted to use it. She proposed cleansing the planet Forli, where anti-Imperium sentiment was still quite high after the recent war."

Arla sucked in a breath, "A whole planet? It's that powerful?"

"It can be made so, purified, refined. I protested Tel's plans to my father, but was horrified when he agreed with her. 'An example will ensure obedience, obedience will bring security, and thus the many will benefit from the sacrifice of the few.' But I couldn't accept his logic, especially after my recent education. An argument followed and I stormed off in anger.

"Later that night I was awoken by a brisk knock at my door. My new tutor, the alien, appeared much disturbed. He told me he had overheard some dragoons discussing some recent orders. Orders to arrest me and seize the anti-aetherium.

"We made plans then and there to escape, and slipped out of the palace together, with the anti-aetherium safely in our hands. My tutor arranged transport to a small world called Eutheri, I stowed away in his egg sac, and you know the rest of the history."

"Your tutor was Rahith?"

"Actually his name is—"

"Or'ryth, Second and One of the Philosopher Brood." The Carth broke his silence.

Arla squinted, trying to recall dim memories, "My father mentioned your name before."

"I have written much that a member of the Galactic Merchants' Compact would find agreeable."

"Oh! The Treatise on Galactic Taxation and its Effect on Trade. We have a copy on the *Profit and Luck*."

Or'ryth wriggled impressed amusement, "Not a work the Prince's father has read, or he would never had hired me."

"But if you support free—"

Arla was interrupted by the opening of the hatch to their little prison. A well-armed dragoon floated through, the muzzle of his repeater carbine scanning the cell as if to ensure none of them had broken free. Behind him, with her customary predatory grace, came Princess Tel Rani.

She wasted no time, and Arla imagined the tiny space had grown several degrees colder upon her entrance, "We're nearing the transit point, dear *brother*." The last word sounded like a curse. "Our navigator requires a destination."

Cal Mor — Arla still had a hard time not thinking of him as Toren — shrugged. "Surely they know their way back to our home world."

"Don't play games with me." Tel Rani's snarl was feral, "You know exactly where you discovered the anti-aetherium, and you're going to lead us there."

"I most certainly will not."

A chilling smile crept up the corners of the Princess's mouth.

"I wonder just how far your so-called principles extend. Private," she nodded towards Arla, "count to ten and then put a bullet in the skull of that one."

The dragoon clenched his jaw and aimed the Morely repeater at Arla's head. She could see his lips move as he counted down silently. The muzzle of the gun was as black as the Kagarath Reach, and infinitely more terrifying.

At 'six' the Prince made a choking noise, "Wait! It's at—"

"Eleven point eight five point two, on the Afarii lane." The Carth's voice rolled like stone over the Prince's. "Prince Cal Mor confided in me before we left the Palace, in case one of us should be killed, its location would not be lost forever."

Only Arla was looking at the Prince for this, so only she saw the flicker of surprise in his eyes as his Carth tutor revealed the location of the secret planet.

Princess Tel Rani chuckled, "Very well. And if this should not be the place, both you," she pointed to Or'ryth, "and you," her other hand crooked at Arla, "will die."

* * *

The Carth was true to his word, and upon exiting the 'lane the Imperium corvette was greeted with a swollen, volcanic planet visible through navigation telescopes.

The corvette's entire compliment of stingwhips, five in all, made the descent to the planet's surface, each filled to the brim with a full squadron of dragoons. The first, Princess Tel Rani's personal gunboat, also carried Arla, Or'ryth, and Cal.

Cal, after a whispered conversation with his former tutor, directed the craft to a large volcanic peak, jutting up from the broken and shattered landscape around it. As they flew closer, Arla could see through the portholes enormous alien faces carved into four sides of the mountain. They were of a race she did not know, and their vicious fangs, curving upwards towards compound eyes, made her shiver.

The little flotilla set down under the gaze of one of these terrible visages and, following Cal's direction, disembarked and made towards an opening just below the fearsome teeth.

"Move." The Princess growled at Arla, waving an ornate revolver towards the opening. "If this is a trap," Tel Rani warned, "she'll be the first to die."

Cal and the Carth said nothing, as around them grim-faced dragoons worked the levers on their rifles, chambering rounds with ominous metallic snaps.

As the party grew closer, dragoons fanning out to either side, the opening revealed itself to be an immense doorway, carved into the living rock, and extending in a straight line into darkness. The air around them was dry and hot, and Arla felt sweat drip down her back, though whether from the heat or the fear she couldn't tell.

She stepped timidly into the opening, but a hard jab from the muzzle of the revolver in the small of her back forced her to move more quickly, and she was soon completely inside the mountain. Several dragoons carried paraffin lamps behind her, and by this weak light she made out the dimensions of the passage. It arched overhead like a Pathlian cathedral, and some distance in front of her it turned abruptly so that she could see no further. Both sides of the passage were lined with concave nooks, and within each of these stood a statue of an alien bearing the same face as those carved on the outside of the mountain.

Arla shivered. In the dancing light of the paraffin lamps the shadows from the statues seemed to twist and writhe. Their extra appendages reached across the arched ceiling as if to enshroud her. In the distance she imagined she heard the clatter of alien claws on the warm stone.

Arla led the entire party, the hundred dragoons, the Princess, her brother, and his tutor, deeper into the mountain. The passage made many turns but never did it branch and she saw no doors at all along its length, only the endless march of statues. She lost track of time, but guessed it had been perhaps half an hour of walking when she rounded another corner and saw a soft orange glow ahead of her.

The glow brightened with each new turn, until soon the dragoons were able to extinguish their lamps as the whole passageway was now lit. One final turn and Arla stopped short.

Ahead of her the passage ended, and it opened onto a vast internal cavern. On either side, falling from a barely visible ceiling far overhead were dozens of glowing strands, which Arla first took to be immensely long glowropes but which, on closer inspection, proved to be thin streams of lava. As they reached the floor of the cavern they became less coherent and flecks of glowing stone splattered the edges of deep channels, carved into the bedrock by decades, perhaps eons, of ceaseless assault.

And stretching before her, like an imperial boulevard on Hasan, was a wide, glowing road, lined on each side with rows of small stone buildings. Each was one story, and all were roughly the same size, but some were ornate, with intricate carvings and grotesque statuary, while others were plain, with smooth columns and unadorned, cube-like walls. All seemed colored a hellacious orange by the boulevard's light, which she saw was caused by two channels of lava, flowing sluggishly away from her, towards the center of the grotto and fed by several of the glowing streams falling from above.

"That is our destination." Cal pointed down the wide road.

In almost the exact center of the vast cavern towered a hulking mound. It looked almost like a fermine hive, haphazard and riddled with imperfections. But as the party marched down the wide causeway and grew closer, Arla could see it was a building. Its stone blocks and columns combined in such a way to make it seem almost like a natural feature of the underground chamber.

Arla looked back. The whole company of dragoons was inside the space by now, their dark maroon uniforms looking black in the fiery glow. The Princess, immediately behind her, scowled, the dragoons flanking her held their carbines level. Behind these walked Cal Mor and Or'ryth guarded by several more dragoons wearing severe expressions. The Carth's undernose was twitching frantically.

Arla turned forward again, puzzled. She didn't recognize those particular tentacle wriggles. Was it feigned distress? No. Happy fear? That didn't make sense.

Then she caught movement in the corner of her eye and realized instantly what the Carth had been doing.

Warning. It was warning.

On an instinct she flung herself to the ground, thinking she could claim she tripped if her guess was wrong.

It wasn't. In the next second the air around her exploded. Gunfire erupted from all sides, a tearing roar that cut through the oppressive underground stillness like a Tornaldian grizz saw let loose in a Chefler pilgrimage tent.

She twisted to see several of the dragoons go down, some soundlessly, others screaming. Arla searched desperately for cover. A hand grabbed her shoulder with a painful, tight grip.

"You're coming with me."

The Princess hauled Arla bodily off the street, across a walkway that spanned the little stream of lava, and into the temporary cover of one of the small buildings. All the while, bullets whined overhead and the remaining dragoons, trying now to return fire against their hidden attackers, rushed to get out of the killing zone. They left a dozen or more bodies littering the boulevard in their haste. Cal and Or'ryth were nowhere to be seen.

Tel Rani was enraged. Flecks of spittle flew from her lips as she shouted at the nearby dragoons taking cover with them, "Push around these buildings and clear those riflemen! And if you find my brother, bring him to me that I might kill him *myself.*"

The troopers jogged off, and then it was just the two of them ducking down in the little alcove of one of the buildings.

She rounded on Arla, who had been eying a quick dash away as the Princess was distracted. Tel Rani's pistol once more pointed at the young trader's face, "And you, the great Prince's little bitch. You'll learn what it means to betray the Imperium. We're bringing order and peace to the galaxy, and you just want chaos. I'll snuff you out as he watches, just as my father snuffed out your pathetic independent Compact."

A flurry of shots sounded from the other side of the avenue and the Princess's eyes flicked away for a split second. Arla kicked out and connected with Tel Rani's knee. She staggered, and before she could recover the young Compact pilot threw herself at her. Both women went down in a tangle of screams and grunts. The engraved revolver skittered across stone.

Tel Rani was strong, stronger than Arla. She delivered a series of vicious jabs, and Arla's neck, sides, and head were soon screaming in agony. She held doggedly onto the older woman, but Tel Rani aimed a rough headbutt downwards and Arla cried out. Her nose was streaming blood, and she jerked her head back. The Princess grunted and flung Arla bodily over, working an arm under her neck and pinning her to the warm stone. The pressure on Arla's neck intensified and her vision closed in on both sides.

The Princess's breath was hot on the back of her neck. "I would have preferred my brother watch you die, but I'll settle for making him see your lifeless corpse."

"My dear sister, I don't think that's a wise choice."

Through her dimming vision Arla thought she saw a shadow on the ground and building in front of her.

"Put her down Tel. I'll not hesitate to deprive our poor father of his favorite child."

The grip on Arla's windpipe slackened, and she drew in a ragged breath.

The Princess growled.

"Ms. Lightrider, can you stand?"

Arla nodded weakly, pushed herself to her knees, and forced her legs to lift her to her feet. She looked up. Above them floated a small skimmer. Its short 'wings and open air design marked it as a planetary vehicle. Its nickel-plated sides and mounted Fetler indicated it was a military one.

Five beings occupied the conveyance, three of them firing rifles over the side at something she couldn't see, one of them piloting the craft, and one of them aiming the Fetler at the still prostate form of the Imperium Princess. Sparks shot off the armor of the skimmer as bullets pinged all around.

Cal's eyes were hard over the barrels of the repeating gun, "Bring us down, Or. Ms. Lightrider, may we give you a lift?"

The skimmer set down between the building and the causeway, affording some cover from rifle fire coming across the street. Arla limped over to the vehicle with a weak grin, wiping blood from underneath her nose. As she came closer she saw a clear Compact Affiliation Sigil on the little craft's side. A pair of dark green hands appeared and helped heave her over the armored gunwale.

As she climbed aboard the Princess spoke, her voice full of venom, "Are you going to kill me now, traitor?"

"No, I'm going to leave you with your failure and with the knowledge that I've defeated you and father once, and I'll return one day to do it again."

"We'll find you. There's not a speck in this galaxy where you can hide!"

"You're wrong, Tel. Give my regards to the Imperator." Cal Mor made a spinning gesture with his hand and the skimmer ascended once more. The Princess's inarticulate screams faded as the craft sped away towards the large, misshapen building in the middle of the chamber.

"Are you all right?"

The Prince was kneeling beside Arla, a torn shirtsleeve pressed against her nose.

"Lean back."

"I'b fine."

"I know. Here, this will stop the bleeding."

She leaned back against the cool metal of the skimmer's armor, "Thangs. For cobbing to ged me."

"Of course."

Below and behind them the gunfire was slackening and Arla looked around the interior of the skimmer for the first time. Besides Cal and Or'ryth there were three other beings on the deck, two Malicks and human male. None of them wore a uniform, dressed instead in a mix of civilian and work clothing, but on the shoulder of the human and the dorsal fin of the Malicks was a cloth band with the Sigil of the Compact sewn in bright gold.

"What is—"

"Not now." The Prince squeezed her arm. "Let's ensure we are out of danger first."

The skimmer angled around to the far side of the giant building, and the Carth piloted it deftly into a wide opening midway up the tower's base. Arla could see the walls of the opening were marked with cuts and grooves. They were rougher than the stone on the rest of the building, as if this portal had been recently carved.

Or'ryth brought the hovering transport to a soft landing on the stone floor, and several figures came out of the darkness to help the little party out. Arla felt hands guiding her towards the rear of the chamber, and hurried whispers from behind her as the Carth acquainted these new companions with recent events.

The end of the stone chamber was pitch black, and she was directed to put her hands on the rough-hewn wall. She felt along the stone until the wall opened up into some sort of passageway. Dank air blew from within it, and she felt a hand on her back.

"Go down this tunnel, we have ships waiting that can outrun any Imperium corvette. We'll come right behind you all after we seal off the exit."

For a moment, Arla stood frozen, not daring to trust her ears. In the dark she still couldn't make out the man's shape, but his voice was unmistakable, was one she'd known her whole life.

"Dad?"

* * *

Shock gave way to confusion. Confusion to relief. And relief to anger.

By the time Arla was safely aboard the Compact fast picket ship with the others, and they had successfully evaded the orbiting corvette and made the transition to lanespace, she'd already gone through every conceivable emotion. She was exhausted. But she was still angry.

"I thought you were dead! I was all alone!"

"You weren't alone. You were never alone. I had my most trusted associate tailing you to protect you, and report back to me how you fared. Dweez!"

There was movement in the cockpit ahead and a figure floated to the doorway. It was a Weeg, and Arla immediately recognized its large, wet eyes. It was trilling its tongue in laughter.

"You're the one from Manrac's, and your ship was the one on Serratt Hold!"

"Yes," came the singsong response.

"But if you weren't the spy, how did the Imperium find us on Serratt Hold?"

Her father clenched his jaw. He had to clear his throat to speak, "Mar Tornald is dead."

Arla felt her stomach drop. The old repair shop owner on Eutheri had been a dear friend, and the first to console her when she thought her father had died.

"He was captured by the Princess's Scourge Troopers. We couldn't rescue him. We believe they forced him to divulge a list of likely places you'd turn up."

She turned to her side, "I would have told you to shoot that bitch where she stood, Cal, if I had known."

The Prince squeezed her hand silently.

Her father pretended not to see and continued, "We've been working diligently to ensure Tel Rani and her father are paid back in full for the debt they have rung up. Or'ryth's mission was the first step in our plan, and it was an unqualified success."

The Carth's nose tentacles wriggled proud embarrassment. "The Imperator, of course, hired me as 'T'ryth,' noted political scientist and author of *On Central Authority: The Necessity of Strong Leadership*."

Jak Lightrider added, "We knew it would be invaluable to have a being inside the Palace, the very heart of our enemy, so we jumped at the chance when the royal papers advertised a space for a tutor of the young Prince. We just didn't realize how valuable Or'ryth's position would be."

"I knew to direct the Princess to this hidden staging planet, because your father was very careful to provide me the coordinates should any unforeseen emergency occur."

"We were tracking the stingwhips through telescopes almost as soon as they left the corvette. Your every step on the planet was watched." Her father smiled tightly, "Imagine my surprise to see my own daughter among the landing party."

Arla frowned. "Who is *we*? What is this group? Why do you all wear Compact Sigils?"

The elder Lightrider grew serious, "We are a rebellion. Not one seeking political power, or to impose our revolutionary ideology on others; but one which simply wants to be left alone.

"The Merchant's Compact may be beaten, but it is not broken. The spread of the Imperium, through force and propaganda and intimidation caught us by surprise and we've become marginalized and scattered as a result. Some of us finally awoke to the true nature of the Imperator's totalizing government, due in large part to the writings of this gentle-being," he nodded to Or'ryth, "and we met to determine what was to be done.

"It was for that reason I faked my own death, for that reason I didn't return to you, dear Arlalei. I was needed as a planner and warrior in this rebellion, and defeating a government is dangerous work. I couldn't bring my own daughter into such an endeavor."

"Fat lot of good that did," Arla shot out peevishly.

"Well, we can't predict the future, and I made a mistake to hide this from you, I see that now. But you still have a choice to make." As he spoke the ship shifted and Arla and the other passengers could see through the portholes that the pilot was pulling them out of lanespace in the middle of a lane, with no transit point in sight.

"No one here will force you to join us and, my dear daughter, I will make no demands on you as your father. If you wish to join, you must do so willingly."

There was a jolt, and the ship transitioned back into aetherspace. Jak Lightrider looked out one of the portholes, and when he tilted his head Arla gasped. Spread out in an otherwise empty stretch of space were hundreds of aetherships. Yachts, tugs, sleek tradeships, and battered planet-hoppers. Their 'wings glittered with starlight. All bore Compact Sigils. It was the largest collection of free traders she had ever seen.

"You may not have noticed in all your travails, but today is actually the galactic new year, according to the standard trade calendar." Her father turned from the porthole to look at the group. "The last five years have been ones of tyranny slowly growing across the galaxy like a Zikaldi fungus. This next year shall be one of liberty, of fighting to take back what was stolen from us. And," he gestured to the fleet outside, "we will not fight alone."

Under the Heel of the Aether Imperium by J.P. Medved © 2014 J.P. Medved

About the Author

J.P. Medved writes fun adventure stories and thoughtful thrillers, from Steampunk works like *To Rescue General Gordon, Queen Victoria's Ball* and *In the Shade of the Ishtar Trees* to political thrillers like *Granite Republic*. You can preview his other works and download free stories at JPMedved.com.

When not writing, J.P. can be found frying anything he can get his hands on in his deep fat fryer, shooting tons of guns, and losing himself in a good book at the most inopportune times — around the dinner table, at baseball games, during heartfelt emotional conversations.

Yellowsea Yank

by William F. Wu

Kanlee Kung finds lies, facades, and secrets at every turn in a steampunk, 1894 China.

East China Sea, Aug. 6, 1894

"Passengers to your quarters!" A uniformed ship's officer strode just behind the travelers at the rail, waving his arms. "To your quarters! For your own safety!"

"Safety," Kanlee Kung muttered. "What's the problem, sir?"

The officer ignored him, repeating his instructions as he moved down the deck.

Kanlee knew hiding out in his quarters was not going to help with any problem. He surreptitiously checked the short-barreled Colt Bloodfinder with brass handles in a shoulder rig he wore under his suit jacket. He was a self-styled private detective and second-rate shortstop on the last leg of a trip from Portland, Oregon.

"To your quarters, everyone!" The officer shouted again. "Move along, move along."

Kanlee ignored the officer in return. He stood on the deck of the steam clipper *Yellowsea Yank*, a sleek, iron-hulled two stacker, and leaned on the rattlesnake-patterned brass rail near other passengers in a chilly wind. He had left his home in the Chinatown of Portland for Shanghai and now strained to see the mouth of the Yangzi River somewhere ahead. In

Shanghai, the bustling port city of many foreign concessions, he would seek his lost cousin Meiping, a nineteen-year-old girl.

"Do you know what's wrong?" Kanlee asked a woman walking past, presumably to her quarters. "Have you heard? I've read there are pirates in these waters."

She was a gray-haired white woman of about sixty years old, wearing an elegant, full-length, gray day dress trimmed with gold lace. Cream-colored lace protected her throat. A short, wide-brimmed purple top hat was tied under her chin by a matching bow. Delicate fingers of silver rose over her hat in the shape of a small leaping doe. Instead of answering Kanlee, she pointedly walked away, apparently unconcerned about the alarms and the crew's frantic movement — or Kanlee.

He ignored the snub, being accustomed to such treatment from those with social status and wealth. He had more important worries. If he failed to reach Shanghai, Meiping might wonder forever if he had ignored her cry for help through a letter sent by a Mr. Lyman Wellstone — with a ship's ticket enclosed for Kanlee. Because he had taken ship immediately, he had not bothered to write a return letter that would arrive no sooner than he would.

Beneath his feet, the deck hummed with the turn of the great screw that propelled the ship. However, the ship's horn sounded long and loud, while alarm klaxons honked specific warnings. Around Kanlee, the ship's crew ran to their emergency stations, shouting to each other, all of them glancing astern.

After three weeks across the Pacific, Kanlee was nearing the country of his father and mother, though not their province. He was twenty-four years old, born in Portland's Chinatown, and was learning part of his trade from a ruthless, retired Pinkerton detective who grew talkative after his third shot of Chinese brandy. Kanlee scraped together a modest living by swamping out a Chinatown saloon and playing on a semi-pro baseball team. Now, in Shanghai, this Lyman Wellstone would help him find Meiping.

Most of the other passengers hurried away from the rail. Kanlee drifted behind the shouting officer and worked his way toward the stern. The breeze whipped at his unbuttoned gray American suit jacket and the plain black tie around his upright starched collar. He fastened the jacket tight around his maize waistcoat and looked behind the ship.

About a quarter of a mile beyond the stern, at the center of the ship's wake, huge bubbles rose in the waves and burst into the air.

At the stern, four men worked a huge crank that gradually turned a platform holding an old 7-inch Armstrong gun. Kanlee picked out the ship's captain, a Boston native named Oxley, at a distance as he strode among the crew, pointing and yelling.

"Full speed on all engines!" Captain Oxley shouted. He raised a long, brass telescope and peered to the rear of the ship. "Full speed!" He called out a new heading to the helmsman, then turned to his chief engineer. "Power those boilers!"

Behind the *Yellowsea Yank*, a giant steel Chinese dragon head broke the surface with a great roar of water. It was painted gold with black delineations. The great mouth, opening on huge, multi-jointed hinges, was almost cavernous enough to swallow the stern of the narrow steam clipper.

Captain Oxley pointed to the crew at the Armstrong gun. "Fire at will!"

They fired. A shell sped toward the steel dragon and exploded harmlessly off the front of its gargantuan head.

Kanlee saw the barest hint of silhouettes, men with their hair in queues and holding rifles at the ready, deep inside the mouth of the dragon, at its steel throat.

Behind the dragon head, Kanlee saw a long, serpentine steel shape with the upper arches of its curves breaking the waves and extending at least as far as the biggest ship he had ever seen. From behind the head, steam rose in huge billows, mixed with black smoke from the fire that heated the boiler somewhere inside. At the far end, the serpentine tail stood high over the waves, ending in multiple points.

The dragon-shaped ship was advancing fast.

The crew at the stern gun fired another shell, which exploded against the front of the dragon's face with no effect.

The dragon mouth slammed down on the oaken stern of the *Yellowsea*

Yank. The bow of the ship came up, tilting the deck. Crew members shouted and screamed. Oxley lost his footing but pushed himself back up.

Kanlee slipped to the deck but already had his Bloodfinder out. He aimed inside the dragon mouth and fired twice. In the darkness of the dragon mouth, he couldn't see any results.

"More coal!" Oxley yelled. He leaned into a brass voice tube that led below. "More coal, damn you!" Then he spotted Kanlee, holding up the Bloodfinder. "Get to your quarters, Chinaman! Get off the deck!"

The big dragon mouth opened, releasing the cargo ship. The stern rose up and the bow dipped forward, splashing hard and throwing crew members across the deck again. Kanlee sailed into the air and fell hard.

Some of the team at the stern gun lay helpless. A few men got to their feet and struggled to crank the artillery piece into a new position.

Ignoring Captain Oxley, Kanlee holstered the Bloodfinder and ran to the stern gun, where he climbed onto the turret. He joined the men turning the crank. None of the white crew members cared what he looked liked now. As the barrel lowered, a crew member fired a shell that flew directly into the dragon's mouth and exploded in a red and yellow burst. Though smoke filled the dragon's mouth, the ship was undamaged.

The dragon mouth opened wider, then chomped down hard again. The stern of the cargo ship was driven down, tilting the deck upward a second time.

Clinging to the big hand crank, Kanlee saw a single figure visible at the top of the dragon head. A tall man wearing a long gown with splits on four sides stood in a yellow mandarin jacket with an upright collar at the neck and wide, short sleeves. His cap was a roundish cone shape, brimless, woven of rattan. It had a ruby-red knob on top and an ostrich feather angling down the back.

Kanlee stared at the colorfully dressed figure, observing that the man watched impassively, neither giving orders nor showing fear. He had no idea of the man's identity, but he was certain the stranger was no pirate.

The dragon mouth opened again, releasing the stern, and the *Yellowsea Yank*'s deck fell level once more.

The impact threw Kanlee to the deck. He pushed to his feet and drew the Bloodfinder. The dragon-shaped ship made a big target, and he emptied the Bloodfinder at its steel head but again saw no effect. He reloaded quickly but did not waste any more rounds.

The *Yellowsea Yank*'s big engines finally built their full heads of steam and propelled the ship faster. With its rear and side-mounted water jets blasting, the ship rose up on its steel skids, skimming the waves. Crew members were heaving baskets, chests, and crates of luxury cargo overboard to lighten the load, even though those goods were not very heavy. Soon the only weight in the hold was the coal needed to power the engines. The *Yellowsea Yank* slowly pulled ahead of the big dragon.

Oxley strode to the edge of the deeply chewed, splintered oaken stern and shook his fist at the receding dragon head. "To the devil you go, you pigtailed bastards!"

The big steel dragon was still on the surface even as the *Yellowsea Yank* pulled away. At the top of the dragon head, the tall man in the ostrich feather cap stood unmoving.

Kanlee ran up next to Captain Oxley. "Captain, you have any idea what this is about?"

Oxley scowled. "You again? Stay out of my business, Chinaman." He stomped away, shouting orders to his crew.

Kanlee decided to forget about the dragon ship. At the rail, he turned away from the stern and looked forward, searching again for the mouth of the Yangzi River.

* * *

In the stone skyscrapers of Shanghai's Italianate and neo-classical skyline, windows glowed like rectangular unseeing eyes. Skywalks, slides, and lift tubes curled and looped above and around them. Dirigibles of rigid design flew at the highest levels above the city, while leather-stitched hot air balloons sailed against gray clouds with their coal burners blazing. In the lower level of the baskets below the balloons, lines of sweating coolies pedaled in unison to keep the rear propellers moving and the deep air rudder angling while wealthy Europeans drank tea and brandy on the upper level.

A chugging tugboat pulled the *Yellowsea Yank* against the current of the Whangpu River from the Pacific Ocean. In the waning light, Kanlee saw the Union Jack and the Tricouleur painted on the biggest dirigibles, flaunting their colonial power. The Imperial Chinese flag, yellow with a blue dragon and red sun, and other designs were also visible.

The sight made him ask himself, what was a lone, boot-strapped private detective and second-rate shortstop doing here? The answer, of course, was that when his father had been dying, he had told Kanlee that as his only surviving son, Kanlee must help his extended family if they needed him. So when he received Meiping's letter, his duty was clear.

Kanlee hoisted the strap of his brown satchel onto his shoulder.

"Young fellow!" Captain Oxley walked up. "I spoke precipitously a while back. Hot-blooded from the attack, I suppose. Can you spare a moment?"

"What for?" Kanlee asked.

Crew members set up the gangplank leading down to a small tender that rolled on the waves.

"I need to make a report about that ship, that monstrous thing. Come with me to the customs house and we'll describe it together."

Kanlee had more immediate concerns. Without a word, he walked down the gangplank, dismissing Captain Oxley from his thoughts. The satchel was his only luggage, with another shirt, a few collars, and changes of underclothing and cash for the trip. Bootstrapping his confidence in this foreign land, he boarded the tender. The deck rocked wildly on the waves, but after a quick stumble, he found his sea legs for the short ride.

His mid-length American haircut worried him some, given that the ruling Qing Dynasty, of Manchus who had conquered China several centuries ago, had made beheading the penalty for Chinamen not wearing a queue. However, he expected to be in the territorial concessions, where colonial law ruled. If the Manchurian authorities decided that the head of yours insincerely, Kanlee Kung, came under their jurisdiction, he would be alone with his Colt Bloodfinder. He could be as insincere as the Yellow Sea tide.

The tender steered past junks with water-jet engines and short airfoil wings along their sides on the way to the stone jetty extending from the Bund. With other passengers, Kanlee walked along the gangplank to plant his feet on terra firma.

"Ah ho, ah ho..." The chant in low, droning rhythm came from overhead, beyond the shouts of dockworkers and the cheery greetings of passengers. "Ah ho..."

Kanlee looked up and stopped. "Hey, what the hell?"

A hot-air balloon angled out of the twilight toward the middle of the jetty. The leather sagged. The coal burner's fire had gone out. The upper level of the basket was empty, but a red-faced Brit foreman and four bare-chested coolies were in the lower level. The coolies chanted as they pedaled hard.

The burly Brit, whose red toupee was slipping on his bald pate, sounded a brass horn powered by air escaping from the balloon. It gave a long, high-pitched tone followed by a short low burst. "Ya bastards, bring 'er in afore I kill ya'll!" He raised a cat o' nine tails and spun a clockwork arm with a rotating elbow to lash the crew.

Outrage burned in Kanlee's veins. He had never felt the lash himself, but he had heard stories all his life in Chinatown about white men's raids and massacres of Chinese immigrants throughout the frontier. This moment made all the stories come alive again.

Passengers who had disembarked ahead of Kanlee scattered, shouting and screaming, as the basket came down.

The basket thumped onto the jetty with the propeller and rudder forcing the basket into a sideways angle. The collapsing balloon fell away from Kanlee.

He found himself approaching the basket, drawn to see how the coolies had fared but worried about what he might see.

"Arr, ya villains!" The British foreman stepped out of the basket. "Ya bloody bastards are lucky the master's not aboard!"

The exhausted coolies, drenched in sweat and bleeding from the lash, climbed out. They stumbled about, gasping for air and muttering to each other in Hoisanese.

Kanlee knew that much of Shanghai's laboring class came from the Hoisan district of Guangdong Province, where the desperately poor — including his cousin Meiping — often departed for Shanghai in search of work despite speaking Hoisanese instead of the Shanghai dialect. They came from the same origins as many of his father's generation of Chinese immigrants to America.

The foreman stepped up and lashed them again at random.

"Stop it!" Kanlee quickened his stride, his anger flaring again in kinship with the coolies.

"Yo, ho — a yeller bastard in white man's clothes, is it?"

"Shove it, limey." Kanlee stepped between him and the coolies.

"It's that way, is it?" The foreman turned the spinning lash.

Kanlee ducked away just as the lash sliced across the back of his head, stinging and sending him staggering forward.

The foreman roared with laughter. "I'll kill ya, ya yeller bilge rat!" He stomped closer with the lethal, whirling lash.

Catching his bowler in his left hand, Kanlee yanked out the Colt with his right while spinning back toward the foreman. The gun blasted and the .45 slug hit the foreman dead center in the chest, throwing him off his feet. He landed hard and his red toupee fell off.

The four Hoisanese coolies stared at Kanlee.

He looked back at them for a long moment, the Colt Bloodfinder smoking. From their shocked expressions, he abruptly realized that with his American suit and haircut, they recognized no kinship with him. He turned and ran up the jetty, with shouts in English, Shanghainese, and French behind him.

Blood red rickshaws waited on the Bund. The first driver in line straddled a two-wheeled engine chugging steam, with the long handles of the rickshaw braced to each side of the engine. He gave a fake grin and shouted in Hoisanese.

Growing up, Kanlee spoke Hoisanese at home and picked up Cantonese from friends, but he jumped into the rickshaw and shouted the address of Lyman Wellstone's home in Yank English.

The rickshaw man put his machine in gear and took off. Kanlee looked back as the wheels of the rickshaw bumped on the cobblestones and bounced him in the seat. On the jetty, European men in suits, white women with brimmed hats, and wealthy Shanghai businessmen in long silk robes and braided queues were yelling and pointing at him.

* * *

The rickshaw driver soon rolled down a tree-lined side street not far from the Bund. He came to a stop and hopped off. The shouts of peddlers and the puffing of their carts joined the chugging of other rickshaws moving up and down the block.

Kanlee jumped to the ground, his satchel swinging and his head aching. Maybe he would donate his head to the Manchus after all.

"Did anyone follow us?" Kanlee asked in Hoisanese.

"No one. But you speak Hoisanese. You from Hoisan?"

Kanlee shook his head. He studied the man for a moment and realized that while the coolies had been mistreated by the foreman, the rickshaw driver seemed to be in business for himself. Kanlee overpaid the driver, an acknowledgement that the rickshaw man had seen he was fleeing from others and got him away from the Bund.

With a big grin, the driver trotted back to his rickshaw.

Kanlee turned to the door in an eight-foot wooden wall that surrounded the Wellstone estate and tugged on the silken bell pull.

In a moment, the door creaked open and a gray-haired Chinaman in a black cap and a long-sleeved, blue gown studied Kanlee. He would be the number one boy, in charge of the servants.

Kanlee stayed with Hoisanese. "I am Kung Kanlee," he said, giving his name in Chinese fashion. "Mr. Wellstone is expecting me."

"He never spoke your name to me." The number one boy considered Kanlee's Chinese descent, American suit, Hoisanese speech, and lack of a queue. "Go away."

From inside, a woman called out in English, with an upper crust British accent. "Ah Wing! Who is it, then?"

"A Mr. Kung, missy," Ah Wing said in English.

"Let him in."

"Yes, missy."

Kanlee followed him to the front door, where he stepped inside and swept off his bowler. "I'm Kanlee Kung, from America."

"Welcome to our home, Mr. Kung. I'm Amanda Wellstone." The young woman lowered her face demurely, displaying a large swirl of golden hair held up with black lacquered hairpins. Petite and curvaceous, she wore a low-cut blue bodice over a cinched waist and an ankle-length white skirt slit in the middle. Thigh-high tabs held the sides of the skirt open like theater curtains, showing off shapely legs above her pointed, black, high-button shoes. She glanced up with quick brown eyes. "Lyman is my brother. Come into the sitting room, won't you?"

"Of course." Eyeing his sashaying hostess with appreciation, Kanlee followed her.

As Kanlee entered, he heard Ah Wing close the door with a solid thump, shutting out sounds from the street. The house turned quiet except for Kanlee's footsteps and those of Amanda. The floor in the sitting room was hardwood, polished to a mirror shine. On the opposite wall, a gaslamp threw a glow of light. A tall, lanky Brit with a bloodless face and thinning brown hair sprawled back in an embroidered wing chair. He wore a white linen smoking jacket over green pajamas.

"Kanlee Kung. I got your letter and took ship right away." He extended his hand to shake.

"I never heard of you," said Lyman Wellstone, ignoring the outstretched hand. He held a pipe made of an inch-thick bamboo stem more than a foot long and a bowl of ivory carved with the shapes of lotus blossoms. "I certainly never wrote you. Be gone, eh?"

"It's your name and address, sir." Kanlee drew out the envelope and dropped it onto his host's lap, ready to be insincere if necessary. "You even sent a bank draft to be drawn on account at the Bank of Shanghai when I arrived, to help defray expenses."

Amanda snatched up the envelope, slipped out the bank draft, and pushed it into Kanlee's hand. "Perhaps I can be of help."

"You talk like a bloody Yank," said Lyman, eyeing Kanlee.

"Yeah, my dad went to California in the Gold Rush. He met my mother there and I was born in 1871."

"You arrived tonight and came straightaway?" Amanda asked.

"That's right. I sailed on the *Yellowsea Yank*."

Lyman waved his pipe dismissively. "Ta-ta, Yank Yank."

"That should come from me, don't you think?" Amanda asked.

Kanlee glanced at her, wondering what she would yank.

"Something about that Fan fellow, I suppose?" Lyman asked. "Bloody pirate if you ask me."

"Fan fellow? This is about you, my cousin, and me."

"Are you still here?" Lyman narrowed his eyes at Kanlee.

"Interesting look," Kanlee said. "Makes you look more Chinese."

Lyman's eyebrows rose in surprise, or maybe just to make his eyes look less Chinese.

Amanda leaned close to Kanlee. "Your cousin Meiping is my handmaid." She turned. "Ah Wing, bring Meiping."

Lyman closed his eyes, with his eyebrows still raised.

"What's wrong with him?" Kanlee whispered.

"Lyman ships out opium for the E.D. Sassoon company. He inherited the family business from daddy dear. Now he partakes of opium himself. He just finished his evening smoke."

Ah Wing entered with Meiping, who wore a light blue servant's gown and kept her hair in two looped braids. She had delicate, pretty features.

She bowed to Amanda and then to Kanlee.

"Do you know me?" Kanlee asked in Hoisanese.

"Kung Kanlee," Meiping said, giving his name in the Chinese manner. "I recognize you from a photograph your mama sent to my family a few years ago." Her manner was formal, which was proper given the presence of the Wellstones. "Why are you here?"

"I just asked myself that question," Kanlee said. "How are you?"

"I am fine, cousin."

"Take us to America," Amanda whispered.

Kanlee gave her a startled glance, then took the envelope from her and pulled out the letter. He examined the loops and curls of tidy English round hand. Lyman Wellstone had never heard of Kanlee and Meiping was fine. Kanlee compared the handwriting in the letter to the script on the bank draft and turned to Amanda. "You wrote these, and even forged your brother's signature on the bank draft. Why?"

"Take us both, won't you? I got your address from Meiping when I learned she had a relative in America, you see?"

Kanlee looked into her brown eyes for a long moment, then grabbed her blonde hair. When he yanked, it came free. Underneath, she had black hair pinned flat. "You're Chinese."

Meiping watched them in apparent alarm.

"'Half-caste,' as Lyman puts it." Amanda took back her wig and tugged it on. "After Lyman's mum died of consumption, daddy started screwing the help. That means my mum, who was Lyman's amah. So here I am, you see? She died in childbirth and daddy felt too guilty to get rid of me — say, to sell me on Foochow Road. Since he died, my half-brother Lyman has tolerated my presence."

"So you pass for Brit."

"Take us to America. Away from this suffocating life I live and freeing Meiping from servitude in this home. We'll go now, while Lyman's asleep."

"What? You have wealth and standing in Shanghai—"

"I have nothing!" Amanda yelled.

"And you lied to me in your letter. Why should I help—"

Awakened by the shout, Lyman grabbed a silken bell pull.

Across the polished floor, a trapdoor crashed open.

"The guards!" Amanda gasped.

A mustachioed Gurkha soldier in a British Army uniform of rifle green rode up through the trapdoor on a whirring belt. He carried a handheld

Enfield-Maxim machine gun with a hand crank, with the twelve-foot ammunition belt trailing. His eyes widened when he saw Kanlee.

Ah Wing backed out of the sitting room.

"Meiping!" Amanda grabbed Kanlee's cousin and drew her down.

Kanlee knew the notorious Enfield-Maxim machine gun by reputation. After observing that the great American Civil War battles were decided by infantry rifle fire, and not by artillery or cavalry, Hiram S. Maxim of America had teamed up with the Royal Small Arms factory of Britain. The result was the most lethal hand weapon to date.

While Kanlee knew he could not beat an Enfield-Maxim with his Colt Bloodfinder, he knew how to slide into second base.

Before the Gurkha started hand-cranking the weapon, Kanlee dropped his bowler and ran toward him with his satchel swinging on its strap. Kanlee threw himself forward feet first, with one leg extended like he was reaching for second base, and his other foot high like he was breaking up a double play. The blast of bullets passed over him. On the polished floor, he slid hard into the Gurkha's legs, knocking him down, and kicked the Enfield-Maxim's barrel upward.

Kanlee scrambled up, grabbed the rifle by the barrel, and ripped it away. Then he angled it back and swung for the fences. The butt hit the Gurkha in the head and he collapsed.

As Kanlee fumbled the Enfield-Maxim into position, he looked down into the floor opening. Jointed steel humanoid figures were riding up a conveyor belt. Their molded shapes included shaved foreheads, braided queues, and sightless eyes. "What the hell are those things?" Kanlee demanded, mystified.

"The Vaucansons!" Amanda called out. "Vaucanson automatons! They guard the opium tins in the cellar!"

Kanlee had heard of such automatons, developed from the creations of inventor Jacques Vaucanson in the previous century, but he had never seen one. With a grimace, Kanlee cranked the Enfield-Maxim and, struggling to control the rumbling recoil, he shot the first Vaucanson. The bullets clanged off. Then Kanlee whirled to grab Meiping and run for the front door, but a second trap door crashed open, blocking the way. Another Vaucanson rose into view.

"This way!" Amanda angled the gaslamp sconce on the wall and opened a hidden door. She pulled Meiping after her.

In the wing chair, Lyman had drifted back to dreamland.

Kanlee backed up, cranking the Enfield-Maxim. Two lines of steel Vaucansons were marching toward him, stiff and expressionless. The bullets sang off the Vaucansons in a metallic melody.

When Kanlee stepped into the secret passage, Amanda pulled a lever and they rode another conveyor belt upward, powered by whirring wheels at the top and bottom.

"What does your brother want those things for, anyhow?"

"Clockwork automatons don't use opium, you see? They don't steal it and they can't be bribed. The Gurkha knows how to wind them up."

The clanking, unseeing steel coolies came through the doorway below them and stepped onto the same belt Kanlee, Amanda, and Meiping were riding.

"Where the hell are we going?" Kanlee demanded.

"Well, really!" Amanda shouted. "Does it matter?"

The Vaucansons with their molded eyes of solid steel rose after them, as the human trio moved up through the second story, to the ceiling where a trapdoor above them opened with a thump.

Kanlee, Amanda, and Meiping stepped out onto a roof where the cool river breeze reached them. The roof was flat, covered with tar into which sand had been rolled to create a waterproof seal. Brick chimneys rose up at the corners and a metal stovepipe chimney stuck up near the middle.

Kanlee aimed the Enfield-Maxim at the bolts holding the conveyor belt roller and cranked hard. The bullets blasted away the fittings. The belt dropped, taking the Vaucansons down into a huge crash of metal.

"Now where do we go?" Kanlee asked.

"I have no idea," said Amanda.

"No idea," Kanlee muttered. He eyed the ammunition belt, which had only about five feet of rounds left.

Meiping looked around helplessly, tossing her looped braids.

A trap door banged open across the roof. Another Vaucanson rose into view, staring with dull metal eyes as insincere as Kanlee's own.

Kanlee glanced around the edges of the roof. No tree branches were close enough for them to reach. When he looked straight down, he saw that the wall was sheer, with no window casings or exterior pipes that could be used to climb down.

The first shining, expressionless Vaucanson from the rooftop trapdoor came marching toward them, followed by others. The roof quivered under the tramp of their steel feet.

Kanlee fired the Enfield-Maxim again, but as before, the bullets glanced off the oncoming Vaucansons.

Kanlee directed Meiping and Amanda behind him to a corner near a chimney, where they watched the Vaucansons advance.

"What can we do?" Amanda wailed.

"How do they find us?" Kanlee demanded.

"What? What do you mean?"

"Those steel eyes can't see. Maybe the Vaucansons got wound up and released, but they change directions to follow us. How do they know where we are?"

"Only the Gurkha knows, and a couple of his colleagues."

"Amanda, they can locate us somehow."

She just shook her head and watched the Vaucansons clank toward them.

Mechanical, Kanlee thought to himself. Clockwork. Wind-up. Tick tock.

They had no sight, no hearing.

Tick tock. They kept coming.

As Kanlee watched their feet stomping forward, he remembered the hum of the *Yellowsea Yank* under his feet. He recalled having to find his footing as the tender rolled on the waves and the way the wheels of the rickshaw had rattled him as he rode down the street. The conveyor belt to the roof had rolled with whirring wheels. He had arrived with engines, waves, and rollers.

The Vaucansons kept walking.

Kanlee felt the roof vibrate as they marched.

Tick tock.

"Don't move," Kanlee whispered in English to Amanda and then in Hoisanese to Meiping.

Kanlee stood motionless with Amanda and Meiping on their corner of the roof, but the Vaucansons were still coming toward them. "No talking, either," he whispered.

"Then shut up," Amanda whispered back.

Watching the Vaucansons close the distance across the roof, Kanlee pulled the ammunition belt loose and took the Enfield-Maxim by the barrel. He stepped ahead of the two young women to make room for his backswing. With a sidewinder throw, he flicked the Enfield-Maxim in a horizontal, spinning motion like the business end of a broken bat spinning away from the hitter.

The whizzing Enfield-Maxim struck the side of the lead Vaucanson's knee, clanged off, and spun into the leg of the next Vaucanson following. The first Vaucanson stopped, diverted by the banging under its feet. The second one in line also halted, bending forward as though it could somehow perceive through its unseeing eyes to find the source of motion.

Both Vaucansons stepped onto the Enfield-Maxim as it settled on the roof with a slight rolling motion, and the next Vaucansons also clanked after it, crashing into the ones ahead. With their sightless eyes and unhearing ears, the followers in the line kept moving forward into the group, crashing into each other, stumbling, some falling. The big jumble grew wider, trapping this little corner of the roof, but at least the Vaucansons were no longer advancing.

"That was it," Kanlee whispered. "It must be built into their clockwork balance. "They're designed — and wound-up — to follow movement through their feet and legs."

"How do we get around them?" Meiping asked.

"Kanlee, listen," said Amanda.

He heard voices above him in the wind.

"Ah ho! Ah ho!" The chant of Hoisanese laborers reached Kanlee from a big basket over his head. They were the four coolies who had seen Kanlee shoot their foreman. A new fire blazed in the coal burner, heating the balloon above them. The brass horn gave its long, high-pitched tone followed by the short low burst.

One coolie threw out a rope ladder. "The rickshaw man told us you were Hoisanese — and you might need help."

Kanlee grasped Meiping's arm and helped her onto the rope ladder, his feet scraping slightly.

Some of the Vaucansons, responding to the new vibrations on the roof, turned and clanked toward them, as unseeing and unhearing as before.

Amanda clutched Kanlee's arm. "You won't leave me?"

Kanlee looked down at her, resenting her wealth, her deception, and her blonde wig. She lived in a mansion, passing for white.

"Yank Yank." Amanda searched his face, desperate yet hoping.

Kanlee stared back as the footsteps advanced. He was a bootstrapping, part-time private detective and semi-pro shortstop. His life had no place for her.

"Please! I have nothing." She swept off the wig and unfastened the tabs on her skirt to let it fall closed around her beautiful legs. "I am nothing," she said softly.

Silver in the moonlight, some Vaucansons kept marching their way.

Kanlee looped one arm around her cinched waist and lifted as he stepped onto the rope ladder. The coolies pulled them up as the Vaucansons plodded after them.

While the balloon carried the rope ladder higher, the Vaucansons that were still on their feet stopped at the edge of the roof. They stepped from side to side, bunching together, searching for more vibrations. The movement of their own footsteps seemed to keep them clomping on the edge of the roof in a shining but clumsy dance.

Then Kanlee and Amanda were in the basket, and she clung to his arm, smiling shyly.

"Where can you take us?" Kanlee asked the man tending the coal.

"The police are seeking you on the Bund — but some ships left Shanghai tonight. When we catch up to one, you must buy passage."

"I will." The cash in his satchel would cover it.

"You'll have to go wherever we go," Kanlee said to Meiping.

"I can't stay here now," she said.

Then Kanlee turned to Amanda, speaking English. "The U.S. government doesn't like Chinese people entering the country. Put your wig back on. You'll have a better chance of entering America as English heiress Amanda Wellstone with your Chinese handmaid."

Amanda slipped on the wig as she answered in perfect Hoisanese for the first time. "I know that role very well."

Kanlee stared at her, speechless in all languages and dialects.

Amanda shifted back to English, with an impish smile. "Ah Wing and the other servants helped raise me with my mum's language."

"What role do you play?" Meiping asked Kanlee in Hoisanese.

Kanlee grinned, sincere at last. "This is our journey to the west — even if we travel east to get there."

Below them, the bright lights of the Bund lit up Shanghai harbor as they flew toward the East China Sea.

* * *

A powerful sea breeze carried the balloon and basket in concert with the crew-driven rear propeller. Kanlee, Amanda, and Meiping said little as they sat in the upper level of the basket, until now always reserved for the wealthy. They were wrapped in woolen blankets from a hollow bench. Kanlee reloaded the Bloodfinder from rounds in his satchel and then had nothing to do but look for lights from ships in the darkness below.

For a moment, he wondered what he would do when he got Amanda and Meiping back to Portland. Then he realized just how far they had to go. Since landing in Shanghai, he had not had a moment to think more than a few steps ahead. Surviving the night was their first worry.

"You lost your hat," Amanda said quietly in English. "That stylish bowler."

"Yeah." Kanlee ran a hand through his hair. "Still got my head."

"An important point, I grant you."

Kanlee found himself wondering about Amanda again.

"When did you decide to leave your family?"

Amanda drew her blanket tighter. "Yes, I fooled you. I wrote the letter and pretended Meiping was in trouble. Before I learned she had a cousin in America, I saw no avenue of escape." She lowered her eyes. "At the time, I was just taking a stab in the dark. I have no justification."

"You said you have nothing. That mansion, the servants? The family business? Your beautiful gown?"

"Do you believe that an illegitimate, half-caste, half-sister is truly a part of the family? That I have any inheritance or means of my own? Do you think I was ever truly allowed into Shanghai's proper colonial society? I shall be an old maid soon, without ever receiving a proper gentleman caller. The mansion is my prison, do you see? Lyman fears if I have a friend outside the family, I might say something about his business — or reveal I'm half Chinese. Yes, my dear brother gave me the money to appear as he believes a Wellstone should, for the occasions when his friends and associates visit our home. He took me out to social events if my appearance served his purpose and he had me entertain at his whim, but my only friends are my mum's people — our household servants." She hesitated a moment. "The servants often took me out with them dressed as a Chinese girl, so I could learn more about life."

Kanlee took a moment to think through what she had said. Living in a mansion with servants sounded good unless she was treated like one — or even worse. He knew her experience was beyond his comprehension, but he was convinced she was sincere. She had been so desperate to escape her confined life that she had risked writing to a total stranger.

A self-styled private investigator and second-rate shortstop understood bootstrapping a new life. He saw Amanda watching him, afraid of how he would judge her.

"We've made our bed now," said Kanlee.

Amanda let out a very small breath of relief.

"Will your brother send anyone after you? To bring you home again?"

"At one time, he would have. Now his brain is so fogged by opium smoke, I doubt it."

"He must have cargo on lots of ships. Doesn't that give him influence?"

"Lyman has arrangements with many ship captains, but the imperial navy has been very tough on my brother's business. Much of the family income has been choked off by a mysterious new ship called Sea Dragon."

Kanlee nodded, ready to dismiss thoughts of Lyman. Then he looked up at Amanda. "Sea Dragon. Tell me about this mysterious ship."

"It's shaped like a Chinese dragon, you see? But the captains say it travels underwater where no one can see it coming. Then it rises to the surface to attack."

"And the big dragon mouth opens and clamps down on the other ship."

Amanda drew in a breath of surprise. "That's what they said. How do you know that?"

"It attacked the *Yellowsea Yank*. But the crew powered up the engines and escaped."

"Many ships escaped this Sea Dragon."

"Your brother only heard from the captains who got away. I wonder how many ships have been taken or sunk."

"That would explain a great deal," said Amanda. "More and more of Lyman's deliveries never arrive."

"Whose ship is it? The emperor's?"

"The rumors say the captain is one of the top imperial ministers. He's a Manchu, but his Chinese name is Fan Feitou."

"Fan. Your brother thought I had something to do with a 'Fan fellow.'"

"I remember."

"What does this Fan fellow do with his ship? The *Yellowsea Yank* is just a passenger and light cargo clipper."

"The captains have heard that Fan Feitou and his ship have been ordered stop the Chinese rebels who want to overthrow the Qing Dynasty. But he also wants to drive out the foreigners. Lyman's thinking is twisted out of all reason. He probably thought Fan sent you to threaten the family business or ask for a bribe."

"Your family business must be very important."

"It's not just Lyman's business. Fan Feitou patrols the East China Sea to watch all the trade to and from Shanghai, you see?"

Kanlee looked down at the darkness below, suddenly realizing this danger could be right beneath them even now. "I see."

* * *

Nearly an hour after they had left the roof of the Wellstone mansion, Kanlee saw the wake of a ship below them, reflected in the light of a near three-quarter moon.

Kanlee leaned over the steps leading to the lower level and called out to the crew chief in Hoisanese. "Ah Jin! Do you see the wake?"

The crew chief, who had introduced himself as Liu Ah Jin, came up from the lower level. He was a very muscular man with a face that seemed oddly gaunt. The wind whipped his queue out in front of him. "That is from the last ship to leave Shanghai tonight."

"We can overtake it?"

"We will," said Ah Jin. He hesitated, as though considering whether to say more.

"What is wrong?" Kanlee asked.

"We cannot take the balloon back against this wind," said Ah Jin. "When we left Shanghai, it was not this strong."

Kanlee understood. "If they will accept us, I will pay what they ask for all of us. You can return tomorrow?"

"We will have a better chance, depending on the wind."

Kanlee looked into the darkness ahead of the wake. "I will have to negotiate with the captain, and the captain will know he has the stronger bargaining position." He glanced at Meiping, who was gazing down at the wake as her looped braids flew in the breeze.

"What time did that ship leave Shanghai?" Amanda asked Ah Jin in Hoisanese. "Do you know?"

"More than an hour before we arrived at your house," Ah Jin said.

"A steam clipper?" Amanda asked. "A cargo ship bound for Nagasaki?"

"A steam clipper bound for Nagasaki," said Ah Jin.

Amanda switched to English and turned to Kanlee. "The *Cardiff Cloud*. Lyman sold crates of opium to the captain. The ship carries light-weight luxury items of record as fast as possible — silk, tea, spices — for Japan. But the real cargo is the opium. That's the profit, so it doesn't have to carry much volume. I overhear Lyman and certain ship captains talk about such matters sometimes, you see?"

"What does that mean to us?" Kanlee asked. He looked out at the spreading wake again, aware that none of his shortstop's skills were going to help them reach the cargo ship.

Ignoring Kanlee, Amanda spoke to Ah Jin in Hoisanese. "They will allow us to land?"

"If not, we will fly until we find another ship," said Ah Jin.

"You have a plan?" Kanlee asked.

Amanda clutched his arm, smiling as she lowered her face demurely. "Trust me."

Kanlee was surprised to realize that he did.

* * *

When Kanlee could look down and see the outline of the narrow steam clipper ship in the moonlight, Ah Jin sounded the brass horn. An answering horn boomed from the *Cardiff Cloud*. The balloon crew responded by moving low over the deck.

Kanlee saw that the *Cardiff Cloud* was a four-stacker with rear and side-mounted water jets. It was up on its steel skids, skimming the surface of the waves with as little of its narrow hull cutting through the water as possible.

Ah Jin exchanged shouts with a member of the ship's crew in Hoisanese, and the balloon lowered the basket onto the deck.

"Bargain quickly," Ah Jin called from the lower level of the basket. "We will keep the balloon up in case we have to leave again."

Kanlee nodded and helped Amanda and Meiping down the ladder onto the deck. He tossed back the blanket he had been using and strode forward with the wind whipping his suit coat. Gaslamps from the pilothouse threw a glow over a stout, gray-haired man in a captain's uniform in the company of several other officers. He wore a short beard along his jawline but had no mustache. Other crew members, including the Hoisanese man who had been calling back and forth with Ah Jin, stood back in the shadows.

"Now, what is the meaning of this intrusion?" The captain spoke with an educated English accent as he glared at Kanlee.

Amanda stepped in front of Kanlee, still gripping a blanket, but now she held it at her neck with one hand and let it fly out behind her in the wind like a cape.

Kanlee, alert for danger but also fascinated, saw that her other hand appeared to be protecting her eyes, but really held her wig in place. She had again fastened the tabs that parted her skirt to show off her shapely legs and the rear of the skirt fluttered out behind her. The indirect gaslight glowed off her blonde wig. Now she had her turn to be insincere.

"Captain Berwick." She gave him a haughty look.

"Do I know you, miss?" The captain gave her a hard look that softened as he took in her appearance.

"Amanda Wellstone of the International Settlement in Shanghai," she said in her aristocratic accent. "My brother Lyman introduced us on one of your visits to our home. You two shared brandy, I believe." Without turning, she added, "This is my bodyguard, Mr. Kung, and my handmaid."

Berwick's eyes widened slightly. He slipped off his hat and stuck it under his left arm. "Of course, Miss Wellstone. I ask your pardon for not recognizing you straightaway."

Kanlee guessed that Berwick's crisp move with his hat came from a background in the British Royal Navy. That meant he had either retired or had been cashiered. Maybe he had started running opium privately when he was still in the Royal Navy, and that had led to his ejection.

"Quite understandable, given the circumstances," said Amanda.

"We have rules and customs about women on shipboard, Miss Wellstone. I must ask you to continue on your way, with my sincerest regrets."

Amanda took a step closer to Berwick. "You are speaking nonsense, you see? Somewhere on this ship you have certain crates."

Berwick met the eyes of one of his officers and tilted his head slightly. The officer steered the other crew members away.

Kanlee maintained a formal look despite his amusement at Amanda bluffing Berwick into tipping his hand.

Amanda spoke in a calm yet commanding tone. "No matter the price you gave Lyman for the contents of the crates, we both know you will see a fine profit for yourself and whichever cronies have joined your enterprise."

Berwick drew himself up. "Your brother and I have a successful arrangement, Miss Wellstone. It has been mutually satisfying."

Kanlee noted that even an opium-running cargo ship captain could stand on a point of pride.

"Piffle. I do not care about particulars and I suspect Lyman cares even less than I. Now, then. You will give me your quarters for the night. My bodyguard shall sleep on the floor inside the door and my handmaid shall stay with me. You shall find a place for my balloon crew, as well."

"Miss Wellstone, I have had business with your family for many years, but even I cannot guarantee your safety on my ship. The crew is full of ruffians and she rides fast to deliver our cargo on time—"

"I grow weary of this. You wish my brother to remain your supplier, do you not? I can assure you he would not be pleased to hear you refused me refuge while I am in distress. Now, have one of your orderlies take us to your quarters and remove your personal items for the night."

Berwick gave her another long look of appraisal, pausing on her exposed legs as the split skirt fluttered behind her. Then he apparently decided to put his business arrangement as an opium runner ahead of all other concerns. With another quick move, he put on his hat as he called out to an orderly.

Within a few moments, Captain Berwick was out of his own quarters.

Kanlee ushered in Amanda and Meiping ahead of him and watched the balloon crew reduce their fire and allow the balloon to make a controlled collapse. Once an officer had joined the balloon crew to find quarters for them, Kanlee entered the captain's quarters and bolted the door behind him.

"Quite a tiresome chap," said Amanda, giving her aristocratic speech an added air of self-parody. "At first I thought he might be eager to please. Then he started posturing in the most ridiculous manner." She sighed and spoke casually. "I didn't like him when he came to our home, but that's why I remembered him."

"You put on an excellent performance," said Kanlee. He walked to a shelf and picked up a half-full bottle of Talisker Scotch. "He can afford a fine island single-malt, I see."

"We're out of the wind," said Amanda. "And out of Shanghai. I'm very grateful."

Kanlee glanced at his cousin and spoke in Hoisanese. "You are well?"

"I'm well," Meiping said in English.

He studied her, startled. "You, too? You speak English?"

Meiping looked embarrassed. "My English not good. Ah Wing, Missy Amanda help me sometime."

"She understands more than she can say," said Amanda. "We never wanted Lyman to know we were teaching her."

"The surprises never end with you two." He gestured to an interior door with the bottle of Talisker. "I see the captain's quarters include a private head. Maybe you ladies would like to use it first." He pulled out the bottle's cork with his teeth.

Amanda dropped into the rough accent of sailors from London's East End and took the Talisker from Kanlee. "Not yet, luv — only after ya gimme a tiddlywink." She put the bottle to her lips and tipped it back. While she took two swallows, her blonde wig came loose and fell on the floor.

* * *

The captain's quarters were cramped. Kanlee reached up for his missing bowler out of habit, then caught himself. He hung his suit jacket on the back of a desk chair, then took off the leather shoulder rig holding the Bloodfinder and draped it on the chair. He removed his tie and collar before taking another swallow of the Talisker while Amanda washed in the head. The burning in his throat helped fight the chill from the extended balloon ride over the sea.

He motioned for Meiping to use the head next and turned up the gas in the single wall sconce. The ship was steady as it plowed through the waves. He judged that he was tired enough to sleep on the floor.

Kanlee took his turn in the head wearing his shirt and suit trousers. When he came out, he found Meiping slipping back in past him, with a slight smile and her head bowed. As she closed the door, he found Amanda standing near the captain's narrow bed, barefoot. Her wig was off and the gaslight shone on her black hair, which was neatly brushed.

"That was a smooth argument you gave Berwick," said Kanlee. "Who owns this ship? The E.D. Sassoon company?"

"Not the *Cardiff Cloud*," said Amanda. "Berwick used to sail for them, but he saved money and then got a loan, you see? He bought this ship from Sassoon and now runs the opium he buys through Lyman as his own enterprise. Opium is so profitable that he paid off his loan rather quickly."

"The owners of Sassoon were willing to sell a ship like this, with all its speed? Why would they let him compete with them?"

"The hold is too narrow to carry the volume they want. Berwick doesn't care about volume. He had the extra engines installed after it was his, to make it faster. Besides, Lyman sells for E.D. Sassoon. To them, Berwick's just another customer."

"The son of a bitch is smarter than I thought."

"Enough of this," Amanda said in her aristocratic accent. "You are my bodyguard, are you not?"

"Of course, Miss Wellstone," he said, playing along.

"Well, then. I suggest that you will guard it best if you guard it up close."

"Is that your instruction to your bodyguard?"

"Your cousin has agreed to sleep in the captain's bathtub, you see?"

Amanda drew her low-cut blue bodice up over her head and tossed it aside. Under it, she wore a vertically striped gold and black corset that cinched her waist. It had semi-circles of white lace and red rosettes along the top edge.

"Has she?" Kanlee strolled toward her, unbuttoning his white shirt.

"I suppose you should know I'm hardly new at this," said Amanda. "In case you have a concern about such matters."

Kanlee stopped in front of her, looking down at her cleavage. "I have no concern of that sort. And I'm not new at it, either." He put his hand under her chin and tilted her face up. "In case you have a concern about such matters, Miss Wellstone."

"Without the wig, I'm Lei Liwah," said Amanda.

"Your real name?"

"My name of record in the rolls of Shanghai is Amanda Wellstone. My mother's surname was Lei. As she was dying, she told Ah Wing that she was naming me Liwah, meaning Jasmine Flower. Who's to say which is my real name?"

"Liwah. I like it. I like Amanda, too."

She smiled demurely and spoke in Hoisanese. "As Liwah, I am very pleased to meet you." She returned to English. "As Amanda, I think my bodyguard should know the body he's guarding, do you see?"

Kanlee reached around her to find the laces on her corset. "I'm pleased to know both of you."

* * *

The rumble of the ship's engine and bright sunlight streaming through the small, high window overlooking the deck greeted Kanlee in the morning. The ship was steady in its drive through the water. He stretched, accidentally nudging Amanda in the narrow bed.

As he came awake, he wondered about the speed of the *Cardiff Cloud* and where they might be on the route to Nagasaki. He had only a rough idea. Grateful to the balloon crew, he hoped they could return to Shanghai without any more difficulty. His next concern would be finding passage from Nagasaki to Portland.

Amanda snuggled close. "And what does my bodyguard think?"

"Your role-play with Berwick last night saved us the price of passage. When we get to Nagasaki, I'll take stock of our new situation."

She was silent a moment. "I mean to ask, sir, what shall come next?"

"On to Portland," said Kanlee.

"Did you sleep well?" Amanda asked, walking two fingers across his chest.

"Like the dead," said Kanlee. He was well-rested but saw another long day ahead. The *Cardiff Cloud*, as a four-stacked, hydrojet steam clipper with a very limited cargo hold, was much faster than most cargo ships. He calculated that the *Cardiff Cloud* by now had passed the halfway point to Nagasaki even if Berwick had it running at less than full speed to conserve coal.

"And last night was…?

"Behind us now." Kanlee decided he needed some strong tea and whatever breakfast Amanda could persuade Captain Berwick to share.

"Well, really." Put out, Amanda threw off the covers and stood, her black hair mussed. She marched away naked, her waist trim, her rear swaying, and her legs slender and toned. "Meiping? I must use the head."

Distant shouts from the crew reached Kanlee just moments before a high-pitched ship's alarm sounded loud and long.

Kanlee, also naked, leaped out of bed and looked out the window, which faced astern. Huge bubbles were rising to the surface of the waves in the distance, coming close in a long line through the center of the *Cardiff Cloud*'s wake. The ship's alarm was still screaming.

Amanda bumped up against him, still naked as she rose on tiptoe. "What's that, then? Bloody whale tallywags?"

"We have to get out there!" Kanlee turned and realized that Meiping, wearing her blue servant's gown as before, was holding out his suit trousers and underwear with her eyes averted. He snatched them and pulled them on, aware that she was smirking.

Amanda slipped her feet into her black, high-button shoes and gathered her clothes.

Kanlee grabbed the corked bottle of Talisker Scotch and tossed it to Meiping. "Come on!"

* * *

Kanlee led the way on deck, still buttoning his shirt with the Bloodfinder shoulder rig awkwardly in place over it, and found that ship's crew members were running and shouting to each other. Unlike the *Yellowsea Yank*, the *Cardiff Cloud* had no stern gun. Kanlee picked out Captain Berwick at a distance as he strode among the crew, pointing and yelling.

"Full speed, then!" Berwick shouted. "Full speed! Power up, to save your souls!"

Amanda stepped up next to Kanlee, holding her unlaced corset in place with one arm and clutching her skirt around her waist with the other hand. Her blonde wig, with its black lacquered hairpins, was tugged down tight.

Meiping, holding the Talisker in the crook of one arm, brought Amanda's skirt into position and fastened it.

"Kanlee, look!" Amanda waited as Meiping drew her blue bodice into place, then took his arm and pointed.

Ah Jin's crew had the balloon basket in a small open area on the deck amidship. The coal burner was blazing and the balloon had begun to swell and rise from the deck with hot air.

Kanlee shrugged into his suit coat and draped his tie around his neck.

The giant steel head of the Sea Dragon broke the surface in a huge geyser. The great mouth opened on its multi-jointed hinges, dark and cavernous.

As before, Kanlee saw silhouettes lined up inside the dragon mouth, men with their hair in queues and holding rifles.

Behind the dragon head, Kanlee saw the long, serpentine shape with the upper arches of its curves above the waves. Steam billowed with black smoke, trailing into the sky. He had never cared much about politics in China, but now he knew that the Sea Dragon was captained by a minister of the emperor, of the conquering Manchu dynasty.

"Hang on!" Kanlee pulled Amanda and Meiping down with him into a crouch.

The dragon mouth slammed down on the stern of *Cardiff Cloud*.

"More steam!" Berwick yelled. "More steam, you bloody fools!" He turned to one of his officers. "Break out the small arms and get them to the men!"

The dragon mouth opened wider, then chomped down hard and hung on.

Kanlee looked for Fan Feitou at the top of the dragon head. Again, the tall man wore a long gown with splits on four sides and a yellow mandarin jacket with an upright collar at the neck and wide, short sleeves. He had on the same roundish, rattan cap with a ruby-red knob on top and an ostrich feather angling down the back.

"Amanda! That must be the Fan fellow."

She hurried forward, holding her skirt with one hand. When she looked, her mouth dropped open. "I don't know who he is — but that's the cap and clothing of a very high-placed imperial minister. I always read the newspapers in Shanghai, you see? And I've seen descriptions of the robes—"

As the dragon mouth clung to the stern, the men inside came jogging out, carrying their rifles with their queues trailing behind them. They wore black and red caps, blue coats, and gray trousers. They were Chinese soldiers in the service of the Manchu emperor.

"Run!" Kanlee yelled. He grabbed Amanda's arm in one hand and Meiping's in the other.

Crew members of the *Cardiff Cloud* began firing their random assortment of rifles, muskets, and pistols from wherever they were around the ship.

Kanlee heard the attackers shooting back, but he was focused on Ah Jin's balloon crew. The balloon had risen, drawing the ropes tight, but the basket was just beginning to lift from the deck.

"Ah Jin!" Kanlee shouted.

"Ah ho! Ah ho!" The balloon crew began their chant.

"Fast!" Ah Jin called in Hoisanese, reaching out.

Kanlee hooked one arm around Amanda's waist and swung her up into the arms of a crew member. Then he lifted Meiping into the arms of another crew member. As the basket rose the first few feet, Ah Jin threw out the rope ladder. Kanlee grabbed the ropes, stepped onto the ladder, and climbed aboard.

"That way!" Kanlee called out in Hoisanese, pointing toward the open sea.

"But the ship!" Amanda shouted in the same language. "We have to help them!"

Meiping looked at Kanlee and Amanda, reluctant to speak.

"We have to get away," Kanlee yelled back, watching the gunfight on the deck just below them. "It won't take much for them to shoot this balloon down."

"We will have the advantage of height," said Ah Jin.

Kanlee swung around toward him, surprised. "You want to stay here and fight?"

"Fan Feitou is no friend to us," said Ah Jin.

"You want to face that gunfire?" Kanlee demanded.

"What if the *Cardiff Cloud* is captured?" Amanda pushed between them, facing Kanlee. "What if the Sea Dragon takes the next closest ship, then the next one after that? We'll have nowhere to land."

"If we're shot down, we won't need a place to land." Kanlee glared at Amanda.

Meiping busied herself tidying Amanda's clothing rather than joining the argument.

As the balloon continued to lift the basket higher, the Sea Dragon's soldiers moved across the deck of the *Cardiff Cloud*, spreading out and shooting at the crew of the cargo ship.

Kanlee reminded himself again that this Fan fellow was a highly placed minister to the foreign dynasty that had conquered China some centuries ago. He had never thought much about political matters.

Amanda placed one hand on his arm. "*Yellowsea Yank* Yank?"

Kanlee looked into her eyes and pulled the Bloodfinder from his shoulder holster. "Take me in range of that dragon head."

Ah Jin shouted new instructions to his crew members, who were already pedaling hard. He grabbed the big air rudder himself and slowly steered the balloon away from the *Cardiff Cloud* on the wind. Then he began to circle back toward the great steel head of the Sea Dragon.

"What are you doing?" Amanda asked in English.

Kanlee held up the Bloodfinder. "It's all I have."

Amanda released his arm and stepped back, drawing Meiping with her, to give him room.

Kanlee eyed the tremendous length of the steel serpent, its alternating curves arching upward from the water and then back down again, out of sight. He looked all the way to the multi-pronged tail as Ah Jin brought the balloon along a successful arc behind the dragon head.

No one on board the Sea Dragon was watching them.

On the *Cardiff Cloud*, the roar of the steam engines, the splashing of the waves against the hulls, and scattered gunfire drew everyone else's attention. The Chinese soldiers gradually drove back or shot down the cargo ship's crew members.

Kanlee had to hurry, because he needed enough of the crew left alive to control the ship. He waited as Ah Jin and his crew lowered the basket slowly behind and above the imperial minister.

As Kanlee readied his Bloodfinder with a full load, he examined his target with curiosity. The man remained fearless, unmoving as he watched the events in front of him on the *Cardiff Cloud*. He neither turned nor leaned forward, but his presence surely must have frightened any crew members of the *Cardiff Cloud* who knew of him.

Kanlee steadied his gun arm on the edge of the basket. In a moment, he would come up close behind Fan Feitou, from a direction in which the minister had not turned since Kanlee had been watching. With the motion of the balloon basket and the movement of the Sea Dragon on the waves, the shot would be difficult and he expected to have only a few chances before the minister would drop down out of sight.

Maybe the wind shifted slightly, carrying sound in a different direction. Perhaps the minister thought he saw a shadow off to one side, possibly from a cloud. In any case, he turned himself around in a stiff motion and then looked up.

Now Kanlee was near enough to call out if he had wished, though he had nothing to say.

Conversely, Minister Fan could have shouted to any of his crew who remained on the Sea Dragon. Instead, Fan Feitou looked up at the basket swaying on long ropes below the hot air balloon and did not react.

Matching his stare, Kanlee looked into the eyes of Minister Fan and found them hard, yet without shine, as though he had no tears.

Kanlee couldn't afford to worry about it. He took careful aim at the minister's chest and fired three shots, bang-bang-bang.

Fan Feitou shook with the impact of each bullet but did not fall. Nor did he frown, scowl, or stagger.

"One more shot," said Amanda, in a surprisingly calm tone. Kanlee aimed carefully just below Fan Feitou's neck and squeezed the trigger. An explosion of metal sprang out, throwing springs, gears, bolts, nuts, screws, and small levers in all directions. As the parts flew through the air, Kanlee finally understood.

"A Vaucanson," Amanda said in a bitter voice. "Not as active as Lyman's, but surely more convincing as a human."

Ah Jin steered the balloon away fast, but both groups of men on the *Cardiff Cloud* shouted and pointed. The men from the Sea Dragon turned and fled back to the dragon mouth. Within a few moments, they had departed the *Cardiff Cloud*, less the ones who were dead or wounded. The huge steel dragon mouth released the stern of the cargo ship after the men had returned, then clamped shut.

Kanlee watched as the big serpentine ship dropped beneath the waves.

"Are they really gone?" Amanda asked.

Kanlee waved a hand at the empty water. Some of Fan Feitou's parts—the smaller, flat metal pieces and some shreds of clothing—drifted on the water. "Maybe they didn't know the minister was a Vaucanson. I think they're going back to their home port, wherever that is."

"Not Shanghai, or Lyman would have heard," said Amanda. "Tianjin, maybe, near Beijing. Or a port to the south."

Ah Jin was already directing his crew to land again on the deck of the *Cardiff Cloud*. Within a few moments, the basket touched the deck.

Kanlee threw out the rope ladder, descended, and then helped Amanda and Meiping climb down.

Across the deck, crew members were helping the wounded and covering the dead. Several stopped to point at Kanlee and talk among themselves.

Captain Berwick came striding up to Amanda, his face distorted with righteous anger. "Miss Wellstone! Did I not warn you last night? That this ship is no place for a lady such as yourself?"

Kanlee remained silent in his role as Amanda's bodyguard, but was alert to Berwick's bad temper.

Amanda drew herself up, ignoring a tear in the front of her blue bodice that made it even more revealing than before. "I congratulate you, Captain Berwick. You and your crew acquitted yourselves in an excellent manner. I feel safe in your care."

Berwick paused, apparently surprised by her compliments. "Aye, well, Miss Wellstone, the fact remains..." He stopped, apparently searching for words.

Kanlee stifled a smile at his predicament.

"I shall commend you to my brother Lyman," said Amanda. "How long until we reach Nagasaki?"

Berwick seemed to weigh his options and let his temper go. He cleared his throat. "Ah, well, at this speed, only another half day, I should think."

"Captain, I was awakened quite suddenly this morning. I am deeply grateful for your hospitality in offering your quarters. May I — pardon my being so forward, but may I be your guest for breakfast? I fancy tea, you see?"

Berwick frowned. "I have much to do, Miss Wellstone, with wounded and dead among my crew. I fear I must tend to my duties."

"I should not wish to add to your burdens, Captain. Perhaps you would like me to be out of your way, in the officers' mess?"

Berwick hesitated only a moment. "Of course, Miss Wellstone. I shall be honored to take you to the officers' mess before I return to my duties."

"And my bodyguard and handmaid shall join me, of course."

"Indeed, Miss Wellstone." Berwick offered his arm. "May I?"

"Thank you, Captain Berwick." Amanda took his arm and walked with him.

Meiping walked behind Amanda as a dutiful handmaid, still carrying Berwick's bottle of Talisker Scotch hidden in the crook of one arm as her looped braids swayed in the breeze.

Kanlee took a moment to watch the East China Sea behind the ship, as the wake spread out behind it. Somewhere in the deep, the Sea Dragon was still lurking.

For now, his contribution to resisting the emperor would have to do. After all, he was hungry.

As though she could hear his thoughts, Meiping turned and tossed him the Talisker.

As Kanlee caught the bottle, he saw his cousin smiling with amusement. He uncorked the bottle and took a long swig to start breakfast.

About the Author

William F. Wu has had over sixty short stories published in the science fiction and fantasy fields and thirteen novels by major New York houses. He adapted his novel *Hong on the Range* for a three-issue, closed-end comic book from Image Comics in the 1990s.

A six-time nominee for the Hugo, Nebula, and World Fantasy Awards, Wu is a news editor in Palmdale, California. He was born and raised in the Kansas City area, and educated at the University of Michigan. He lives in Palmdale with his wife, Fulian Wu, and their son Alan. For more information, see WilliamFWu.com.

Doubleplusunhate

by George Donnelly

A father in an Orwellian future teaches his precocious son Oldspeak — until his wife discovers their crimethink.

"I love you, Dad."

Marshal turned from his portscreen and looked at the boy. Unspeak. The rigid seat back pushed the thin slice of metal into his buttock. He pulled himself up from a slouch and looked back to his portscreen.

The boy climbed onto Marshal's lap. He knocked the portscreen from Marshal's hands and it clattered to the bare cement floor. Anger rose within him. "Doubleplusun—"

The boy stared up at Marshal. His smile was wide and mischievous. Marshal studied his face. The deep blue eyes, the round face, the wide smile — Liker. Like... me.

Marshal jerked his head back as the realization struck him. "Doubleplusunhate. Doubleplusunhate Jak." He grabbed the boy and hugged him tight. Jak wrapped his thin sticks of arms around his father's neck. A jumble of emotions stirred in Marshal's gut but one word percolated to the top: defense.

* * *

"Jak forgetted goodpharm morewise. Ungood!" The woman smacked the back of her hand across Jak's face. Behind them was a gray wall. A small

97

window provided limited access to the steel city behind them. The buildings followed one another in silence, none reaching higher than the other.

Jake's face turned red. He tilted his head to one side and swallowed. He looked at Marshal. Marshal sat against the wall at the tiny kitchen table. He faced the window but kept his eyes to his portscreen.

"Hate!" yelled Jak. "Hate! Doubleplushate! Goodpharm ungood. Kill me, inner me. No! No morewise." He turned to his father. "Dad. Tell her."

His mother grabbed the boy by the shoulders and twisted him until he stood with his back to her. She pushed him towards the door. "Learnplace unlater, Jak! Go!"

"Dad," said Jak. His face fell and the beginnings of a frown formed around his mouth and eyes.

His mother glanced at Marshal. Her eyes were red and swollen. Her hands shook. She cleared her throat, grabbed Jak's bag from the floor and jammed it into his chest. She pushed him and he fell to the ground.

"Dad, please." Jak looked up at him from the floor. Water welled up and over his eyelids.

Marshal sighed. He put down the portscreen. The memory flashed in his mind. Jak's eyes. Unhateful. Knowwantingful. Unfrowning. Goodpharm ungave it. Goodpharm unlived Jak's... Marshal searched for the word. He imagined a ball of swirling, cereal-colored light inside of Jak. Soul. The Oldspeak came to him. His eyes darted from side to side and his forehead broke out in a sweat.

"Hate uncontrolled Jak! Hate Oldspeak!" yelled Jak's mother. She looked at Marshal. Her face was taut. She raised her chin and sneered. "Marshal crimethink." She nodded to herself. "Marshal unperson. Ownlife ungood. Oldspeak forbidded." She arched an eyebrow and took a step towards the door.

Time stopped for Marshal. He planned this day. He didn't want it but he expected it. He loved Johness. She once had Jak's same smile. But he loved Jak more. Why did I have to teach Jak Oldspeak? The feeling of the archaic language in his mind shocked him but he knew the answer.

"Joycamp fixwill Jak," said Johness. "Fixwill." She laid her hand on the doorknob.

Marshal stood up and threw his portscreen at the wall next to Johness. He was behind her. Marshal pulled the hunk of pointed metal from his back pocket and pushed it into the side of her neck. He stepped away from her and she fell backwards with a dull thud. Crimson liquid pooled on the gray floor next to her wriggling body.

Marshal thought back five years ago to when he first encountered the Oldpseak book in the domicile of a prole unperson. "Dictionary," it said in silver letters against a navy blue cover. The sharp, dry pages of forgotten words stirred an unexpected need in him. He steeled his resolve. Doubleplushate crimethink ungood. Ownlife. An ugly word. He translated it into Oldspeak. My own life. Jak's own life. He took in a rapid breath as the image of a tree sparked in his mind.

"We go." He pulled the boy up from the floor.

Jak's chest convulsed. "Mom," he whispered. Her body was still. He leaned down and caressed her cheek. "I love you."

A man scowled at them in the doorway. Jak startled and the man saw Johness's body. His eyes went big and he took a step back.

Marshal kneeled down next to his wife's dead body. He extracted the makeshift knife. He ran to the door and forced the shiny metal deep into the man's chest. The man fell back into the corner and stared at the floor. Marshal reached for Jak's hand.

Jak took a step back. His mouth hung open and he shook his head.

Marshal grabbed Jak's upper arm and looked him in the eye. "Freedom, Jak. Freedom! Forest. New life. Unforget!"

* * *

"Slowful walk. Unfacecrime. Inair." Marshal smoothed out the wrinkles in Jak's shirt and pushed his hair to one side. "Untense." The sidewalk was crowded.

Jak nodded and let his breath out fast. His pace accelerated.

"Slowful." Marshal scrunched up his face then let the muscles fall.

Freedom. He stared straight ahead and made for the movestop in lockstep with Jak.

At the movestop, a group gathered. People and transports streamed in all directions. Crowds gathered for the quick morning ration in a sprawling square cornerwise from him. Big Brother's cartoonish visage streamed from building to building in a digital display of omnipresence. People dressed in white, silver, tan and sky blue laid eyes on him. Facecrime! He raged at himself for his lapse.

The white transport eased to a stop in front of them. The doors slid open. Marshal redoubled his grip on Jak's small hand. His heart leapt with joy and he struggled to contain his ungood emotion.

"Killer!" The ragged voice came from behind him. "Unproceed killer Marshal."

Marshal froze. Jak's grip tightened and trembled. Marshal sneered at his own incompetence.

"Killer unproceed. Thinkpol come," said the neighbor. The giant screens on the buildings changed. Big Brother's face appeared larger now. His eyes raged and a giant finger pointed down at Marshal.

The crowd formed into lines and moved away from the pair. The square fell silent. Passengers filed out of the back door of the transport. The front doors closed mere centimeters from Marshal's nose.

"Dad. I love you."

Marshal didn't want to look down at his boy but he steeled himself. His heart crushed. Gravity pulled hard at the boy's eyes and mouth. I doed crimethink. I doed... did this. He imagined the boy in joycamp.

No. The thought catalyzed a chain reaction of decision within him. Marshal whipped around and shook a finger at his accuser. "Oldthinker!" he yelled. He narrowed his eyes and strode towards the older man. "Blackwhite ungoodpharm oldthinker bewill unperson!"

The man staggered back, his eyes wide. "No," he whispered. "Doubleplusgood duckspeaker. Ingsoc bellyfeel."

Marshal turned and ran down the block. They turned left, ran down another block and the crowds were there again. They boarded a transport and stared straight ahead. Marshal rubbed his thumb into the palm of Jak's hand. Bewill good. Bewill good.

About the Author

Rebel. Troublemaker. Accused terrorist. Idealist. When not dreaming up new rebel heroes, **George Donnelly** hikes and bikes Colombian mountains and unschools his 8-year-old son Clark (who is named after Superman but actually likes Batman way better). George is from Pennsylvania but has lived in Chicago, Osaka, Kobe, Bogota and Medellín, too. He's a firm believer in human rights, universal fairness and abundant hugs before bedtime. He's got two rescued kittens on the payroll as well. Connect with him at GeorgeDonnelly.com.

Get Kidd to Bounty

by Jack McDonald Burnett

When a freezing fugitive enters her life, war veteran Karren Considine is faced with a deadly choice.

Karren Considine raised her beer bottle to the *shit-fucking goddamn Government*. She even took a pull when the other five drank. Her boundaries were the weaker for the two beers she'd had before the present one. Still, she resisted anything more demonstrative than the camaraderie fellow drinkers could expect in a gloomy pub. She wouldn't herself propose a toast to the *shit-fucking goddamn Government*, in irony. Or, for that matter, otherwise. But it was best not to dwell on her feelings about the Government that evening.

The pub was dark and sullen. There were lights over the bar itself: hot lights, after a while, she could attest. She'd repaired to a small two-person table, one of the tall ones with the tall chairs, because the lights over the bar had been so hot. It was below freezing out and winter howled at the pub door, but there was warmth enough at her table. She didn't need to be baked at the bar.

The decor was wooden, with all the variety that suggested. Wooden tables and chair backs, wooden floor showing the grain and smelling like peanut shells and spilled beer, dura-plast outer walls made to look like the same wood as the floors. The padding on the back of the booths and the back of the chairs was a faded maroon, and not all the same shade. It was someplace to eat pub food at mealtime, and someplace to drink when you'd had a shitty day.

Karren shared the pub that night with a party of three, there specifically to bitch about the Government, and a party of two, one of whom, Karren gathered, had lost her job that day. The now-unemployed woman and her companion were lending their full-throated accompaniment to the first party's bitching about the Government during recent rounds. The woman must have worked for the Government, or for some outfit with a Government contract — oh, hell. It could be just about anything. She might have lost her job because of over-regulation. Karren could speak with some authority about over-regulation. She could also speak with authority about other ways the Government can make your life a little bit worse. Not that she would, in public.

"I lost my job today," the woman said to the pub. Karren suppressed a self-congratulatory smile, and waited to find out why. "Gover'ment says my company has to pay me a certain amount, an' health insurance. They can't afford it no more. I tol' 'em, I'll work for less, an' no insurance, but they're not allowed. So I get nothin'." The party of three thought this was the worst thing they'd ever heard, to go by the expletives they let fly. Another toast to the *shit-fucking goddamn Government*. Karren took a more discreet pull, this time.

"How about you?" one of the party of three said. Karren flushed, hoping they weren't talking to her — but of course, they were.

"Just having a beer," she said.

"Just having a beer," the man said. "What do you do for a living? May I ask?"

Karren sighed, but didn't make a show of it. "AI horses," she said. "Repair and maintenance."

One of the other men in the party of three said, "Robot horses! Holy shit. You must be about the only one does that."

"Around here," she said.

"Get a lot of Government work?"

She breathed in and out. "No, hardly any. Mostly the other side of the law from them."

"Other side. You talking about criminals? German Trotter and his thugs?"

"'S right," she said. Was she slurring a little?

"Why them? I mean, why they like the robot horses?"

"It's so they can shoot," the unemployed woman's companion chimed in. "Can't shoot a gun from a sled, you'll fall off."

"Is that why?"

Karren thought better of answering, but then did anyway. "Might be part of it. Biggest reason is AI horses ain't gotta be chipped."

There was intake of breath from two of the party of three. "I hadn't thought of that! Holy shit. That's something. They use robot — sorry, AI horses because they can't be tracked. I would never have thought of that."

"So, you pretty much have a Government-proof business, don't you?" his buddy said.

"I wish," she said.

"Why do you say that?"

She had vowed not to get into this. Not out loud. But here it came. "Because they passed a new law. Just found out today. I gotta install a chip on every horse I service, starting in a week and a half."

There was silence, for several beats. Then, a general commotion, punctuated with commiserating talk.

"That might make AI horses kind of less popular," someone observed.

Karren snorted. She raised her nearly-empty bottle high in the air. "To the Government," she said, resigned to toasting.

The others ignored her lack of adjectives, and chorused, "to the *shit-fucking goddamn Government!*"

* * *

Later on, the bartender put some news on. There would be nothing there about the new law that was going to sink Karren's business and ruin her livelihood — there was trade sanctions against the settlement on the moon, there was Justice trying to run down a fugitive, there was Patriot Day celebrations, thoroughly organized and heavily scripted. All more important than some one-off law about chipping AI horses. Karren was grateful. She didn't want to think about it, and that meant she didn't want to hear about it, either.

Karren left shortly after the news was done, before the man and the unemployed woman, but after the party of three. One of the three had hit on her first. She thought it was sweet, but it was also alcohol-induced. The man — boy, really — was in his early, maybe mid–20s, with barely a reason to shave every day. Karren's mostly unattended dark hair already had some grays in it, at 33. By the time she'd been the boy's age, she'd been a Marine corporal, and that seemed like a lifetime and a whole war ago. She could have babysat him twenty years ago. She was unwilling to do so tonight. She had some feeling sorry for herself to do, back at home. She let him down easy.

She shuffled out into the icy wind, which had picked up considerably during her drinking. She wound the scarf she'd had hanging limply over her shoulders around the lower half of her face, tucking the remainder over her shoulder to keep her neck warm, too. She slipped, but righted herself — ice, already. Roads and walks in Surfeit generally weren't heated. Just plain dura-plast, which iced up pretty quick. Despite the wind and cold, she was glad she had walked. She didn't own a sled — bad for business, people seeing her scooting around a foot off the ground. Her own AI horse — a heavily-modified, Frankenstein hunk of junk, but reliable transportation anywhere the ground wasn't frozen — was safe and warm at home.

The pub was opposite a train station. After the war, Karren had come to Surfeit because it was the kind of place where people got around by walking and by train, by lococycle and by Wheelhaus. By sleds, which were still earthbound, really, when you got down to it. And, of course, by AI horse. Firmly on the ground, in any case. Surfeit's sky was empty, most of the time. The odd vehicle overhead, almost always going from one more crowded place to another. You stopped in Surfeit if you lived there. You usually didn't if you didn't.

Cold as it was, it was clear, and there were no fewer than three moons in the sky. One whose disk was about the size of a dime, two that were blobs of reflected light.

There ought to be but one more train that night, she thought, checking the time. There had been one only a few minutes before, which the boy and his party had likely caught. She felt a pang of missed opportunity. Why did she always have to be so sensible? She could have brought a twenty-something guy home with her that night. She could just as easily have felt sorry for herself when he was asleep, or gone. She had always "saved" sex for relationships involving other intimacies. Seeing as how she had determined not to start any relationships for the foreseeable future, she could have indulged herself this once.

Her mood was more sour now than when she'd ordered her first beer.

She crossed the tracks, and on the other side, short of the platform, there was a canvas or cloth bag, left behind by somebody. Karren didn't envy whomever had dropped it on their way onto the train, having to come back for it, if they even knew for sure where they'd—

It wasn't a bag, it was a person. Collapsed, from the looks of it on his way to the platform, balled up in a vain attempt to stay warm. No jacket, no scarf, no boots.

* * *

She hurried over to the man.

He was alive, but he was barely even shivering anymore. His eyes were closed, a tortured look on his face. The lines were distinct, making him look about late 30s. He had mousy brown hair past a well-receded hairline. He was dressed in a flannel long-sleeve shirt, denim pants, walking shoes with white socks.

She had to get him someplace warm. Her house and garage were a ten-minute walk. She scooped the man up and turned back to the pub. She hadn't been obsessive about fitness since she was in the Corps, but the man was on the small side. She could feel the cold of his body through her jacket. She wanted to check his hands, but they were tucked into his long sleeves, and she didn't want to uncover them 'til they were warm in the pub.

Presently they arrived back at the pub. The man and unemployed woman were still there. She called for a towel from the bartender, and blankets, layers. The bartender hurried into the back and then reemerged with towels and a blanket. Karren propped the man up in a seat at a table. He was conscious, had awoken groggily during their walk back to the pub. The man's shoes were frozen, but his socks still soaked through. Karren carefully removed them and dried the feet. That towel, now damp, she set aside. Ice had also stuck to his clothes when he'd been prone on the ground and as it melted, it got the clothes wet. Karren didn't think that was as urgent as his extremities.

She wrapped a second towel around the man's head, carefully drying his ears — his hair had collected ice as well. She had him take his hands out of his sleeves, and she dried them and wrapped them in a third towel. "Do you have one more towel?" she asked the bartender. He hurried into the back again.

The man was sucking in breath through clenched teeth, no doubt from the feeling returning to his hands. Karren asked him what had happened. His teeth chattered and he shivered violently, which Karren knew was a good thing; it meant he was warming up. He shook his head. Karren draped the blanket over his shoulders, and he drew it tightly around himself.

The bartender arrived with another towel, and Karren made to wrap the man's feet. Instead, the man tried to stand. "I don't think that's a good idea, pal," she said, but he was up and staggering toward the bar. He didn't get very far before he sank to his hands and knees and began to crawl instead. Good that he wasn't trying to walk on possibly frost-bitten feet, but what was he doing?

As four people stared at him curiously, the man dragged himself toward the side of the bar. "What do you need, buddy?" the bartender asked. The man didn't reply, instead rounding the bar and crawling behind it. It became apparent the door to the back kitchen and storage area was his goal.

The bartender protested, but it was so strange to see the man doing this, nearly frozen to death, that nobody moved.

Finally, Karren made her way to the side of the bar, intending to help the man or find out what he wanted. As she reached the side of the bar, in walked three Justice cops in full armor. They always wore full armor while on duty, but you still noticed — that was the point. Karren stole a glance in the direction of the crawling man, and he had almost, but not quite, made it through the door to the back. She turned her attention to the new arrivals.

Two cops wore all-black, stretch-tight material over bulky padding at the shoulders and elbows, midsection and thighs and shins. The other had the same getup, with a scarlet stripe from his shoulder to his opposite hip. They each had helmets with opaque face plates. One of the all-black cops lifted his up. He was a doughy, chubby-cheeked boy, the kind who tries to catch on with Justice because with Justice, nobody makes fun of him.

"Looking for a man, late 30s, about a hundred and sixty-five centimeters, thinning hair, big forehead. Probably had a flannel shirt and denim on. Seen him around?"

Karren looked at the man and the unemployed woman, and then they three all looked at the bartender.

"Ain't been in here today," he said. "Got a card or somebody I can call?"

"Just call Justice. Anyone who answers will be able to help you. That goes for you three, too."

The scarlet-striped cop had begun to stride slowly but deliberately around the pub. Everybody watched him, including his two fellow Justice cops. He ducked down the hall leading to the restrooms. They heard both doors creak open. He reemerged and headed for the bar.

Karren knew why he had the scarlet stripe. His name was Makepeace, a Sergeant. He was the highest-ranking person in Justice who wasn't a paper pusher. If their freezing friend had attracted the attention of Sergeant Makepeace, hiding him was a bigger deal than any of them thought.

Karren wasn't rightly sure why she hadn't spoken up that she'd seen the man. If nothing else, the Justice people would take care of his hypothermia and potential frostbite. It was just that she thought of the man crawling toward the back room, presumably knowing these cops were coming for him. Maybe he'd raped and killed a woman. She doubted it very much, but it was possible. It was also possible that he'd nearly frozen himself to death and dragged himself across the dirty pub floor because being apprehended by the Justice cops wouldn't be justice at all.

Whatever. If Makepeace found the shivering man, he would bring his wrath down on the bartender, not her. Whatever horrors Justice and the Government visited on its citizens were none of her concern. She'd earned her peace and quiet in life fighting for that very Government, and if the bartender or anybody else didn't like it, they should have fought at her side.

The bartender was a little shifty as Makepeace approached the bar. He rounded it and looked behind it.

"Don't suppose you have a warrant?" Karren said. It just came out. She wasn't in the mood to defer to Government authority after the day she'd had.

The unbidden words chilled her as they lingered over the bar. They had been retrieved from a memory of years ago, the last time she'd said it.

Makepeace turned his head so his faceplate faced Karren. He glared at her (presumably) for a moment, then slapped the bar, making Karren jump, as intended. She darkened. Makepeace patted the bar, gently now.

"This place," pat, pat, " is open to the public," Makepeace said. Since he didn't raise his faceplate, the voice had a mechanical echo.

"That part of it isn't," Karren said. She kept her eyes on Makepeace's faceplate, but at the corner of her eye she saw the bartender squirm a little.

Makepeace regarded her for a few more beats, then he opened the door to the back. He peered inside. After forever, it seemed to Karren (and probably the bartender as well), he released the door and let it shut.

He turned to Karren again. "Thank you for your service during the war, Ms. Considine," he said. Justice cops could pick up your identity, and just about anything else, from your fone. That she had fought in the war would have taken a GovStream query, though. The hairs on the back of Karren's neck stood up. "I'd be out of a job, if it weren't for veterans like you." He rejoined the other two cops as Karren flushed. The woman who had lost her job was looking at her sourly.

"This suspect is dangerous, even if he doesn't seem so at first," the cop with a face said. He was staring down the bartender. Karren thought the bartender might crack, and say the man was in his back room. But he didn't. "Make sure you let us know if you see him."

That seemed like the trio's cue to leave, but Makepeace chimed in. "Justice is authorized to use any means, including deadly force, to prevent obstruction of one of its operations," he said. "Business owner, bystander, Marine Corps veteran, it doesn't matter. Think hard about turning our fugitive in if you should encounter him." Hard to tell, but Karren thought Makepeace glanced at her one more time before the three turned and left.

Don't suppose you have a warrant. Justice had answered that question years ago by hauling off someone dear to her, right out of her own home. Someone she should have protected.

Someone who would still be with her if she could manage to keep her mouth shut.

Karren exchanged another look with the bartender. Then she rounded the bar and opened the door to the kitchen. She immediately spied the blanket she'd put over the freezing man, looking like it covered a pile of... something. The man was balled up under it. She knelt down and told him the Justice cops had come and gone. He rose to his knees, teeth still chattering. The towels around his head and hands were still there, but loose.

"Did they ask you about me?" His speech was clipped. Part of it was how cold he was. Part of it wasn't.

Hunched down, Karren circled the man's shoulders with her arm to lend him support if he wanted to stand. He stiffened.

"I would rather that you didn't touch me, please," he said, urgently, in that clipped cadence. That convinced Karren: he was Spectrum. Repulsed by touch, monotone speaking voice, and he'd yet to make eye contact with her. She backed away, and now knowing what she knew she saw on his wrist the tell-tale cloth medic-bracelet with a charm on it worn by sufferers of certain medical disorders. She couldn't make out what was on the charm, but she had no doubt it identified him as Spectrum.

"Sorry. I see the bracelet, now," she said. She rose, and the man got to his feet, unsteadily, but she didn't try to hold him up. He began to stagger back out into the pub. She trailed behind him.

He sat at a table and tightened the towel around his head. Karren sat across from him, and helped wrap his hands back up. "You need to wrap your feet up," she told him. He nodded, and Karren went and fetched that towel. Two towels on the floor by an unoccupied table — it was a wonder the Justice cops hadn't noticed, or hadn't thought it was suspicious.

"What happened?" Karren asked.

"Civil disobedience," the man said. He introduced himself as Kidd. Michael Kidd.

The man and the unemployed woman left. The bartender shrugged and said he was closing for the night. Karren asked if he had any room for Kidd to stay and stay warm for the night. The bartender glared at her. "I'd like to keep my pub, and myself out of jail," he said.

"I have room," Karren said to Kidd, "but getting there is the issue. It's a ten, fifteen minute walk. Fifteen in this weather."

"What if they come there looking for me?"

"You hide," she said.

Karren asked the bartender if he at least had a sled or a Wheelhaus she could borrow. She'd bring it back first thing. The bartender said they could borrow his Wheelhaus, drop Kidd off, she could bring it back, then walk herself back home. It was much better than the notion of having to walk Kidd to her place, so she agreed, gratefully.

They rode to her place, Kidd making himself unseen as possible. Karren went in with Kidd and showed him where everything was. He was to sit still on the couch, warming up beneath that blanket and those towels, 'til she got back. When Karren took the Wheelhaus back the bartender asked after his blanket and towels, and Karren promised she would return them the next day.

When she reached her place again and came inside, Kidd had been a good forty-five minutes under the blanket and towels, and he was grateful to be able to take them off. Karren thought it quaint that he'd kept them on after they'd become uncomfortable, but when you were Spectrum, you were very literal, very detailed, very rules-oriented.

Karren wanted to know the details of Kidd's "civil disobedience," but Kidd wasn't offering. He said he wanted to take the train to the next province over, Bounty, where he would be safe. Karren was skeptical, first, of the idea he'd be safe in Bounty. Different local Justice department, but there was no good reason Bounty cops wouldn't hand him over to Surfeit's if they happened upon him. And no reason Bounty's Justice cops wouldn't hunt him down themselves, come to that, if Kidd was "wanted" badly enough in Surfeit.

For now, he was safe, and warming up. It looked as though there wouldn't be any lasting damage to Kidd's hands or feet. They worked out how and where he would hide if there came a knock on the door, and Karren left him on her loveseat to fall asleep or not as he wished.

For her part, Karren had difficulty sleeping. Twice she dozed only to be roused by what she thought was a knock on her door. That was preferable, she decided, to the times she heard knocking at her door in her dreams, and didn't wake up out of them.

* * *

The next morning, Karren was able to tease some details out of Kidd.

"We were protesting," he told her. "When you're Spectrum the Government can commit you to HealthCare for what they call 're-education.' Most of the time, you never come out." To Karren's mind, that brought into question the effectiveness of the "re-education."

"I've seen Spectrums here in Surfeit before," Karren said. "They don't seem to be hiding."

"Keep out of trouble and they'll let you be," Kidd said. "Protesting isn't keeping out of trouble, I guess. Protesting re-education gets you committed to HealthCare for re-education," Kidd said. The whole setup was chilling, and Karren could understand wanting to protest it.

"Justice broke us up and they were arresting everybody. Me and my two friends, we got away, got on the train headed to Bounty. But they were waiting for us a couple stops down the line. I lit out on foot while they were busy with my friends." The weather had turned even uglier, and Kidd had only made it as far as where Karren found him.

"Which in its way was lucky," she told him. "I guarantee they were watching the train. If you'd boarded it, assuming they didn't catch you in the act of doing that, they would have had you within a stop or two."

This prediction did not have its intended effect on Kidd. "I'm warmed back up and the weather is better," he said, as though Karren knew neither. "I need to get on the train and get to Bounty."

She remembered Makepeace's interest in Kidd. A man escaping from Justice cops trying to arrest him — would that be enough to get Makepeace personally interested? Maybe... But if Kidd boarded the train, it didn't matter whether it was Makepeace or a rookie Justice cop after him.

"You won't make it," she told him, finding herself getting frustrated. He was no concern of hers, now that he was saved from freezing to death, but she reeled at his unwillingness to believe he had to avoid the train if he wanted to avoid "re-education."

"Kidd— Michael? Michael, Justice is looking for you. Sergeant Makepeace is looking for you himself, and he only gets involved in priority cases," she guessed. She felt safe saying so. "They'll have people watching the train. That's where you were last night, and they'll figure someone with your— they'll figure that a Spectrum will try the train again. You'd be handing yourself over to them."

"I have to get to Bounty," he said simply.

"I understand that."

"I can't walk, it's too far. I have to take the train."

"Michael, quit thinking of the train as an option." But he wouldn't.

She let him go. She nodded at him in lieu of shaking his hand and wished him good luck, knowing it wouldn't do a damn bit of good, and let him go. Even told him which direction was the train station.

And that was that. At a certainty, Kidd would be picked up by

Makepeace and Justice, and that would be the last anyone would hear from Michael Kidd.

That, she could live with. She'd done more than her share of trying to convince him not to take the train. He'd made the choice to try it anyway. Whatever he got, he was earning.

Trouble was, all she could think about was Makepeace slapping that bar to startle her. Ten years earlier, when she was the one with the uniform, somebody did that to her he'd regret it. But not now, and not Makepeace. Now, Makepeace was getting exactly what he wanted. Makepeace was going to win.

Kidd wasn't out the door more than five minutes when she went after him. Coaxed him back into the garage and said she'd help him get to Bounty. She'd take him herself.

* * *

"How?" If not by train, Kidd meant.

She swept her arm around her garage. "Give me half an hour to get one of these running," she said, indicating three AI horses belonging to customers, in various stages of disassembly. "We'll go on horseback." Presented with a viable alternative to the train, Kidd agreed.

Karren had the one good winter jacket. She was small, one and a half meters, fifty-five kilograms. Kidd was small, too, compared to the average, but he had ten centimeters on her, and was broader by a little bit. She had a spare jacket for him that didn't fit. He would travel with the bartender's blanket draped over him instead.

They set out, each on a "robot horse," as the public inevitably called them — Kidd on a "loaner," her on her own machine. Steady in any terrain, the horses' feet took the measure of the ground before stepping, and learned just how long a step it needed to be. Legs could lengthen and shorten as necessary to keep the rider steady. There wasn't much of the bouncing up and down you would have with a live horse. You sat on the fuel tank, at least on Karren's and the one she had slapped back together for Kidd. You held on to a "mane" that was malleable, soft, and fit your hands.

The "head" of the things housed lights for night riding but otherwise just gave the machines the shape of real horses. The machines' AI brains were forward of the fuel tank, under riders' hands as they gripped the manes — where a real horse's heart would be. Keeping the "brains" out of the machine's extremities was safer — the things' heads stuck out like a target, same as real horses.

Kidd hadn't thanked her for the horse — not that it was hers to lend him, technically — but he did ask whose it was. "Customer," she told him. "A good one. Has what you might call an unofficial fleet. I've always got his spares, keeping them up for him."

"Did you ask if you could borrow it?"

She mumbled, "Wouldn't bother him with that," or words to that effect. She told herself, if not Kidd, that German Trotter would be all for her using one of his spare horses to help a fugitive from Justice, particularly Makepeace.

Yeah, right before he had her beaten soundly for "borrowing" his property.

They hadn't gone far, perhaps fifteen minutes, when it became clear to Karren that something had to be done about Kidd wearing the blanket. They were getting too many curious looks. She couldn't imagine anyone from the outskirts of her town running to Makepeace and Justice, but it was surely better to be inconspicuous than memorable.

Next town over, Crail, there was a consignment store. Karren had them stop and look for a winter jacket that would fit. They got lucky; there was one for sale, big on Kidd, but manageable. A dull orange, used for hunting, most likely. Karren said if he wanted, which he did, Kidd could ride with the blanket covering his legs.

Karren wasn't thrilled with how twitchy the owner of the consignment store seemed to be, nor her husband. They seemed anxious to have Karren and Kidd leave. When their transaction was complete, Karren led Kidd outside to the horses. She waited the time it took her to count to thirty, and then she marched back into the store. The owner was on the fone, and looked wide-eyed at Karren. Karren rolled her eyes and left again.

"Store owner called Justice on us," she said to Kidd. "We'll have to leave the road."

She led them up the slope north of Crail, the hard ground crumbling now and then under their hooves, tree cover starting to pick up. The mechanical noises the horses made got higher pitched as they went uphill, Karren imagining it was a protest of some kind. They turned and started east again at the edge of the woods, the borderland between the woods and the prairie the road and track cut through. If they were seen, it was a simple matter of turning left and heading into the forest, where the density of trees would let them get lost.

The woods north of the train tracks were God's own country. You could smell pine needles instead of dust and asphalt. The soil was more malleable, richer than the blasted moonscape the tracks and towns were built on. Plenty of shade. Plenty of green. Plenty of birds. Plenty — the very trait after which both Surfeit and Bounty were named. Standing in the middle of Crail, it was easy to think the names were ironic.

They rode in spotty tree cover until Karren judged that they'd gone as far as the next station east of Crail. They emerged from the woods and there it was, due south. The slope north of Crail had become gentler, and they weren't as far above this station as last. This one didn't have what you would call a town associated with it. There were settlements some ways to the south, which was the idea behind a stop there. Karren held up a fist to stop them, then dug out a pair of binoculars.

Through the glass she saw what she feared — a Justice cop with a slash of scarlet on his uniform. He was in the company of three other cops. They had come upon the train platform. They had dismounted and were no doubt asking the people within the station's orbit whether they had seen Karren and Kidd, complete with detailed descriptions. The manpower Makepeace was using to get Kidd back staggered her. But she knew enough about him to guess he would consider a fugitive a personal insult.

Karren thought real hard about pointing Kidd in the right direction and telling him to ride to the mountains, cross them through the valley the train track knifed through, and there, you'd be in Bounty. The horse he was riding wasn't hers, though. How would she get it back, if she didn't lead it? Should she give him her machine? That wasn't an option.

And there was more to it than that. She believed Kidd's story, saw how Kidd struggled to express himself and untrack his mind when he got to thinking of something like taking the train. Leaving him to get caught by Justice wouldn't be just. The man didn't need "re-education." He could make his way just fine in the same world as everyone else, as long as everyone had a little patience with him.

To top it off, leaving him in the hands of Makepeace wouldn't be just. And it wouldn't sit with Karren anyhow.

You go ahead and slap that bar one more time, she thought in his direction.

Kidd was rigid in the AI horse's saddle — didn't even dismount to stretch his legs. He was single-minded about getting to Bounty. She appealed to him again on the matter.

"I'll be safe in Bounty," Kidd said. "I have an address. An address I memorized." That was the first Karren had heard of it, and her eyebrows arched. He recited the address. "There's people there who will keep me safe."

Realization bloomed on Karren in a flush of her cheeks. Kidd wasn't just trying to escape Surfeit, regardless of whether Bounty's Justice cops would treat him any better. He had someplace to go, probably someplace they took in folks who needed to be hidden.

Here she was helping him out because he didn't need "re-education," and she'd assumed he was single-minded to the point of being a dullard.

She asked about it as they headed eastward, but Kidd was stingy with details. Probably for the best, anyhow, Karren reasoned. She did learn enough to confirm that Kidd's "address" was where he would find a haven for Spectrums being persecuted by the Government. And more than just Spectrums.

"People stay there?" Karren asked.

"'Til it's safe, or 'til they can get off world."

"I'm sure you'll be fine."

"They told me there were lots of people like me there, but my friend Jake told me there were lots of criminals, too."

"Don't worry about it. If you hide from the Government, they consider you a criminal. Doesn't mean you're dangerous, or even bad."

"My friend Jake said if the Government ever found the address, everybody there would be in even more trouble than when they started."

"That's probably true."

They headed in that direction, toward Kidd's haven. Eastward through the woods, even though Karren knew, like anybody who rode in that part of Surfeit knew, it was a dangerous route. She laid a hand on the left side of her ribcage as they rode, feeling the bulge that was her pistol, hidden by her jacket. She hoped her pistol would stay harnessed there.

* * *

They passed, far to the north, a station, and they could hear the train idling there. Presently it got underway again, screeching and wailing. As she was listening to that, two men rode up behind them.

Karren heard them at the last second and turned her mount to face them. She called out to Kidd, and he stopped and turned himself. As close behind as the two men were, there was no missing the clicks as they readied their firearms. Nor when they were so close, the whirrs and grinding noises of their own AI horses.

Keeping her motion fluid and slow, Karren switched from holding her horse's mane with her right to her left hand. With luck, the two men didn't see it as anything but her balancing herself.

"Afternoon, folks," the closer man said, gun leveled at Kidd. He had on a wide hat the brown of Karren's leather bomber jacket. The other man had on a smaller black hat, and was covering Karren.

"We're not carrying anything valuable," Karren said, buying time.

"You're riding on something valuable," brown hat said.

"They're not ours."

"Well, they ain't ours, either, at the moment," the man said. "But if you'll please dismount, slowly, we'll see about that."

"Hey!" Black Hat said. "You're the lady fixes horses."

The other man turned to look at him. "She's who?"

"She fixes AI horses." To Karren he said, "You fixed mine 'bout five, six months ago."

"Thank you for your business," Karren said. She readied herself. This was not a positive development.

"So you're a customer of hers," Brown Hat said.

"That I am. She even souped 'er up a little, and I didn't even have to ask."

"That's always part of German Trotter's work orders," she said. "He paid me for it."

Black Hat wondered aloud at the smallness of the world. Brown Hat agreed, fixing Karren with a glare that at once menaced and seemed apologetic for what he would have to do.

"Look," Karren hurried to say. "I get a lot of work from Trotter. I identify one of his men to Justice, that dries up."

"Is it true you have to start chipping these things now?" Brown Hat asked.

Karren ground her teeth. "That's the new law. I don't see how they'll enforce it." They would enforce it the way they enforced everything else: relentlessly, and as obtrusively as possible. Audits, inspections, even supervision at her garage for a time, if they felt it warranted.

Brown Hat chuckled. "You don't?"

"We aren't going to run to Justice to tell about you," Karren said. "We're riding out here because we're wanted by Justice ourselves."

Brown Hat was obviously unpersuaded. "Why don't you two dismount, slowly, while we give your argument some thought?"

Kidd looked at Karren. She nodded to him, and he began to climb down off his horse. She turned her horse broadside, and got down so that it was between her and the two men.

Before she had even let go of the mane with her left hand, she had drawn her pistol from her shoulder harness with her right. Black Hat was telling her to move out from behind the horse at the same time she was drawing.

She aimed around the horse's neck, under its "head," and fired at Brown Hat. She got him in the arm, the one that held his pistol. He dropped it.

Black Hat fired at her, and struck the horse with a solid, metallic thunk. She shot back, over the horse's fuel tank, other side of the neck, hitting the man in his shoulder. Blood and flesh splashed out at the impact, and he cried out. Karren made a frustrated noise, not used to missing. Wasn't even his gun shoulder. Ten years earlier, she would have put one right in the middle of Black Hat's single eyebrow.

Brown Hat was dismounting, hoping to pick up his pistol with his off hand.

Kidd was hunched down, hands over his head. Karren wished he would move for better cover than his arms.

"Leave it!" Karren shouted to Brown Hat. He held up, putting his good arm over his head. "Kidd, go get that man's gun!" Kidd wouldn't move. And the man was making for the pistol again, from a crouch, arm over his head. She was keeping every part of herself she could hidden from Black Hat, behind her horse. She fired at the ground in front of the man trying to retrieve his gun. He held up again.

As inappropriate as it was, she thought about how she had just lost a couple customers.

Black Hat shot, and she heard a ripping — she'd been hit, in the leg. It didn't hurt yet. He'd grazed her. She counted off the time it should have taken her to pop up and fire back. Once that time had passed, and a good many beats more, she sprung up over the horse's fuel tank and fired. She hit Black Hat in the head, this time. He spilled off his mount.

"I give up, I ain't going for my gun!" Brown Hat said.

Karren turned and stalked over to the man's gun. She unloaded it, then handed it back to him. "We didn't want any trouble," she said.

She rounded her horse and looked at where it had taken the shot. The horse would still run, for a while, but it was leaking fluid. She clambered for her binoculars, and trained them south. Two Justice cops were riding their way, the sound of the shots attracting them, Karren supposed.

"Kidd! Get back on your horse. We need to go!" He did as he was told, and the two of them struck out east, a good bit faster than they had been riding before.

* * *

Spooked by their almost getting robbed, Karren decided they ought to leave the woods and cross down south of the tracks and road, so they did. There was nothing this far out but the track and road. There were two more stops for the train, then at the foot of the mountains the track would split, part bending north, serving the mining communities near the mountains, part continuing through a mostly-natural valley between two peaks into Bounty.

Makepeace would be watching the valley pass into Bounty. Hell, he'd probably be watching everywhere, but their best option was to turn due south and make for the entrance to a tunnel through the mountains. It would add another fifteen kilometers to their trip, but they were OK on water, and she had enough extra lubricant to make up for the leak for a while. And somewhere even in this near-wasteland there would be a general store with saddlery where she could buy something to stanch her mount's bleeding.

She was right about the general store, and they saw it from a kilometer away. Despite the burning daylight and their need to get to the tunnel, Karren had them approach cautiously. The biggest moon had risen, from the east, looking full for now, with the sun still a few hands high in the sky. By the time the sun set, the moon would reflect precious little sunlight.

With no sign of either cops or robbers, Karren and Kidd stopped at hitching posts outside the store. Out this far, the place would service as many real horses as AI ones.

The man who owned this store wouldn't be calling Justice on them, Karren reckoned. Living and working a few kilometers off the beaten path, which path itself was many kilometers from anywhere, and you probably had less regard for the Government than she currently did.

The owner had more lines in his face than the blasted, craggy ground outside his store. It was mostly hidden by a shock of white hair up top and a bushy white-gray beard. His hands were hide-tan, his forehead pasty white: a life working outside, always with a hat on. He looked at her as she picked through stuff, but not with any measurable interest.

Presently Kidd brought her two bottles of water. She brought the water, some jerky and some patch for her mount up to the counter that the owner leaned on. He seemed about to move, or somehow acknowledge her, when somewhere nearby a fone chirped. The old man looked in the direction of the sound and furrowed his brow. Karren gathered the fone didn't ring much in the store. She nodded to Kidd and they waited for the man to take his fone call.

"You Karren Considine?" the man said. Karren's heart sank. She nodded. "It's for you."

She glumly slung the fone over her right ear, and right away heard, "Ms. Considine? This is Sergeant Howard Makepeace, Justice."

"Lieutenant," Karren said.

Makepeace seemed thrown. "I really am a Sergeant."

"Then it should come naturally to you to address me as Lieutenant."

"Oh, yes, your war service," Makepeace said. "I apologize, Lieutenant Considine. As I'm sure you're aware, not much of the war made its way to Surfeit, and not many people emigrate here, and I obviously just find myself outside my comfort zone where you're concerned. Still, that was inexcusable of me."

"Do you have something to say to me, Sergeant?"

"I do, Lieutenant Considine. I want to urge you to stay there where you are, at Old Man Foster's store, you and Michael Kidd. We're no more than ten minutes behind you. I would like to avoid prolonging this pursuit, if I can."

"What's in it for me?"

"There's no reward, if that's what you mean. But as far as I know, you've yet to commit a crime. If you say so, I'm willing to believe you encountered Michael Kidd after we searched for him at that pub, so you haven't obstructed justice. Even the man you shot to death had his gun on you first, by the account of his wounded partner. At most, at present, you're guilty of no more than taking a long ride with what I'm sure is a borrowed mechanical horse."

Shit, Karren thought. *I thought I'd been obstructing justice all along.* She knew better than to wonder how Makepeace would know about the "borrowed" horse, she just appreciated it for the additional threat it was.

"You haven't gotten to the part where you tell me what's in it for me." She was hurrying and paying for their merchandise as she spoke.

"As I say, you've yet to commit a crime. If you leave the store, you will be doing so against what I'd call my urging, to be polite. That, I'm afraid, Lieutenant, would constitute obstruction. What's in it for you is not being charged with a crime."

Makepeace's offer made a whole lot of sense, Karren thought. Maybe she didn't make a whole lot of sense herself, anymore, but that the warning came from Makepeace was the main reason she was going to ignore it. The transaction complete with Old Man Foster, she quickly said into the fone, "tell me what Kidd has done." Then she unlooped it and tossed it to Foster, miming to him to keep the call engaged. She hustled Kidd out the door and they mounted. She impressed upon Kidd their new urgency, and they made off at almost a trot. Karren was pretty sure Foster wouldn't have kept the call going. And if Makepeace said ten minutes, it was probably five — although, in that case, why call? She felt the smallest of rushes of hope, as she convinced herself that Makepeace and the Justice cops were at least twenty minutes behind.

* * *

There was little Karren could do about the likelihood that some Justice cops had gone ahead, through the air probably, and would be watching the tunnel they'd started out for. She had not seen any air traffic headed toward the tunnel, but she wouldn't have seen anything airborne when they were in the thick of the woods, or in Foster's store. It was less likely, even if just slightly, that they wouldn't be watching the next tunnel south after that one. So she and Kidd rode, their mounts' footfalls crunching now and then as they dislodged or stepped on chunks of rock, past where they would have turned for the first tunnel. Another forty kilometers, give or take, to the next one. Plus the eight, ten kilometers she estimated they were west of the foot of the mountains. They could do it before nightfall, if they covered fifteen or so kilometers each hour.

"I knew somebody, a long time ago," Karren said, as the sun sank and it grew even colder. "Your address. I wish— your address. I wish he'd had your address."

"Who was he?"

Karren half-smiled at Kidd's Spectrum directness. "Just someone I— someone I thought I was protecting. Tried to make sure Justice had a warrant to search his things. I think—" She looked skyward, sniffed once. "I got him into deeper trouble. Learned a lesson about people who have all the power they ever wanted. They use it. Anyway, I wish he could have gone to your address."

"Do you know what my address is? What's there?" Kidd asked.

"Hope," Karren said. "Most people, they hope they can make an honest living, hope to be left alone, hope they can keep the people they love with them. Your address is for people who don't have any of that. It's what you ain't got, but you need more than anybody. It's the most valuable thing you'll ever own, Kidd."

* * *

Though they felt like they were going fast, in the hazardous terrain they were only covering about twelve kilometers each hour. Or so her mount's instruments told her. At that rate, they would have to cover too much ground at night to be safe. No moons likely to help with light enough to see by. She had Kidd stop, about fifteen kilometers from Foster's store. It was the first time she'd remembered the patch she'd bought, so she dismounted and set about field dressing her mount.

"We're not going to make it to the tunnel I set us out for, not before nighttime," she said as she worked. "What we need to do is head due east from here to the mountains. Find someplace to hole up for the night, keep out of sight if Makepeace keeps looking for us through the night." She smoothed the patch over the first bullet hole.

Kidd regarded her stonily. It was frustrating. "We find shelter from the wind, and stay together, we shouldn't get too cold. I've got rope, that'll keep the snakes off us. We keep going in the morning."

She had no idea if Kidd was processing any of her babble, not because he was Spectrum, but because he was exhausted, like her. At least he had dismounted with her, to stretch.

Karren finished her repairs, and they remounted. She led them toward the mountains. On some other planets, "mountains" would have been a generous description. The range that separated Surfeit and Bounty, though not up to other worlds' standards, was enough of an impediment that you had to go through them rather than over them, including by air.

"Once we're in Bounty," Karren said, "we'll have to figure a way to lose whoever's trailing us. We can't lead Justice to your address."

"I'm not supposed to tell anyone where it is."

"You told me."

"You were worried about me."

Karren didn't know what to say to that.

Upon reaching the foot of the mountains, they crept south, Karren on the lookout for some nook where they could camp for the night. She found one after not too long. It sheltered them from any night winds on three sides. Nearby was a shelf flat and wide enough where Karren could set the horses down on their sides, minimizing the already slim chances they would be spotted.

They ate jerky and drank water around a small warming fire as the sun set, neither saying much. Once night had fallen, Karren snuffed out the fire, and had them situate themselves inside the nook. She spread the blanket lengthwise over both of them, and it covered from knees to collarbones, enough to insulate their cores some. Kidd was rigid, staring straight up, but Karren could tell he was also tired. Before he slept he opened up a little more: about growing up in Surfeit, about a girl he had once had something like a relationship with. About his escape.

"They rounded us up, me and my two friends side by side, and they were putting handcuffs on us behind our backs. Whoever was doing mine was fumbling and having a hard time, and before he finished, my friend Jake got jostled or pinched or something and he made a huge ruckus. I got slammed and staggered back away from him, away from them, and I just turned and started running. I didn't stop for a real long time. It was really cold." That was the end of the story. Karren thought the escape brave, and said so.

"And I don't mean 'for a Spectrum,'" she added. "I mean it was brave."

Kidd took the compliment as impassively as he did everything else, and soon after, he was asleep. Karren was awfully uncomfortable, and also had forgotten to ring the rope around them to keep off snakes, so she was up and busy and then restless for a time before she, too, fell asleep.

She still woke during the night to the sound of knocks on her door.

* * *

At first light she woke Kidd, and they stretched and worked their kinks out. Karren retrieved the horses while Kidd packed up what little they had out. The sky was bright, but they remained in the shadow of the mountains for some time, and both were very cold. They clopped north slowly, blowing out white breaths and aching.

As if sensing that they were near the tunnel, Kidd mumbled "thank you," softly enough that Karren didn't hear and asked him what he said. Kidd reddened, but he said it again. Karren smiled. The effort that went into that "thank you" made it one of Karren's favorites, ever.

"Don't thank me yet," she said. "Justice cops still likely watching the tunnel, and if we make it through, you aren't going to be safe yet. Thank me when we get to your address."

Kidd said OK, he would. He seemed pleased with himself for the effort made expressing his gratitude. Or pleased that it made Karren smile.

After two and a half hours, they finally had the opportunity to warm up in the sunlight. Karren was starting to feel her toes again when she saw the tunnel. She didn't say anything to Kidd, but she planned to simply clop up to the tunnel entrance, look both ways, then enter. There wasn't any opportunity she could think of to do anything different.

This tunnel wasn't well-traveled, Karren knew. It was at most twenty-five meters wide and five tall, ground traffic only. Airborne traffic had to use tunnels farther north, which were much taller and wider, or follow the course of the train tracks. As they approached, they saw widely spaced pockets of parties on horse, AI horse or sled coming and going.

They were just coming up on the tunnel entrance when Karren heard a shot. Behind them, she thought, though it was hard to tell with the echo from the mountain. Karren turned her mount broadside to where she thought the shot had come from. She couldn't see the source anywhere. She wondered if it was somebody hunting up above.

Another shot, same indistinct location. It occurred to her that nobody would be shooting elk or whatever right near a traffic tunnel. The shots were meant for them.

"OK, Kidd? I want you to ride through that tunnel. Fast as you can. I'm going to stay here at the entrance and see if I can slow the cops up some." Kidd looked concerned, whether about leaving Karren or simply going someplace unfamiliar on his own, Karren didn't know. "I'll be ten, fifteen minutes behind you."

Another shot. Were they getting closer? It was impossible to tell with the echoes.

"You can do it. You'll be OK." He twitched a smile at her, then furrowed his brow and concentrated. A nod from Karren sent him trotting into the tunnel. He negotiated the light sled and horse traffic, going faster than it, for which Karren was grateful. She had been concerned Kidd would fall in behind somebody because of all the "no passing" signs posted in and around the tunnel. Just as Karren lost sight of him, there was another shot.

She happened to look up, above the tunnel, and she saw somebody duck behind an outcropping of rock. She scanned that level and saw another cop, mostly hidden, the barrel of a gun sticking up. Were they shooting at them, and missing? From that close?

Karren looked to her right, as a sled-train emerged, puttering from the tunnel. Across the tunnel mouth, there was Makepeace. Scarlet stripe, no helmet, stationary. Watching her.

She understood cops watching the tunnel. They'd watch for Kidd any way into Bounty. She didn't understand why Makepeace himself happened to be here, of all places.

She looked up again, just as one of the cops poked out and fired into the air.

They were firing into the air. Watching.

She trotted across the line of traffic and approached Makepeace. He stood still.

She pulled up and halted, keeping five meters between her and him. No more shots.

Makepeace said, "Why are you doing this, Lieutenant Considine? I'm genuinely curious." Neither he nor Karren moved. He watched her, and she watched him back. "You help this man you've presumably never met evade Justice, almost getting yourself killed at least once, and getting placed under arrest, which is next. As you would say, what's in it for you?" Neither Makepeace nor the cops above the tunnel were moving. Karren said nothing.

"Is it guilt? Shame? For fighting a war on the side of the very Government you feel is mistreating Mr. Kidd so?"

Karren pulled her gun, leveled it at Makepeace. "What's going on here, Makepeace?"

"You've seen the Justice officers up above the tunnel entrance, haven't you, Lieutenant?"

"I've seen them, and I see them staying put. Not going after Kidd. What, is there a platoon of Bounty cops waiting for him on the other side?"

"What kind of world do you think this is, Lieutenant? Is it one where people don't get shot for brandishing a weapon at the police?"

"Or is it your men on the other side?"

"Is it one where you can move heaven and earth to help a fugitive evade Justice? With impunity?"

"Why are you letting Kidd go through the tunnel?"

"Is it one where you don't get the credit you deserve? For fighting for it ten years ago? I fight for it every day of my goddamn life.

"Tell me about the world you live in, Lieutenant. Who's in charge? Who gives the orders, and who obeys? I want to hear about it. Tell me about it, and you'll live through this."

Nobody moved. Makepeace's gun was at his side. Karren's was aimed between his eyes.

"You talk too much, Makepeace," Karren said. "Why are you letting Kidd get away?"

"Tell me who has the power, in the world you live in, Lieutenant."

"You want him to get where he's going? That it?"

"I want you to—"

There was a loud, braying sound. The AI horse's "horn." Makepeace jumped.

"How does that feel, you—"

She didn't finish. Because all at once, she got it. She figured out what they'd done. The cop who Kidd said couldn't get the cuffs on him. She got it.

"You bastard!" she screeched. She swung her mount around and galloped toward the tunnel. One of the cops above fired into the air again.

She got in front of a party on real horses, and nearly caused an accident. As she put them behind her, she saw Makepeace coming after her. She put her head down and rocketed into the tunnel.

There was a huge explosion — really just a gunshot, Karren realized, but thunderously echoing in the tunnel. The horses in the party she'd almost crashed with whinnied. Somebody screamed.

Another shot. At the same time she heard it, she felt it, somebody swinging a sledgehammer with full force into her back, bottom of her rib cage. She lost all her air, and flew off her mount. She landed hard on the shoulder opposite the side where she'd been shot, then rolled right onto the spot. She wailed, and cursed, rolling over so she was on her forearms and knees.

She looked back to the tunnel entrance, her eyesight blurry. But she made out Makepeace, with his scarlet stripe, joined by another cop. They were conferring. Tears leaked out of Karren's eyes. She tried to scream in pain, but the breath hurt, so she ended up keening.

When she was able to focus enough again, she saw Makepeace approaching her at a walk. Two other cops were waving their arms at people wanting to enter the tunnel, keeping them back.

She blacked out to the sound of running footfalls, approaching her from inside the tunnel.

She came to a moment later with somebody trying to shake her awake. If she'd had the strength, she would have beaten whoever it was bloody. She expected it was Makepeace, and she growled.

"Karren. Karren."

"Stop shaking me!" she whined, and she saw it was Kidd, come back for her.

"I heard shots. Were you shot?"

"Kidd," she gasped. She flailed at his hand, then tried again, and grabbed his wrist. "Kidd." She brought up her other hand, so it was holding his. She felt him squeeze.

"Are you gonna be all right?" He sounded panicked.

"Kidd," she said. "Mi— Michael. Run. Run as fast as you can and don't stop for anything. Get to your address, any way you can."

"You've been shot," Kidd said.

"I'll be OK. They'll arrest me, but they'll fix me up. Go. Kidd, please. Go. Run."

"I don't want to leave you!"

"You ha— have to. Go. Michael, go!"

He staggered backward, stood still for a moment, then turned and leapt up onto his mount. He took off like a shot.

Makepeace arrived. Karren was half curled into a ball, half favoring her broken ribs and wound, her arm out as though to protect her from Makepeace. He knelt down to her, and as he did, she crumpled.

* * *

Makepeace checked for a pulse, and found none. He waved at a cop to come join him, help him with the body.

Between them they carried Karren back to the tunnel mouth, and set her down. The cop who had joined Makepeace called for an ambulance, non-urgent.

Makepeace looked down at Karren, then up and into the tunnel.

Another cop was trotting toward him. Before he could say anything, Makepeace asked him, "Still got a signal?"

"Sergeant!" someone called. Makepeace cupped his palm to his ear. "These people want to talk to who's in charge!" The party with the real horses. They looked agitated. One of their horses looked lame, probably turned or broke its ankle when it was scared by the shots.

"You're in charge!" Makepeace called back.

"Sergeant?" The cop who'd trotted over to him.

"Right. Andrews. Signal?"

"Yeah, Sarge— er, Sergeant, we still have a signal—"

"Good. Let's hope the retard can find the place." Makepeace started to walk away.

"It's coming from right here, Sergeant."

Makepeace stopped. He turned. "Beg pardon?"

"The signal is coming from right here where we're standing, Sergeant."

Makepeace looked down at Karren.

He knelt down and turned her over. Her arm hit the ground, and her palm opened. The bracelet with the Spectrum charm Kidd had been wearing was tangled in the fingers.

"Shit-fucking goddamn *mechanic*!"

Get Kidd to Bounty by Jack McDonald Burnett © 2014 Jack McDonald Burnett

About the Author

Jack McDonald Burnett is an attorney and a prize-winning author of short fiction. His first novel, *Amethyst: Stocks and Mods Book One* will be published by Combat Haiku Press in 2015. Find him online at CombatHaiku.com. Jack is a charter member of the Libertarian Fiction Authors Association.

The Intruder

by Robert S. Hirsch

Will he defeat the tricky home invader? Or lose his life when his swarmbots are exhausted?

I ran after the bastard.

My swarm was pulled in tight to allow me to fit through all the other people in the street without decimating my supply of the tiny bots. The fleet of four million Gyphers were in surveillance and obfuscation mode. Scuttling black dots were all over my body comprising the swarm. I could be seen running, but SecureForce cameras and personnel would be unable to identify me by my facial features or identats. The remainder of the swarm was dedicated to transmitting visual, infrared and location data to my goggles.

Soon SecureForce agents would catch up to me. No one runs in Creatia. It's not illegal to run, but if you are, it's presumed that you did something illegal. It's not like in Troy, where liberty is presumed and conflict is dealt with on a private basis.

I was going to do something illegal. I was going to kill that man. What kind of person invades someone's body and forces them to do things?

Rounding the corner, I found myself in the middle of a multitiered Anthracyte cloud. My face mask prevented the white swarm of bots from getting into my mouth. Those Anthracyte idiots act like sheep with their two year old featureset that they paid twice as much for. Then they show off their "new" features. Four of them were in a symbiotic cloud, made up of the combination of their monochrome, white swarms. They were passing thoughts to each other as if this was something new. Anthracyte swarms are good for imagery and that's about all.

I pulled in my botnet even tighter and ran through the white puffball, losing most of my vision for a moment. I came out on the other side and continued running.

I cleaved a subswarm and sent it out on reconnaissance. The recon went autonomous and soared high, looking for the intruder. A side window opened in my goggles and it transmitted a 270-degree spherical view from the subswarm. Thermal imaging was overlaid on the natural image and the people became more distinct. The recon swarm moved three or four times the speed I could run and soon it found him. The subswarm identified the man by his identat that the house surveillance recorded. My goggles highlighted him in white in the side window.

I lucked out. The man had an Anthracyte swarm. How was he able to use it to infect my wife? There are no applications that create zombie swarms that can do that. Anthracyte makes swarms that are fully SecureForce compliant.

Jailbroken. Damn.

Still, even jailbroken, Anthracyte swarms didn't have hardware as capable as Gyphers. They focused on delivering content, there were no apps for body invasion and control.

The recon led me to him in a park. I recalled the subswarm and melded it into the mothercloud enveloping my body. Signaling the botnet into defense mode, I lost my extra-sensory vision. Instead, I gained gleaming black armor that covered my entire body except my goggles and face mask.

I ran around a large boulder in the park and there was my man. I flashed back to the scene in my house.

I had come home and sent my swarm to the recharging station. I walked to the bedroom. My wife was there, on her knees, in front of a man with no visible swarm, who was undoing his shorts. She saw me, tears streaming from her eyes and red in the face. But she leaned forward, eyes still on me and her mouth opened.

"Jon!", she said in a mangled way since she didn't close her mouth.

Rage filled my body. Without my swarm I was powerless. But so was this guy. Where was his swarm? I grabbed the house wand and slammed it across the man's head. The man screamed in pain as the house wand splintered in metal and plastic bits. I didn't care at all that I could no longer control the features of my home without my swarm on. I hoped every shard went into that man's face.

My wife breathed out in relief as she sat back. I stared at her. Looking closer, she wasn't just red in the face and body, but she was covered in small red marks. Suddenly, white bots were leaving her skin through those same pores. They came out in multiple colors, finally coalescing into a white cloud that covered the intruder.

"Jon… it was horrible. The pain!" She started to cry.

I kneeled beside her and rested a hand on her shoulders. Her skin had tiny droplets of blood all over it. Her hands, her neck, her face were all covered with tiny drops of blood that smeared when I touched her.

"They moved inside of me, in my skin. I had to do what they wanted, I moved with them so it wouldn't hurt."

She started to cry.

I looked at the rapist, fury once again rising in my belly. The white bots had almost finished repairing the damage I had done. In a few seconds, faster than I could respond, the man sprung up and jumped out the window.

That man was now standing in front of me. His swarm billowed out, making it difficult to see him.

I sent a small stream of only a few bots to penetrate his cloud. They sent back a reconstruction of what was inside. I had to be careful because of the delay of the representation. I could improve the lag time by sending in more bots to compensate. Sending in more would degrade my armor, this was good enough.

And then it wasn't. Two more bodies showed up in the cloud. In a second, the cloud imploded creating a white second skin on three people. That was fine, Anthracyte armor sucked.

I formed four projectiles from my swarm, taking the supply from my back and shoulders. Aiming with my hand, I fired a projectile along my arm and fingers at the middle body. It hit with enough force to break the poorly constructed armor.

The humanoid dissipated completely. Decoy! The swarm that made up the decoy congealed into the two other bodies.

I reformed the remaining ballistics into a long thin serrated blade that extended from my hand and ran at the two shapes. I swiped at the left body and watched it dissipate just after the blade struck.

I turned to face the intruder. The man who would have forced my wife to pleasure him if I had not happened to come home. The entire white cloud had coalesced on his body. It formed Anthracyte armor up his waist, over his shoulders, and finally his head. His swarm created a gleaming white mask, turning his head into the shape of an exaggerated skull. The armor on his shoulders, arms, and legs thickened, forming body musculature like some comic book character. A six-foot sword grew from his hands, with no obvious reduction in his coverage of armor. My word! He must have had a huge number of nanites.

I launched my blade directly at the skull. He easily knocked it to the side with his sword. It was a stupid move. Organizing bots like that for highly kinetic moves exhausted their energy until they could recharge. Each move like that depleted my supply of nanodrones. I was down to half, most of which were acting as armor on my front side, leaving me rather vulnerable on my back.

His huge blade slashed at my left side. The bots moved to intercept. I was unharmed but the force of the blade contacting my armor sent me stumbling to my right. He wheeled around and went to attack my right side before I could regain my balance. The sword struck again. This time only some of my swarm placed themselves in time to block the blow and the weapon pierced my skin, drawing blood.

He struck me again on my barely protected chest with the sword which was now enlarged to a ridiculous size. I could hear the man laughing. He went to swing again.

I created another ballistic, far smaller than my previous one. It wasn't intended to kill, just distract or harm. I straightened an arm, giving the projectile a surface to increase speed. I shot his foot.

The gigantic blade had finally started using bots from other areas of his body. The intruder's heel was exposed. Now it was a bloody mess.

The man howled. He raised his knee and grasped his foot. I almost laughed watching this huge, skull faced man hopping around, holding a foot.

I initiated Thor's Hammer and got a burrower ready. Almost all my remaining bots formed into a large hammer. I swung it, knocking the man off his good foot. The hammer was massive to whatever it impacted, but it was virtually weightless to me. The weakness was that after only one or two swings, the nanites that make it up become exhausted. I only got one swing. After impact, the tiny bots fell to the ground like dust.

I launched the burrower at the man's heel. I wasn't going to watch what happened next, though I could hear it well. The rest of my swarm formed into a leech shape, finding exposed skin. He screamed as it entered his body and looked for a specific target. I had given it an objective of boring into anything that gives off electrical energy between 40 and 200 times per minute. I listened as the man had one hell of a heart attack.

I walked back around the boulder, naked and vulnerable except for my street clothes and headed home.

The Intruder by Robert S. Hirsch © 2014 Robert S. Hirsch

About the Author

Robert S. Hirsch is an engineer turned writer, who has been in a midlife crisis for most of his mid life. He came to Troy, New York to go to RPI as an eager teenager who wanted to make things. After a stint in Hollywood making creatures for movies, he finished his bachelors, masters and even a Ph.D. in 1998. Since then, he has continued to work in the area, recently completing about 25 years of engineering experience. Currently, Robert lives in Troy, with his wife Gladys and his two children. His first book, *Clash of the Fae*, is available now.

Workaday

by Jonathan David Baird

It's just another day in an HR-oppressed engineering office until some unusual cargo appears.

It took supreme effort of will to not break my gaze from the screen in front of me and look up at the stupid bitch standing in front of my desk. She stood silently holding what looked to be a large rolled up piece of paper in her hands, most likely a CAD print-off. She was always on about CADs and how they wasted paper. "Mr. Henderson, why do you insist on printing this off?" Her voice was high-pitched and demanding. "How are we expected to stay green when you refuse to abide by the simplest office protocol?"

I refused to look up and acknowledge her. "There is no we. You don't work for Epikouroi. You are merely the EPA person who tells us what to do with our waste." I looked up and into her eyes and spoke to her the way I would speak to a child. "The Engineers have to have the CADs or they cannot do their jobs." The bitch stalked out of my office mumbling about worthless plebs and quarterly government mandates.

When I looked back down at my desktop I noticed the screen flickered a bit and my mouse icon wiggled slightly — time to get to work. Somebody from Epikouroi's HR had just logged into my desk remotely. I think HR could fix their snooping so that people would not be able to tell when they were spying, but maybe the paranoia of waiting and watching for the telltale signs of a remote user logging into your system was much more conducive to keeping us all on our toes. I am sure there was some sort of study about that, and I bet the HR people were all atwitter over how the study showed this and that about controlling our work habits.

I wasn't all that concerned. HR had it worse than us. There were so many of us that needed to be watched that HR couldn't watch us at all times, but all the upper level HR employees at Epi had cameras trained on them to make sure they were doing their job harassing us. I am sure the guys that watched HR had someone watching them as well. Who knew where it all ended? I have heard rumors that somewhere up the line there are supervisors working for our parent company Phylakes who have had their brains compartmentalized so that they watched themselves. I was sure that probably wasn't true. It couldn't be true.

Anyway, Gold Star for me, as the HR guy or girl logged in just as I was finishing one of the endless TPS reports and sending it down to the IT department. Making me look like I had actually been productive for once. Back to work.

Ten minutes later, Polly from the next cubicle over stormed in and passed my desk. "Stop whatever you are working on and come with me."

"I can't. HR is logged in, if I don't keep working they'll report me."

"Never mind that." Polly grabbed my arm and dragged me out of the cubicle.

"Where are we going?" I struggled, but Polly had a firm grip.

"Shipping. We need you to translate."

I was flustered. Yes I had a very good rapport with the hoi polloi in shipping, but I have never actually been down to their department. I didn't think any of us office workers went down there. Mostly we spoke to them on the phone or communicated by email.

"Polly, are you sure it is wise to go down to shipping. Have you ever been down there?"

"I was just there, that is why I came to get you. Shipping has a major problem. No one has been able to get them to see reason."

We entered the freight elevator and traveled down past the lobby and into the depths of the building. We were in a new territory for me. A place I had never been, although I had been curious about what they did down here.

It was dark. It took a minute for my eyes to get adjusted to the low light conditions. The room was cavernous and filled with boxes, materials that had just arrived or products which were leaving the factory floor. Along one wall was a series of docks. Each of the docks had a shipping container backed up against it. Just a little light filtered in from around the containers where they did not fit perfectly into the docks. Computer screens flickered in the distance, phones were ringing off the hook, and no one was answering them. At one of the docks, ten or twelve men stood stock-still, all seeming to look into the container there.

"These men need to get that up to R&D." Polly pointed past the group of men. "Can you get them into gear?" Polly was almost pleading.

I understood her consternation. She was up for a performance review this quarter and any delay or work stoppage in her department would look very bad on her evaluation.

We walked up behind the men and I could just make out a large glowing sphere. Sitting atop it was what looked like a giant hookah. The hookah was stamped with the letters L.I.B.E.R. and was strapped securely to a wooden pallet. It was the only thing in the shipping container. Snaking out of the glowing sphere were twenty to thirty hoses and each of the men were puffing on them. No smoke was escaping when they exhaled, but there was a shimmer in the air around them.

Why must dock workers the world over always test out each new item that comes into the warehouse?

"Hey guys let's wrap up the smoke break and get this thing up to R&D."

One of the dock workers ambled over to me with a hookah hose in his hand.

"Try some liberty." He offered me the hose halfway giving it to me and halfway sticking it up to my mouth. As it waved under my nose I got a whiff of something. I suddenly lost control of myself. I grabbed the hose, sucking deep on it.

My mind exploded — not literally, but I wasn't on the loading dock any longer. I could sort of make it out, the men around me and Polly standing just behind me, but they were more like shadows than real people. At that moment I realized that I had been living in a dream my entire life. The constant drudgery, the fear, even the job were merely vaporous illusions. I was not the sum of what I did or who I knew.

I had taken drugs before, during college, hell it was mandatory to use hallucinogens in college. If you did not conform to the expected norm you certainly would not have expected any sort of promotion or benefits. Nonconformists did not make good middle managers. This wasn't like any drug. You knew somewhere deep inside that the drug high would wear off. Even if you were freaked out, some small part of you knew the LSD trip wasn't "really" real. This was real. I knew it was real.

I stood on the edge of a cliff with waves crashing onto the beach below. Sea spray hit my bare chest. I was wearing a loincloth and holding a stone-tipped spear. Life surged through me. I could taste the clean, crisp air. The shadowy presence of the dock and my co-workers was slowly receding into a dark cave behind me. I was free and alive, more alive.

Suddenly I was back. Polly had struck the hose from my mouth. She was shaking me, trying to wake me from the effects of the hookah. The sensation however was not of waking but of falling back into slumber. Each time she shook me I fell deeper into sleep and began to have the nightmare about Epikouroi industries once more.

"No!" I wasn't sure I had shouted, or if I dreamed I was shouting. My shadow self struck back at Polly. Moving was like pushing through thick molasses, but I pushed her away. I could just make out her falling as I fumbled for the hose. It was an eternity before I grasped it again and could get it back to my mouth. Instantly I was awake again. The shadow Polly was at my feet. She was cringing and had her arms up as if to ward me away. I had just enough sense of the dream world left to pick up one of the loose hoses and offer it to Polly. She tried to brush my hand aside. I was still half in both worlds and just enough in hers to shove the hose up to her nose in the same way that I had been offered freedom. She ripped the hose out of my hand and began huffing.

Polly did not fade. She became more solid, more real than she had ever seemed in the nightmare we had shared.

We both stood on the edge of the cliff in tanned leathers of our own making. A distant memory of restrictive suits and ties was dissipating. I was distracted by the call of a bird, yawned a little, and it was gone. We had just awakened moments before and stepped out into the invigorating air. The world stretched out before us free and unhindered, nothing was beyond our grasp.

"Polly, I had a really vivid dream last night. I think you were in it, but I can't remember it now."

Workaday by Jonathan David Baird © 2014 Jonathan David Baird

About the Author

Jonathan David Baird has worked as an archaeologist for the past fifteen years throughout the Southeast. He has a master's degree in English (literary arts) from Fort Hays State University. His focus of study was the development of late Victorian Gothic horror. He has a second master's degree in American history focusing on the early frontier. Jonathan was recently elected District Soil and Water Supervisor in Burke County, North Carolina — the only registered Libertarian to win an elected seat in North Carolina in 2014. He is currently working towards a PhD in Humanities. Jonathan blogs at NukeMars.com.

Fluorescence

by J.P. Medved

Will you keep the lights on?

To me, my grandmother had always been associated with light. Not the golden ethereal light one thinks of angels having or, indeed, the harsh whiteness of a hospital, or even the sterile fluorescence that everyone else in the country endured. Grandma's light was warm. It seemed natural, like the sun.

Before I was even old enough to understand what terms like "state-ordered," "black market," "environmental concerns," "contempt of court," and "the greater good" meant, I understood what it was that made grandma's house so cheery, safe, and comfortable. It was the light.

I could play with my dolls for hours on her floor, late in the evenings, and never once get a headache, like at my parents' house. I never had one of my "episodes" at grandma's house. Hers was the only home I could fall asleep in with the lights still on. I would nod off on the floor, or while watching one of the old time cartoons she had saved for her grandkids, and as she would carry me softly to bed, I would drowsily mumble, "Grandma, keep the light on, please."

Her whispered response was always the same, "Of course I will."

But then, I've always been sensitive to light.

The doctors called it Optic Nerve Hypoplasia and said I was "photosensitive." I just knew I got a lot of headaches. In fact, I got so many headaches I was held back a grade for missing so much school.

My parents tried everything they could — expensive medicines, weird glasses, even some strange guy called a "psychotherapist." None of it worked.

But one thing did work. Something all the doctors and experts and "psychotherapists" in the world couldn't provide — a trip to stay with my grandmother and an evening basking in the warm, cozy glow of her modest home.

So when my parents told me that policemen had been to grandma's house, and that we all had to travel downtown to see her, I knew immediately why they had come.

They had come for the light.

I remember very little from that day. I remember a large room, filled with people sitting in rows. I remember my grandmother, face ablaze, bellowing to a man in black robes about the "Damn fool, one-size-fits-all hogwash!" It was the only time I'd seen my grandmother angry. I remembered hearing the words "Energy Independence and Security Act" and "multiple transgressions."

And I remember the end, being maneuvered out the big wooden doors of the imposing stone building by my parents and finally, painfully, wresting my wrists free from their grip to run, breathless and weepy, into the arms of my grandmother as she stood flanked by tall men wearing blue.

She looked right at me, inside that courthouse, her dry eyes a counterpoint to my wet ones. She only told me one thing that day, and it was the last thing I ever heard her speak, because later, when we tried to see her at the correctional nursing home facility, my parents were informed that she was refusing all visitors.

In a deeply solemn voice she said, "Keep the lights on, child."

I could only nod and say one thing in response, "Of course I will."

And I intend to.

Fluorescence by J.P. Medved © 2014 J.P. Medved

About the Author

J.P. Medved writes fun adventure stories and thoughtful thrillers, from Steampunk works like *To Rescue General Gordon, Queen Victoria's Ball* and *In the Shade of the Ishtar Trees* to political thrillers like *Granite Republic*. You can preview his other works and download free stories at JPMedved.com.

When not writing, J.P. can be found frying anything he can get his hands on in his deep fat fryer, shooting tons of guns, and losing himself in a good book at the most inopportune times — around the dinner table, at baseball games, during heartfelt emotional conversations.

The Death Shop

by George Donnelly

When uplift is declared in her protectorate, will Ailsa keep fighting for her daughter? Or will she give up?

"This damned thing won't connect!" Ailsa rapped the palm-sized device on the sidewalk. Her long, dirty blond hair hung in a greasy stiff ponytail across her shoulder. She brushed it back.

Texa stared at the giant viewscreen across the street. An advertisement for Xemura Pharma flashed across it. The small girl's rheumy eyes blanked out. She sat cross-legged on the pockmarked sidewalk next to her mother. Beyond the viewscreen sat the wall. Guardians patrolled its heights with weapons ready.

"Did you hear me?" Ailsa whispered. She glanced down the street towards the feed line. "Do you have any other ideas? You are a bright little girl. I believe in—"

"With hope, you can do anything!" Texa whispered the words in unison with the mouth movements of a character onscreen. "Mommy!" She turned to Ailsa. "The audio subscription?"

Ailsa firmed her mouth. Her eyes tightened. "You know the answer, baby girl."

"Why don't you get us some money?" Texa furrowed her brow at her mother.

Ailsa looked away. A heaviness grew in her chest and her face burned with shame. She let the handheld device fall to the ground and opened her mouth to take a deep, calming breath. *I can fix it. There is still time.*

A lithe boy with a silver visor over his eyes ran around the corner and palmed the device. Ailsa grabbed his wrist and pulled him towards her.

"Don't you dare!" she yelled. "I just put it down, that's all!" She pulled the device from his hand and buried it in her gut pocket.

The boy's visor slipped down his nose. She ripped it off of his face and he screamed.

"Didn't your mother teach you not to steal?" Ailsa yelled.

His face seized up. His eyes were all white. "I didn't have a mother, lady. Please, put it back. I just got it this morning and I still got a debt. I can see for the first time in seven months. I can't live without it!"

She looked at Texa and grinned. Texa shifted her eyes towards her mother but did not look away from the viewscreen across the street.

She slipped the visor back on the boy's face and arranged his bangs. He cocked his head to one side and smiled at her. "You didn't have to do that, you know. It's worth something."

Ailsa shrugged. She turned and stared at her daughter.

The boy took a seat in front of her. "What's your name?"

"What right do you have to my name?" Ailsa asked. "Private information."

To her right, the end of the feed line crawled in their direction. Guardians flew in and parked their scooters in the street in front of them.

Texa growled. She got on all fours and crawled up the block so she could see the viewscreen again.

"Are you in the feed line?" asked the boy. "My name's Henry, by the way."

Ailsa stared at him. There was the current again, like a low hum in her brain. She shook it off. "Henry? That's an old-fashioned one. How did you get a name like that?" She looked up the block at Texa.

"If you want to eat today, you better get in line," said Henry. "The Gards are here to close it off, you know." He stood up and walked towards the end of the line.

She pursed her lips. "I know how these things work." She stood up and walked to Texa. She grabbed her arm. "It's time to go little girl. I have a bad feeling about this."

Down the street, Guardians blocked access to the feed line with their bodies. A shriek sounded in her ear and she crashed to one knee.

"This Xemura Feed Line is now closed. Do not attempt to join the queue. Do not move out of line. Everyone currently in line will receive a five-hundred-calorie ration courtesy of Xemura Pharma. Violators are subject to a three-day sustenance suspension. Stay in line. Remain calm. The Republic will care for us."

The viewscreen in front of them went all-white. Ailsa noticed out of the corner of her eye that the other viewscreens on the block changed, too. Black letters appeared. "The Republic Trust is our protector!" they said. The Guardians on the wall looked down on them.

Texa turned to her mother and slapped the sidewalk. "Mom!" she whined. "The viewscreen!"

Ailsa felt the rage rise in her, too. She exhaled purposefully then smiled at her daughter. "There's nothing—"

"Five-hundred calories a day ain't enough for no man!" The deep, throaty yell came from behind her.

Ailsa pulled Texa to her feet. Texa refused to put her feet down and run. Ailsa held her against her chest. She ran around the corner. Texa scratched her face.

"My show's not over! Take me back! Take me back!" Texa screamed. There was blood under her fingernails.

Ailsa grabbed Texa's hands and squeezed them together. Blood trickled from the gashes on the young mother's face.

"I'm sorry, baby, but things are about—"

A rising chorus came from the street behind them. "Our fair share! Our fair share! Our fair share!"

Ailsa's neck muscles tensed. Her head arched backwards and a desperate ache spread throughout her back. "Don't worry, baby girl. We're almost there. Try to calm down. Do the breathing—"

"Warning," said a genderless voice in her ear, "this is now an illegal assembly. Disperse or be terminated."

A Guardian scooter zipped past them and stopped in their path. Henry stuck his head out of the front window. "Get on. I can save you!"

Ailsa stopped dead and scowled at him. *What more do I have to lose? Better to try than to die like an animal in the street.* She climbed into the backseat and sat Texa next to her. Texa's tiny body collapsed and her head bounced against the car door.

"Go!" yelled Ailsa. "Go!" The inside of the scooter stank of sweat and rotten food. There was a small plaque on the rear of the front passenger seat. "Sponsored by Xemura Pharma," it said.

Henry jammed his feet into the accelerator pedal and they took off into the sky.

"We beat it! We got—" started Henry.

The termination registered in her ear as a piercing but low scream. She grimaced for a brief second then smiled at Texa and caressed her soft, blond hair. "We made it, little one. Just out of range," she whispered. She let herself feel the exhaustion that tugged at every bone in her body. *Now what?*

The scooter dived forward. Ailsa's chest slammed into the bench wall in front of her. She caught Texa and struggled to expand her lungs.

"Henry!" she yelled.

A shiny cobalt skyscraper grew in front of them. She reached forward and pulled Henry's limp body to one side. His feet came off the pedals. The car leveled off. The building was still in front of them.

She grabbed the wheel and turned right but the inertia carried them sideways into a deep blue window. A nasty crunch sounded followed by a long screech. Their bodies were thrown hard against the crumpled driver's side of the vehicle. They began to fall.

* * *

Ailsa fought raw panic to grab the wheel but the rest of her body would not come. The windshield screamed as air fought to pass through its broken lines. The approaching city below beckoned them on. Ahead and below, she spied the next protectorate over and the high wall that separated them. The other protectorate was a crater-filled wasteland of rock, dirt and rusting machines.

Ailsa looked back at her daughter. Texa was lodged against the back window. Her eyes were closed and her shoulders were rotated inwards. She was silent.

But we've come so far. "With hope, anything is possible." Texa mouthed the words in Ailsa's mind's eye.

She tensed her arms and pulled her body closer to the oncoming cement. She stiffened her abdomen but her feet fought her.

Ailsa felt the weakness. This is better. She won't feel a thing. Ailsa relaxed.

The scooter slowed and leveled off. Ailsa rolled over into the front seat.

A shrill siren sounded in her ear. "You have highjacked a Guardian vehicle. Ailsa Santamaria and Texaco Santamaria, you are hereby sentenced to thirty hours of correction. Do not attempt to exit the vehicle. Place your hands on the back of your neck and close your eyes."

* * *

Ailsa limped out of Protectorate 13477. It was a thick, gray stone building that sprawled across the block. The windows were blackened and the street was empty. Ailsa cradled Texa in her arms. She was still asleep from the post-correction satiators.

A lone delivery truck carried a light load down the potholed street. Ailsa trundled down the hard steps. She found a viewscreen and sat down across from it on the cold cement.

"With hope, anything is possible," she whispered. She sneered. What if there is no hope?

She jiggled her baby girl. Texa's eyes were open but there was no spark in them. "Come on, baby, wake up." She started to sing. "My little girl, oh, my little girl. She is so happy and sweet. I so love her, I so love—"

Ailsa's voice choked off. She lost herself in the viewscreen soap opera but held tight onto her little girl. *No one can take her from me. Never.* The thought echoed in her subconscious.

* * *

Ailsa looked away from the viewscreen. It was dark. *Damnit! I lost all day here.* She pulled the device from her gut pocket. *The Gards hadn't thought to look for it. Still no signal. That pirate ripped me off.*

The thought of Texa protruded into her mind. Ailsa didn't want to look down at her but she forced herself. Texa's eyes blinked. Ailsa caressed her face. "Don't worry, little one. I will figure a way out of this for us. With hope, anything is possible, right?" *I'm hoping, but I don't know why.*

The corners of Texa's mouth creased and she licked her lips.

Ailsa walked blocks to reach their favorite spot near the feed line. Hoverbots scooped up the last of the dead bodies into shiny green dumpsters. Her ear buzzed with the warning to stay back. *Hungry men, that's all they were. And now they were dead, killed like dogs in the street without dignity.*

Ailsa made her way to the short feed line and within an hour found a picnic bench in the cavernous basement of the feeding facility. She sat Texa on the edge of the bench between her legs and stuffed bite-sized chunks of bologna on white bread into the drugged-up child's mouth.

A viewscreen came on and Texa popped awake. "Mommy!" she said in a slow, faraway voice, "You paid for the audio. It's working."

A Guardianship spokesperson came onscreen. "Welcome to this Guardian feeding station, brought to you by Xemura Pharma," the white-helmeted woman said. "You will find this food nourishing and tasty. Even the little ones love it!" she added in a sing-song voice. Her image morphed into smiling children frolicking on a grassy knoll next to a stream. "This feeding station is made possible—"

The viewscreen froze. It turned black. White words scrolled across it. "Wait until the end of this message for the keyword," it said. The sounds echoed in her mind as she both read and heard them.

"Guardian protectorate number 13477 is hiring three Guardian trainees," it continued. No one moved. All eyes focused on the viewscreen. There was complete silence.

"You must be a full citizen in good standing without debt and able-bodied between the ages of fourteen and forty-five. Childcare, education, occupational training for you, a full two-thousand calorie daily feed allowance, clothing and accommodations are included with the position as well as an honorary stipend."

The viewscreen showed a map. "To apply, proceed to grid 115, street 4, entry 7. The keyword is elixtography. Remember, the Republic will care for us." The screen went dark and the lights came on.

Ailsa grabbed Texa and ran for the door.

"But, mommy, my sandwich!" yelled Texa. The sandwich hit the floor and was gone under a dozen pair of feet.

Ailsa grabbed Texa's head, laid it down on her shoulder and pointed the face inwards. She covered Texa's eyes with one hand and held the other tight under her buttocks.

She pushed and she ran.

* * *

There was already a long line at the protectorate. Ailsa grabbed a spot and kept her toes always directly behind the heels of the person in front of her. No one is line-jumping on me.

Ailsa moved to put Texa down.

"No!" Texa screamed. "I want up!"

Please don't start. Not now. Not when we have this chance. Sure, it's a slim chance. If you look at it too closely, it's no chance. But it's still a chance. And any chance, even no chance, is better than the alternative. She picked Texa back up. "Happy now, little girl?" Please be happy. If we can't catch this chance, I don't know what we'll do.

Texa nodded, her eyes far away.

Ailsa's heart melted. A doubt entered her mind. She tapped the shoulder of the man in front of her. "Is this the line for the trainee position?"

The man looked back at her, his eyes wide open. "How dare you touch me! How dare you touch me!" He pushed her and she fell back into the people behind her. Several of them fell to the floor like dominoes. Ailsa struggled to get off of them without hurting Texa.

A helmeted Guardian approached them. "You two, out! Now!" He grabbed the man and Ailsa and dragged them towards the narrow front door.

"I only asked him if I was in the right line!" yelled Ailsa. She glimpsed the hard, stubbled face and blank eyes of the Guardian through his helmet. He had a growing double-chin and his abdomen stretched the white fabric of his suit.

"We don't have time for troublemakers or line-jumpers at this protectorate." He kicked the front door open and pushed them out into the night.

Ailsa and the wild-eyed man collided. He kicked her and she fell down the steps, back first. In mid-air, she grabbed tight onto Texa and nestled the girl's head into her soft chest.

Ailsa's back hit the sharp concrete steps and she gasped for breath. Texa screamed.

"Stay away from my mommy!" Texa yelled. She got up and walked over to the man. She shook a finger in his face and curled her upper lip. "Don't you touch her again."

* * *

Ailsa fought her own body as she lowered herself down to the sidewalk just a few feet down from their usual spot. Where they normally sat lay a body covered in dirty white rags next to a mix of tan feces and pale green vomit. A fat, black rat fed on the brew.

"Mommy, are you going to be okay?" Texa asked. The girl fixed her eyes on the viewscreen across the street. They went blank and her face relaxed. "With hope, anything is possible," she whispered with rising intonation.

"Don't worry, baby, I will—" She let out a tiny whimper as she stretched her back. "I will be okay." She turned and smiled at Texa. A stench of graphite and bologna mixed with a deep sewer musk reached her nose. She started to move, then remembered Texa and gave up hope.

Texa giggled. The darkness in her eyes lifted for a moment as her cheeks curved upward.

Ailsa sighed. I can't blame her for wanting to escape into the screen. But what future is there for a child addicted to it and without any education? She closed her eyes.

A man tapped her on the shoulder. "How about a meal, angel?"

She looked up at him out of the haze of her dream. He looked like a god to her.

"A meal, what meal?" she asked.

"Five clients, five tickets. Come on." He snatched her hand and pulled her up. He was portly, with short, dark hair that sat tousled above his lined face.

She groaned as her back reorganized itself.

He narrowed his eyes. "You alright, angel?"

"I just hurt my back, that's all."

"Don't worry, we'll get you some numbers." He grinned. His teeth were black and gray. A front tooth and two smaller bottom ones were missing.

Ailsa frowned. "I'm just so hungry. Do you have a lot of food?"

"It's the all-you-can-eat, angel." He leaned down and picked up Texa. She laid her head on his shoulder and kept her eyes on the viewscreen. "And one order of the usual entertainment for this one!"

"Mac, I need to see the food first. I need to know…"

He turned around and smiled at her. "You know I always take care of my girls." He coughed and spit phlegm on the sidewalk with a deep, gurgling noise.

Ailsa plodded after him. This is not the chance I wanted but maybe it's the only one I deserve.

* * *

A Guardian walked into the room. He took off his helmet, stomped his feet and raised his eyebrows at her.

Ailsa lay on the narrow, lumpy bed. She stared up at the dust-encrusted ceiling. She struggled to purge her mind of disgust and fear.

"What's it gonna take?" yelled the Guardian.

A tremor ran through Ailsa. She raised herself up to look. It's the same one. "Hey, I still need a job," she said. "Maybe we can work something—"

"I only have a five-minute break so be quick about it," he said. He opened the velcro flap on the front of his suit and exposed himself. He stared at her with dead eyes.

She got off the bed and kneeled in front of him. She caught her reflection in a mirror that lay to her left. She was naked and emaciated. Her small breasts clung tightly to her chest just above the outlines of her rib cage. She studied her face and found it pleasing. Her shoulder-length dirty blond hair was freshly washed. It hung around her head like a flowing halo. Am I really here? Again? Is this all there is for me? What about my little girl?

Ailsa despaired but resolved to try anyway. "If you can get me into that trainee position, we can work out a more regular arrangement," she said. She looked up at him and softened her face.

He pursed his lips in contempt. "This is the position you seem to be most qualified for. Now I have four minutes. Take care of the Republic and it will take care of you. He smirked then scowled down at Ailsa. "Be quick!"

Ailsa did what she had to do.

* * *

Ailsa lay naked under the gray, threadbare sheet. She hurt. She didn't like to hurt. It reminded her of things she wanted to forget. The current still pulsed through her but it was much weaker now.

The door slid open and Mac stuck his head in. "Last one. Texa is asleep and I've got my eye on her, no worries there."

"Just give me five minutes," said Ailsa. "The last one…"

"Yeah that one is, uh, okay. Five minutes. I'll try to send this one to someone else." He paused a moment to look at her hair and opened his mouth. He snapped it shut, turned and closed the door behind him.

The door slammed closed. It jarred her awake. "I said five minutes, Mac. Just—"

She turned. It was the wild-eyed man from the protectorate.

He grinned. He had no teeth. He scratched an open sore on his cheek.

"No. No. Just get out," Ailsa said.

His eyes went wide. His lips flapped open and his body began to shake. "But I paid," he said in a gentle voice.

She sat up in bed. "I'm sorry." She cleared her throat. "Are you going to be violent?"

"No, no, of course not. I just..." He blushed.

"Let's get it over with," she said.

"Yes, ma'am." He stared at her as he undressed.

She threw the covers back and looked at herself in the mirror. She was bleeding.

Just get through it, just get through it. Almost done. Then we eat. All you can eat. Her spirit jumped and a smile pushed the sides of her mouth up.

* * *

The wild-eyed man struggled to get his shirt over his head. "Are you going to be alright?" he asked.

Ailsa curled into a fetal position, her head on the soft pillow. She felt safe, relaxed. The bed was cool. She ignored the pain and focused on the good feelings. My little girl can eat now. I can eat now! A feeling of joy welled up in her and nothing else mattered.

She nodded to the man. "What's your name?"

"Milton." He pulled his pants up and fastened his belt tight around his thin midsection. "I'm real sorry about when I pushed you earlier, over at the protectorate. I got freaked out and I didn't..." He looked away. "I can't always get my meds."

"You have your meds now?" She lay on her side and twirled her hair around her right index finger.

Milton nodded with a small smile. "Oh, yeah. Five days worth."

"How did you afford them?" asked Ailsa.

There was a pounding at the door. "Thirty seconds, bud." It was Mac.

"It's the— What's your name, if you don't mind my asking?"

"Call me Lizzy." She raised an eyebrow and smiled at him. She let her hair flop forward over her face and she giggled.

Milton's toothless mouth hung open. "If I hadn't just..." He gulped. "Well, I would want to do it again. Have you done any modeling?"

She looked down and pouted. "I did plumber training but with all the bots, who needs a plumber?"

Milton finished slipping into his shoes. He nodded. "I was a scientist, a long time ago."

"So how did you earn the money for your meds, and for me?"

"Oh, The Death Shop," he said. "They—"

The door flew open. "You're over, sir," said Mac. "Time to go."

"No, wait!" cried Ailsa.

* * *

"Wait, Milton," Ailsa yelled. She ran out the door of the brothel with a sleeping Texa over her shoulder and her shoes in one hand. She stepped on something sharp and fell onto her butt.

"Ow, my back," she whispered. A dull ache shot up her spine. "Milton!"

Milton walked a few steps back towards her. "It's 4 AM, Lizzy. I have to go to work. Gotta pay for my next date with you." He turned and walked away from her.

Ailsa picked herself up with one hand on the back of Texa's neck. "What is The Death Shop?" she asked in a loud whisper.

Milton's eyes went wide. "I can't— No. No!" He took a step towards her. "Quiet! You mustn't— It's..." He shook his head violently.

Ailsa took a step back. "I'm dying here, Milton." Her eyes watered up and sparkled. "My baby girl... We need money!"

Milton scowled at her and crossed his arms. "Seems like you made some money tonight."

Ailsa's shoulders sagged forward. "That's no life, Milton. What about my little girl? What kind of life can she expect if I can't even feed her?" Ailsa collapsed to the ground and sobbed. "I just... We have no future, Milton! I need help!"

Milton rolled his eyes upwards and sighed. "Okay, okay, I'm sorry, Lizzy. I'm sorry!" He grasped his hands together in front of him. "But I have to go!" He ran a few steps then turned back to her. "At least we're not in uplift. We have time." He shrugged. His shadow bounced and elongated in front of her as he ran away up the deserted street.

* * *

A moist hand slapped the back of Ailsa's neck. She picked her head up from the table at the all-you-can-eat restaurant and looked to her right.

"Mommy," said Texa through gritted teeth, "the viewscreen's not working!" She folded her arms and grunted. The plate in front of her overflowed with meat chunks and carb strips.

Ailsa looked around through half-open eyelids. The viewscreen monopolized the wall about fifteen feet to her left. It showed 5:59 PM. A scribble of black and gray lines ran across it.

Texa smacked Ailsa's cheek. "Mommy! Do something!"

Ailsa took a deep breath. Her stomach was empty and dry. She still hurt down there. Her ear crackled. "Texa, I need you to just—"

"Alert." The word appeared on the viewscreen in white on a black background a millisecond before it was spoken into her ear.

"By order of the High Council of the Republic Trust, protectorate 13477 is hereby scheduled for uplift. The Guardianship instructs you to report to grid 115, street 4, entry 9 for immediate invitation to the accommodations of your choosing."

Uplift. Ailsa's back straightened. Terror displaced her brain fog.

"You will receive," the message continued in Ailsa's ear, "1,250 calories per day, viewscreen access and complimentary audio subscription for the duration of your stay."

Texa scraped her fingernails on Ailsa's tricep. "How much longer?" she asked through gritted teeth.

Ailsa's mind refused to process the new information. She ignored her daughter, and the pain in her arm.

"When your health is restored and your retraining complete, you will be able to resettle in a place of your choosing other than protectorate 13477. Report within thirty minutes to avoid additional correction."

The screen went black and a timer counted down thirty minutes.

Everyone screamed.

* * *

Ailsa stepped out into the twilight. A dark orange sun was setting straight ahead. People ran in every direction. Some carried suitcases. Others barely had any clothes on. She shivered.

Texa smiled up at her. "Why is everyone so crazy?"

Someone hit them from behind and they went flying into the street. A foot landed on Ailsa's back, right in the spot that hurt. She lost sight of Texa.

"Texa! Texa!" she yelled. She got onto all fours but the herd kicked her onto her back. Feet fell on her face and her abdomen. She reached out, grabbed an ankle and twisted.

She hit another person behind the knee and got up. "Texa! Texa!" she screamed.

A hand grasped her shoulder. She turned around. It was Milton. Texa sat on his shoulders.

"I've got her," he said. He grinned like a champion steer. "We'll hide at the shop until the chaos settles."

"No!" yelled Ailsa. "We have to get out of this protectorate. They're—"

"Uplifting. I know," he said.

"Well? How do we get out of here?" she asked. I can't let her go through an uplift.

His mouth went flat and he scowled at her. "Where are you going to go? They'll track you. They've already disabled all the vehicles and the walls are well-guarded. It's the same everywhere, anyway. No food, no work, no mercy, no love. This'll be my fourth time." He narrowed his eyes. "And what's in it for me?"

She stared at him, her eyes wide and her mouth open.

"Come to The Death Shop with me," he said. He held out his hand and she grabbed it. Her eyes glazed over.

* * *

"How does it work?" Ailsa asked. Milton stood next to her. Texa slept with her head on his shoulder. They stood in the entryway of a narrow and dark storefront. Outside it was quiet.

"It's really quite pleasant," said the shop attendant, a female-styled android with a bob cut and Asian eyes. "I am Aiko and it is a pleasure to meet you. I am here to gain your informed consent and meet your needs throughout the process. Do you understand?"

Death. Is that really our only way out? "Yes," said Ailsa. "Tell me more."

"At The Death Shop, we honor the end of your time with dignity. Mix and match any of more than one thousand virtual reality scenarios in our exclusive holodeck. Pass away your final moments in bliss, light pain, heavy pain or feel nothing at all!" The machine wore a low, amber top and a tasteful gray skirt.

Aiko's mouth pulled back from her silicon teeth in something approaching a smile.

We could run right now. We could run. She was silent a moment. The Gards would catch us. And then we'll be dead anyway. But it will be long and painful. "How much does it cost?" Ailsa asked. A doubt rose within her. She thought about how little money she had in her pocket. She stole a glance at Texa's face. She won't even know it happened. We'll just put on her favorite show.

"How much is your budget?" asked Aiko.

Ailsa felt in her pocket. "Maybe a few coins, that's it. I have some money on this device," she pulled the non-working computer out of her gut pocket, "but it won't connect to the grid."

Aiko's eyes rotated to look at Milton. "We can take trade." Its head angled to the side and it smiled again. "Show us how much you have."

Ailsa dumped everything in her pockets on the table. There were a few copper- and silver-colored coins and the remaining meal coupons. "Is there enough?"

"The four all-you-can-eat coupons will buy you the deluxe option," said Aiko. "Please, have a seat. We will sign the paperwork, then you can have thirty minutes in the fun room before it is time."

* * *

Ailsa set the stylus down. "I clicked 'OK' on them all. Are we done now?"

Aiko's motorized body groaned as she hobbled over to Ailsa.

"It's just that I'm getting hungry again and my daughter's going to want a viewscreen as soon as she wakes up."

Aiko stood very still. A whining sound came from inside of her. "Your contract is approved. Thank you for choosing The Death Shop. We are honored by your trust. Please, come this way."

* * *

Texa opened her eyes. She blew out the candles on her virtual birthday cake and chirped with glee.

"Did you make a wish, baby?" Ailsa asked.

"Yes, mommy. I want to visit Disneyland and have a lifetime audio subscription. Do you think we can do that someday?"

Ailsa's eyes unfocused as she contemplated her daughter. She's only seven. So much life ahead. But what will it be like for her? Scraping for food and... that, with those men? No. No! Better this. Then nothingness. It's better.

"You know what? Right after your show, we'll do just that."

"Really, mommy? I love you. You're the best mom I could ever—"

Texa's favorite show came on the viewscreen in full definition. She turned her attention to that and was silent.

A cold, rubbery hand touched Ailsa's arm and she jumped awake.

"It is time," said Aiko. "Your daughter is already in the chair and sedated."

Ailsa did a double-take. "What do you mean she's already sedated? I want to say goodbye to her. I want us to fall asleep together. You promised we could do that!"

"I humbly apologize," said the android, "but your daughter is now in place and we are only waiting on you." The machine tapped its wrist.

"Where is Milton? I want to talk to him."

"Who is Milton?" asked Aiko.

Ailsa sighed. Always the same thing. No one knows anything. She took her seat in a reclining chair next to Texa. She caressed Texa's soft cheek. It's really the best thing for us both, baby girl. A twinge of regret grabbed her gut. I'm a failure.

Aiko moved her hand toward a red button. "The world will miss you," she said. The android took a deep and perfectly executed bow.

"Wait," said Ailsa. "What do your other customers do now?"

"You selected the option to feel bliss, so lay back and enjoy your happy moment," said Aiko. It attempted to smile again.

"Mommy?" Texa woke and took a deep breath. Her eyes remained closed. "Anything is—"

The red button clicked and Ailsa felt herself plunged into a warm pool of pure joy.

Why did I ever worry about any of this? She sensed Texa next to her. She turned.

That's when the pain began.

* * *

Aiko carried the bodies of Ailsa and Texa out of the death chamber, through the rear hallway and into the alley out back. She dropped the corpses into a shiny green dumpster and returned inside.

She locked the door behind her and pressed a button.

A man approached the dumpster. It was Milton. He raised up the dumpster lid and looked inside. He smiled without showing his teeth.

He turned and pounded on the blue door of The Death Shop. Aiko opened the door. She smiled at him.

"Do you love me, Milton?" she asked.

"You are my beautiful Japanese princess."

"Do you want me?" She cocked her head to the side and let her top fall off of one shoulder.

"I want you. But right now—"

She straightened her head. "I know what you want. Here are the coupons."

Milton grabbed them and turned toward the dumpster. "I'll call—"

"Baby, I need you now!" the android yelled. The sounds of women moaning came from its speakers. It leaned forward and opened its mouth.

Milton let out a long breath. "Look, Aiko, you're a machine. Your urges are all in your programming. Or something. You can wait a few hours. I've got to take care of this."

She tilted her head to one side. "I will pout for you. Just imagine that I am pouting." She bowed slightly and closed the door behind her. Milton was left alone in the alley.

* * *

Milton pulled the two-wheeled cart up to the back door of grid 115, street 9, entry 36. He dropped the huge wooden handles to the ground and the long plastic bags in the cargo area shifted.

He entered 1–9–8–3–4–7 on a keypad next to the door and a screen revealed itself in the wall.

He tapped the screen twice and selected Dr. Vernor Xemura. It's my only chance to have her again. He might hide her but if I don't do this, she'll be gone forever. He clicked 'Call.'

A harried man with bushy brown hair and a black beard answered. He squinted at the screen. "I'm not buying right now. Thank you." He hung up.

Milton growled. Too distracted for his own good.

He dialed again. "Now just hold on, Dr. Xemura, how are you today and I hope you are well, by the way, wherever you are right—"

"Get to it, Milton. I'm very busy here," said Dr. Xemura.

"I have a special one," said Milton.

"I'm not buying!" He hung up.

Milton dialed him again. Oh, yes you are. "Look, these two are special. Young females. Healthy. They just fell on hard times. I don't need much, just—"

"Time elapsed?" asked Dr. Xemura.

"Not more than twenty-five minutes."

"Price?"

"Same as last—" started Milton.

Dr. Xemura hung up. Milton redialed. Always the cheapskate.

"It's two for one, Doctor! Two-for-one. You get the lady in the prime of her life, plus, you can take title of a child."

Dr. Xemura moved his face closer to the camera. "Details."

"No more than eight. In good health. A slight leg deformity. Very fond of audio subscriptions!" Milton added in a sing-song voice.

Dr. Xemura brought his hand to his chin. "Pre-pubescent," he muttered to himself. "And the two of them for the usual price?"

"That's a special deal, just for you, Doctor. Because you're my favorite," said Milton with a smile.

Dr. Xemura grimaced. "Close that mouth, man. I'll send someone immediately."

* * *

Ailsa opened her eyes. Everything was white. She stood up and looked around. Where am I?

She reached for the ceiling. It was hard and she couldn't completely extend her arm when touching it.

She turned right and put both hands out in front of her. There was the wall. She turned around and walked three steps in the other direction. There was the wall again.

She found the corner, and another wall. There were no seams.

Her pulse accelerated. She felt hot. What is this? There was a buzzing in her head and she struggled to think.

"Do not move," said a computer voice.

She ran forward and slammed into an invisible wall. She fell to the floor, her nose bloodied.

She reached out for the wall. It was transparent. What the…?

"Do not move!" said the computer voice. "You have injured yourself. Self-inflicted injury will be dealt with most severely."

She looked up. "What is this place? Who are you? Where am I? How did I get here?"

There was only silence and a bright white light that came from everywhere at once. She looked out through the transparent front wall. There was only more white.

She sat down cross-legged in front of the transparent wall. How did I get here? She remembered the uplift, that disgusting but somehow comforting man… and then what?

Something metallic clacked on the hard plastic floor behind her. She turned around.

It was a metal tray of food.

* * *

"I need to know what's going on!" Ailsa yelled. She went to the back wall and pounded on it with her fists.

"The tray must have come in here, somewhere," she muttered. She felt the back wall, starting from the floor and working up, then over and down again.

There was an indent. She ran her finger over it again. It moved. She got her finger in the space and pushed up. A hole opened up.

She shoved her fingers in and moved them around. The surface was rough, waxy and wet.

She pulled her fingers back out and smelled them. They stank of raw beef and rotten blood. Her stomach turned and she felt bile in her throat.

She laid her head on the floor and looked out the slit. Metal shelves sat beyond a white table. The shelves held nondescript brown boxes. Behind glass doors sat transparent jars with varying color tints.

She shifted to the left. There was a door, a big door. Shiny and metallic, it had a bulbous, circular glass window in the middle of it surrounded by a black circle.

There has to be a way out of here.

She stood up. She pushed the wall, here, there and everywhere. Nothing gave way.

She sat down in a corner and began to cry. "I'm never going to—" she started.

Texa. The thought electrified her. My little girl! How could I forget you?

She stood up. She grabbed the metal tray, dumped its contents in a corner and rammed it into the slot.

She pulled up on it. Nothing.

She pushed down on it. Nothing. She stepped on the tray. The wall slid up, then fell back down into place.

She levered it up again. She pushed on the wall and a thin panel fell onto her.

She knocked it to one side and stepped out onto the waxy, white table. The big door was only meters away.

* * *

The big door with the bulbous, glass window swung open with ease. Ailsa stepped through. It was cold and dark on the other side. Her bare, wet feet touched smooth, icy metal. She shivered.

Ailsa stopped and listened.

She turned a corner and went though a set of double doors. A panel of small lights lay ahead. She raced forward and slammed into a transparent wall. She fell onto her back. A screeching, whirring noise came from her right.

She looked. A hooded figure in a formless white lab suit ran towards her. It leaned down and grabbed her shoulders. Ailsa looked into the visor and saw a female face frozen in terror. It was her own.

She screamed. The figure seized her by the ankle and dragged her back towards her cage.

Ailsa slammed her head on the white table. The figure threw her into the cage. The panel was secured. Her eyelids closed and she fell into a troubled sleep.

* * *

"Mommy? Mommy! Wake up!" It was Texa's voice.

Ailsa opened her eyes. She was reclined on a thin bed. In front of her, two hooded figures with reflective viewplates moved around a spacious white room.

Around the edges of this new room lay deep, white tables with curious, reflective machines that Ailsa didn't recognize.

"Who are you?" Ailsa mouthed the words but she didn't hear herself say them.

She felt an itch on her nose and moved a hand to scratch it but it would not come. Her legs were immobilized as well.

She looked down. There were no straps over her limbs. Panic rose within her. What are they going to do to me?

"Mom!"

She whipped her head to the left. There was Texa. The skin around the girl's eyes was pink and soft now. Her eyes sparkled. Her face was smooth and relaxed. Her beauty was rendered all the more fragile by the expression of panic on her face.

Ailsa smiled. "My baby girl. Are you okay?" she whispered.

"What is this mom? Where are we? Who are these people?" she asked. The look in her eyes made Ailsa's gut feel empty.

Ailsa swallowed hard. "I don't know." Her voice rasped and she struggled to pull enough air into her lungs. The room began to spin.

One of the figures turned around. It stood absolutely still in its white lab suit and reflective helmet. It held a long, thin tube in its hand. It looked at Ailsa, then approached Texa.

"Don't you touch her! Don't you do anything to her!" yelled Ailsa. This is my fault. How could I let this happen to us? She willed her body to respond. Her left hand came up and she grabbed the figure.

It whipped around and smacked her hard across the face.

Ailsa struggled to recover. Her cheek burned. She sat up.

The figure jammed the tube into Texa's abdomen. It pulled it back out with a jerk.

"No!" whispered Ailsa. "What are you—"

She felt a hand on her leg. The other figure jammed a similar tube into her thigh.

"Mommy!" Texa's scream activated every maternal alarm in her brain.

A burning rose up through her leg and into her gut. Her heart seized. Ailsa struggled for breath.

"Mommy!"

She reached out her only good arm towards the figure, then collapsed.

* * *

I demand to know. I demand to know!

Ailsa jolted awake and stood up. Her stomach ached. It was empty and dry. Her leg gave way and she fell back to the chilly, plastic floor.

"I demand—" Her throat seized up. "I demand to know!" she yelled. "Where am I?"

She was back in the original cage, or one like it. She crawled to the transparent window and pounded on it with both fists. She strained to look out the edges. All white. Nothing.

I am going to get a reaction from them, no matter what.

She pulled her head back and slammed it into the transparent wall. Then again. And again.

Thick, warm blood ran down her face. She smeared some on the wall. She outlined a heart with her finger, then drew jagged vertical lines down the middle of it.

She pulled her head back again. A man with bushy brown hair and a black beard appeared in front of her.

"You may call me Dr. X. You are now a member of my laboratory here in Surrey." He pulled a pipe from his mouth and continued, "There are very strict rules in this laboratory. You must not harm yourself."

Ailsa felt a weakness in her chest. "Why am I here? I don't belong here." She gathered her strength and prepared to yell. "I demand to see my daughter, now!"

He took a step towards her and his image shimmered. Their noses were mere centimeters apart. "Let me be very clear with you. You are now my property . You will follow the rules. There will be no self-harm! You are a valuable piece of research equipment in my laboratory. In fact, you are the foundation. The girl depends on you. There will be no more—"

"Call me Ailsa," she whispered.

"Your name now is 1176892 and you have no daughter." His nostrils flared and his image dissolved for a moment before reappearing.

"I am a full citizen with enhanced rights of the Republic Trust!" Ailsa whispered. "You can't do this to me!"

"Your rights," said Dr. X in an even tone of voice, "were extinguished at death." The image looked to its right and a whoosh of air hit Ailsa.

A light chill ran down her arm. She laid her head on the hard floor. Extinguished... at... death? The words ran through her mind as she lost consciousness.

* * *

"She's had a reaction to the initial injection." Dr. Zora Collins wore sky blue scrubs and her platinum blond hair was tightly wrapped in a bun on the back of her head.

Her hands shook but she looked straight into the viewscreen.

Dr. Xemura looked up at her. "Surely, Erik can deal with this?"

"He's not here. What should I do?" Zora looked around at the tiny office. It made her feel compressed and cloistered. It was all wrong.

Dr. Xemura leaned back in his chair and smiled at her. "Relax. I know this is all new for you, Zora, but I can assure you that such reactions are entirely within the normal range." He turned back to his tablet.

"I'll give her a dose of anti-inflams and something for the pain, then. Collins out." Zora turned to leave. *Maybe then the little girl can get some sleep.*

"You will do no such thing!" yelled Dr. Xemura. He stood up and dropped his tablet onto a pile of metal folders on his desk. The camera followed his face.

Zora jumped and closed her eyes. *Relax. He doesn't know.*

"Have you understood nothing that I have taught you here, Dr. Collins?"

She turned to face him, her head held low and to the side.

"This is a research institution. We perform Republic-sanctioned research on validated—"

Zora looked up at the viewscreen and squared her face. "An adult is one thing, but a child… And to cause her unnecessary pain…"

"That will be quite enough! This is not a hospital. This is a research facility and unless you have been named its executive director, then I suggest you watch your words."

He sat down then looked back at Zora. He leered and raised an eyebrow. "After all, you would make a fine research subject yourself." His laugh echoed in her ear.

* * *

"I need your attention, Texa," said Ailsa. She found herself in a white room again. This one had a viewscreen.

"Right after this show. Just five minutes," said Texa.

"Now!" said Ailsa.

Texa flashed angry eyes at her mother. "We finally get the audio subscription and you can't let me watch?" She groaned. "What? What? What do you want?"

Ailsa's eyes unfocused. Texa's face glowed with health. *I've never seen her like this before. She's positively radiant.* A pang of regret and frustration gripped her. "We have to get out of here, baby," Ailsa said with some reluctance. "I need your help. How do you feel?"

Texa shrugged. "I'm happy, Mommy. The food is better and I have the audio subscription now. Thank you so much. I'm sorry. I'm mean. I'm a dummy."

"You're my beautiful little girl." Ailsa caressed Texa's cheek. "But don't you see? They have us in a cage."

"Can I watch now?"

"We're getting out of here," Ailsa whispered. "When I call you, you come with me immediately, no matter what is on the viewscreen."

Texa nodded. She pointed to the viewscreen behind her.

"Just be ready."

Ailsa examined her thigh. The wound was tender and swollen. Texa's abdomen was enlarged and firm. She tapped it hard.

"Can you feel that, baby?"

Texa did not answer.

"Texa! Did you feel that just now?"

"What?" Texa replied.

Ailsa rapped the swollen flesh again.

Texa shrugged.

Two food trays popped into their plastic cage, one after the other. Ailsa pushed them out of the way. She laid down, raised up the flap and looked out. A small, blond woman worked with a lime green knife.

She dumped the contents of one of the trays in a corner.

"Mommy! What are you doing? Don't mess it up! They don't like that," said Texa.

Ailsa jammed the tray into the slot and stepped on it but the wall would not move. She tried it again and again. She kicked the wall.

"I'm getting out of here," she yelled, "whatever it takes!" She threw the tray against the wall. "With hope, Texa! With hope, anything is possible!"

"Mommy! Please, I can't hear!" said Texa.

Texa's obliviousness enraged her. Humans are to be free, not caged. They can starve me. They can fuck me. They can make me live like a dog. But they can not cage my girl. No. No more.

Ailsa grabbed the tray anew. She shoved it into the slot. She jumped on it. The tray bent. "Damnit!" she muttered. She threw herself against the wall. The wall bounced her back. She grabbed the other tray and slammed its edge into the section of wall she knew should give way. She hit it again and again. Runny green and brown food splattered everywhere. A crack opened.

"Mom!" Texa yelled.

Ailsa felt the current but it was sluggish and uncertain. She took three long steps back, then ran and threw herself against the cracked wall.

Something snapped. She burst through and fell out onto the waxy table.

Dr. Zora Collins stared back at her, her eyes wide.

* * *

"You're going to help us get out of here," Ailsa said. She grabbed the green knife, jumped off the table and pointed it at Zora.

Zora opened her mouth but nothing came out.

Ailsa turned to the cage door. "Texa, now. Come on."

Texa crawled to the cage door and looked out. She gave her mother a dark frown and exhaled hard out of her nose. "Promise me you'll get the audio subscription wherever we're going."

"Texa, I—"

"Promise me!" Texa said.

"Okay, alright. I promise. Just be reasonable. It could take me a day or two."

Texa climbed out of the cage. "Hi." She smiled at Zora. "Are you escaping too?"

Zora's face went soft. She stared at Texa's abdomen. "Of course. Yes. But first, why don't I give you—"

"No!" Ailsa took a step towards here. "No more giving us stuff. We leave. Now." She jabbed the knife at Zora. "You go first."

Zora led them out the door with the bulbous window, through the chilly room of brightly-lit machines and to a plastic wall. Through the wall, Ailsa saw that same panel of small jumbled lights as before. She struggled to decipher anything meaningful from it.

"Are you sure about this?" Zora asked.

"What do you mean, 'am I sure about this?' Would you be? Open it," Ailsa said. She touched the blade of the knife to the back of Zora's neck.

Zora froze. "Please…"

"Open it! No more screwing around."

Zora reached down and pulled up a zipper. The plastic wall split open with a deep ripping sound.

They stepped out into bright sunshine.

Ailsa covered her eyes until they adjusted. She opened one and looked out through two fingers at Zora. She held the knife at the ready.

A cool, wet wind slapped her in the face. She smelled salt and minerals and grime. She furrowed her brow and looked around her with both eyes open.

There was indigo blue ocean, everywhere.

* * *

Ailsa ran to the edge of the deck. The metal-plated flooring shifted and buckled under her bare feet. The water was very far down, too far to jump. She grabbed Texa and pushed her back to the door of the shimmery plastic tent they just came out of. "Stay here," she said.

She walked around the edge of the tent. The water was unbroken on all sides for as far as she could see.

Ailsa ran back to Zora. "Where the hell are we!"

Zora narrowed her eyes and looked away. "We're on a research platform in international waters."

Ailsa put the knife to her throat. Her hands shook. "Where? What's near here?"

Zora eyed the knife but refused to look directly at it or Ailsa. "Relax," said Zora. She cleared her throat. "We're in the Celtic Sea, just a few hundred kilometers from St. Agnes."

"A few hundred kilometers? St. Agnes? Where is that?" Ailsa put her hands on her knees and leaned forward. She took deliberate breaths as the information sank in. She took one final deep breath before righting herself.

"Alright. How do we get out of here then?" she asked Zora.

"You can't," said Zora.

* * *

"Who else is here?" Ailsa asked Zora. She walked to the edge of the platform and looked down but could only see the support structure below. "Are there more floors to this? How far down does it go?"

"I want to help you," Zora said. "I really do. But—"

"You want to cover your ass."

"We're being watched." Zora moved her eyes up and to the left. "Don't—"

Ailsa whipped around. Above the shimmery tent was a pole with a black ball on top of it. She looked back at Zora and frowned. "I shouldn't have looked."

"No," said Zora. She shrugged.

"Texa," said Ailsa, "come on. We're finding a way out of here. There must be a boat or something. She lay down on the edge of the platform and looked over the edge.

Underneath was a complex metal structure but no ladder or other obvious means of safe transportation to the surface of the water, hundreds of meters below. Nor was there any boat moored down there.

Ailsa stood back up. She walked over to Zora and slashed her arm with the knife.

Zora screamed. She held her arm tight against her body. She stepped towards the tent.

"There is a way off of this thing," said Ailsa, "and you're going to tell me what it is!"

"Mom, what are you doing?" asked Texa. Her mouth hung open. She stepped back and entered the tent.

Ailsa's face flushed. The vibration of the current activated a feeling of hot shame in her. "Just sit down by the tent door, baby. Outside the tent! Mommy... Mommy has to get us out of here. Turn around, baby, I don't want you to see this."

"No!" yelled Texa. She took a step closer to her mother. "She's nice. She's helping us."

"Just be quiet." Ailsa struggled to focus on Zora. "Why would they put a platform out in the middle of the ocean, this high up with just a flimsy tent on it? Just for us? Why? Why!"

Ailsa grabbed Zora's arm and jerked her closer. She dug her thumb into the cut on Zora's arm. Zora grimaced. "Ow! Please!"

Ailsa put the knife to Zora's neck. "So help me…" She stared deep into Zora's eyes. "So help me! Look at my little girl and tell me you wouldn't do the same. Tell me!" she screamed.

Ailsa slashed the thin blade against Zora's cheek and a tiny gash opened. Blood oozed out. Zora touched her cheek, saw the blood on her fingers and sobbed. She hugged her arms to herself and took a step towards the edge of the platform.

Ailsa kicked Zora's feet out from under her. Zora fell hard on her back and gasped for air. Ailsa sat on her chest and held the blade just above the pale skin of Zora's neck. Ailsa watched Zora's chest heave. Just beyond the woman's head was the rolling ocean. She hesitated but then she remembered being strapped to the table, helpless, as the people in suits accessed her body without her permission.

She started to push down into the pudgy flesh of her neck.

"Okay! Okay!" yelled Zora. "I'll tell you!"

Ailsa continued to push.

* * *

Zora opened a flap of metal in the floor near the entrance to the tent. "Stand over here." Her hand shook as she pointed to a safe spot.

Ailsa and Texa looked at her. "What?"

Zora gestured at them. "Over here." She swallowed hard.

"Don't try anything," Ailsa said.

The mother and daughter stood up against the tent. Zora pushed something inside the metal flap. There was a screeching metal groan. The floor of the platform split in front of them. It slid apart and a winged vehicle rose up from below.

"Please, let me go with you," said Zora.

Ailsa grabbed Texa and ran to the vehicle. Its cigar-shaped body was a matte dark metallic blue. There was a pilot's bench and behind it three rows of two seats each. The wings unfolded. They were wide and deep but very thin.

Ailsa belted Texa into the second row. Ailsa sat down next to her. "Take us to London!" she said.

Nothing happened.

Zora crossed her arms and rolled her eyes. "You need a pilot."

"Turn on! Close hatch!" yelled Ailsa.

"Mom," Texa said, "we don't know how to use it. We need…" She turned to Zora. "What's your name?"

"Go!" yelled Ailsa. Her face was red.

Texa rolled her eyes. "She already knows where we want to go. And I like her."

Zora walked over the edge of the vehicle. "Well?"

Ailsa slunk down in her seat and crossed her arms.

Zora got into the pilot's seat. In front of her was a steering wheel, four large buttons colored red, blue, green and yellow. Dials and digital readouts surrounded them. She strapped herself in. "Turn on," she said. "Hatch down. Destination: London."

Ailsa sat up straight. "Hey, why does it work for her?"

Texa giggled.

* * *

Zora sat absolutely still. She strained her wrist to pull the slim communicator out of her back pocket. She cleared her throat, then stopped herself. *If they're resting, I shouldn't make a sound.* She listened for any sign of movement in the back seat. There was nothing.

"Broadcast. Rising. London," she typed. "Two Xemura refugees, lab specimens, human female and female child, need exit strategy near XLS1 now. Immediate reply. Confirm."

"What's your name?" It was the girl. She leaned forward between the two front seats and looked at Zora.

Zora put on her serious face. "You need to strap in, young lady, before—"

"I just want to know your name," Texa said. Her brash grin burst through Zora's defenses.

"Zora," she said with a smile.

"My name's Texa."

"Yes, I know. Now sit—"

"Who are you messaging?" the child asked.

Zora's chest seized up.

"And what are you so afraid of?" asked Texa.

Zora sighed. "This is a little complicated for a little—"

Texa frowned and crossed her arms. "I can understand more than adults think I can."

A reply came back. "Black car, southeast corner of XLS1 five minutes, sharp. Refugees only."

Zora took a deep breath. She put the communicator away. Now all I have to worry about is what Vernor will do to me.

* * *

"It's a good thing we brought Zora, huh, Mom?" said Texa with a resentful grin.

Ailsa was silent. I'm ditching her as soon as we land. The low squeal of the aircraft zooming through cloudy skies relaxed her. She closed her eyes again and let her shoulders fall.

"This is Xemura 8342," said Zora, "requesting permission to enter Republic airspace."

"Destination?" said a genderless voice.

"London, Xemura Life Sciences Building One," said Zora.

"Approved," said the voice, "Engage auto-pilot now."

"Auto," said Zora. She looked back at Texa and smiled. "It'll be just another few minutes."

"Xemura?" asked Ailsa. She opened her eyes and leaned forward. "Is this whole thing…? No, we're not going there!"

"No other destination is credible," said Zora. "This craft always flies back and forth between XLS1 and the platform."

"'Always'? So you've done this to other people? And what happened to them?" Ailsa asked.

Zora said nothing.

"See?" Ailsa whispered to Texa. "She's no saint. She's done—"

Texa put her face against the glass. "Look, Mom. It's beautiful."

Ailsa leaned over her daughter and looked out the window. Her mouth opened in wonder. Below them, the indigo ocean met the gleaming shores of England.

"It's so shiny!" said Texa.

"The Republic is very technologically advanced," said Zora. "It provides—"

Ailsa reached around and smacked the side of Zora's head. "You won't feed that bullshit to her."

Zora swallowed hard. "The Republic has given me—"

"Enough!" yelled Ailsa. "Set it down over there."

"But I have to go to XLS1," said Zora. "That's where the auto-pilot is taking us."

"Turn it off!"

"Auto-pilot off," said Zora.

The ship jerked. "Auto-pilot must be on under Republic order 892–330. Request denied. Resuming original course to Xemura Life Sciences Building One."

* * *

"She what?" Dr. Vernor Xemura yelled. He stood up behind his thin metal and glass desk in his darkened office on the eighty-third floor of Xemura Life Sciences Building One in London.

"She's gone and so are the subjects," said the male voice.

"I'm sorry, Mr. President," Xemura said with a formal tone. "I have a pressing matter. I will return your call shortly." He tapped a button on his desk.

"The relevant video is available to you now," said the male voice.

Xemura watched the video footage. "Doesn't she realize how important this is? This is a personal betrayal. Thank you."

"But how do we—"

"Disconnect," said Xemura. "Connect Hanshin."

"Yes, sir," said Hanshin. His voice was deep and guttural.

"A hovercraft is missing from the CS32 facility. I need you to track—"

"Actually, sir," said Hanshin, "it's landing on the roof in forty-five seconds."

The corners of Dr. Xemura's mouth twitched upwards. "Dispatch a team. I want Dr. Collins secured in an interrogator and I want the cargo returned to CS32 immediately."

* * *

"I don't want to land there!" yelled Ailsa.

The hovercraft slowed as it approached XLS1. Men in black with helmets and long rifles filed onto the roof. They waited next to the circle with a letter 'H' inside.

"Don't make me kill you!" yelled Ailsa.

The engines cut out and the craft jerked downwards before the thrusters kicked in with a roar and lowered the vessel gently down to the hoverpad.

The soldiers surrounded them.

"Mommy?" whispered Texa. She wrapped her arms around Ailsa's neck. Her bloated abdomen got in the way and she screamed in pain.

"It hurts now?" asked Ailsa.

Texa grimaced. "A lot."

"Open—" started Zora.

Ailsa climbed into the front seat and jammed the knife up against her chest. "Get us out of here! Now!"

Zora looked at her with dead eyes. She hit the red button and the hatch opened. The soldiers pointed their rifles at them and approached.

Ailsa searched the panel with her eyes. She hit a yellow button that said "Manual" under it and grabbed the co-pilot's steering wheel. The craft hovered just above the deck and moved slowly towards the soldiers.

"Damnit!" yelled Ailsa. She searched the panel again. She hit the red button and the hatch slowly closed. A soldier reached them and got his arm inside. He grabbed Ailsa's neck and squeezed.

Ailsa's breath rasped in her throat. The soldier pinned her to the seat. Her hand would not reach the panel. Zora hit the red button before the hatch finished closing on the soldier's arm.

Out of the corner of her eye, she spotted a green button. Ailsa extended her fingers but they would not reach. She brought up her foot and jammed it into the console.

The craft jetted straight up into the air. It bumped into a lime green blimp and careened wildly into gray sky. The scream of the wind deafened her. The soldier in black pulled himself up and got his arm into the cabin. He pulled a pistol from under his arm and aimed it Ailsa.

Ailsa buried her knife in his throat. Blood spurted on her and he fell away. She dropped the knife inside the cabin and tried in vain to wipe the blood from her hands and face.

An alarm sounded. Ailsa held onto the steering wheel but her body floated up. "What do I do?" she yelled.

Zora reached over and hit the yellow button again. She closed the hatch. The craft righted itself and glided smoothly towards XLS1 again.

Ailsa searched the floor for the knife. It was under her seat. She grabbed but it slipped from her fingers. She reached around the back of her seat, clutched the knife and jammed it through Zora's arm. It lodged in the seatback. Ailsa hit the yellow button again and accelerated the ship forward.

Zora screamed. Her eyes got big. "How— How could you...? She stared open-mouthed at the green metal that protruded from her upper arm."

Ailsa hit a blue "Land" button. The engines cut out and the craft hurtled toward the ground below. She looked out the window. Below them, four lanes of aircars crawled south.

"What do I do?" Ailsa yelled to Zora.

Zora's eyes were closed and she breathed deliberately.

Ailsa hit the blue button again and the engines restarted. She was thrown against the steering wheel.

Texa slammed into the seat in front of her.

Zora pulled the knife out of her arm. She screamed and set it between her and the wall of the craft.

Ailsa looked around in a daze. The craft continued forward, skimming above the tops of the four-lane airway.

Zora grabbed the controls and guided them back in the direction of XLS1.

Ailsa turned around. "Are you okay, Texa?"

Texa lay on the floor. She did not move.

"Texa!" Ailsa yelled. She turned to Zora. "Set us down, now!"

"Or what?" asked Zora. She narrowed her eyes at Ailsa. "You have nothing more to threaten me with."

The black towers of XLS1 took shape ahead of them through puffy, ash-colored clouds.

Ailsa stared at her. "You would do the same thing in my shoes."

Zora scowled and narrowed her eyes.

"Anyway," said Ailsa, "you need treatment now. I'll just keep fighting you till you bleed out up here."

Zora took a deep breath and let it out. She veered the craft to the right. They circled down in a corkscrew pattern. She hit the blue button. "This is the best I can do. You don't belong in a cage but this is the wrong way to do it. Dr. Xemura is a reasonable—"

Ailsa reached across and hit the red button. The hatch opened. She grabbed Texa and hopped out into the smoggy, gray London afternoon. A burning sensation erupted in her calf and she fell to her knees.

* * *

Ailsa picked herself up. She waded out into the street-level traffic with an unconscious Texa in her arms.

A white truck honked a complex and angry melody at her. It swerved to avoid her.

A billboard driver didn't see her until the last moment. He turned hard to the left and clipped her with his rear bumper. Ailsa and Texa flew to the ground.

A black taxi stopped. A portly, giant man with curly, raven hair emerged from inside of the tiny car. "Hey, you! You hit this woman and her child," he yelled.

The billboard driver stuck his head out the window and looked at Ailsa. Ailsa stirred.

"She'll be fine, mate. I'll leave her in your more than capable hands," said the billboard driver. He started his rig back up and continued down the road.

The taxidriver looked at his cab. Other vehicles honked at him. His work console lit up the inside of his vehicle. He looked back at Texa and Ailsa. They weren't moving.

* * *

"I've got an emergency here, darling," said the taxidriver. He sat in the front seat of the cab. A nurse appeared on his viewscreen. "Two—"

"Please," whispered Ailsa from the back seat. "Just get us out of here."

"What's your name?" asked the taxidriver.

Ailsa struggled to sit up straight. "Drive, just drive!" she yelled. She looked at the viewscreen in his headrest. "Gabriel," it said.

Gabriel turned around.

"Gabriel," she said. She leaned forward and looked him in the eye. "My daughter and I are escaping from this… corporation… this Dr. Xemura."

"Xemura?" Gabriel asked.

She looked at the headrest viewscreen again. Gabriel's last name was written in tall, fat letters: XEMURA. Ailsa held her breath.

She grabbed for the door handle and pulled. It would not open. "Let us out!"

She looked through the rear window. The black-suited soldiers ran towards the small cab.

Gabriel turned around. "I'm going to help you—"

Ailsa narrowed her eyes at him. "Who are you?"

"Don't worry about that yet, darling," said Gabriel. He punched the accelerator and they flew up into the air.

* * *

Gabriel descended against an approaching bank of storm clouds and parked the car high in the alley between two darkened red brick factories.

Ailsa reclined in the back seat. She hugged Texa tight to her. "Why are we stopping?" she asked. It was dark outside. All she saw were broken windows. The darkness inside the old factories made her shiver.

Gabriel twisted his giant frame in the driver's seat to look Ailsa in the face. He smiled without showing any teeth. "I need to know everything."

"Why? What do you want from us?" Ailsa studied his face. It was strong and tired.

"Tell him, Mom," said Texa. "I think we can trust him."

"Quiet," she said to Texa. "What are you to him?"

Gabriel sighed. "He's my brother."

* * *

"Why is that guy's brother driving a cab?" Ailsa asked.

The three of them lounged in Gabriel's living room. The couch was too shallow, the seat cushions bowed and peppered with dark spots but it was comfortable and cool. Their backs were to the front door.

Texa bounced in her seat. She looked at the ceiling and back down. "Can I watch your viewscreen?" she asked.

"Sure," said Gabriel. "Viewscreen on," he said. "Go ahead and tell it what you want, darling."

Across from the couch, giant moving images appeared in crystal clarity.

Gabriel got up, turned right and walked to the kitchen. He pulled out some bread, mayonnaise and sliced meat. He carried them over and set

186

them on the coffee table in front of the couch. "Help yourselves."

Ailsa glared at him. "So, your brother…"

"Oh, right," said Gabriel. He sat back down. "Well, when we were kids, he was the Hawking. Brilliant in science, aced all the tests, teacher's pet. The whole thing."

"Mom," said Texa, "the audio subscription still works! I can hear the sound great. Thanks, Mom. I love you." She smiled and kept bouncing with her eyes glued to the viewscreen.

Ailsa smiled at her. She raised her eyebrows at Gabriel.

"He won a science competition. He was adopted by Monsanto. And they educated him." He sighed. "But I haven't seen him since. I see his ads and all that. But not him."

Ailsa fixed herself a sandwich. "I am so hungry," she whispered.

"So, he kidnapped you and your girl?" Gabriel asked.

"Not exactly. We… died," she whispered.

Gabriel frowned at her. "He killed you…?"

"We went to this… place." She waved a hand in front of her face and turned away from him. "Anyway, it doesn't matter. We died. We were dead."

Gabriel nodded and waited for her to finish. "I'm glad you're still with us, darling. You have a beautiful little girl. You are a beautiful young lady."

Ailsa blushed. He thinks I'm cute. She arched her head to one side and twirled an index finger in her hair. She thought about what she must look, and smell, like after the ordeal. She stopped and looked away, ashamed.

Gabriel smiled back. "Where's her dad?" he said in a low voice.

"He was killed," Ailsa said. "He was out getting us food and some punk killed him for five coins." She finished her sandwich and sat back. "That is much better. I don't even remember the last time I ate."

"You don't have papers do you?" he asked.

She shook her head tightly from side to side. "Our protectorate was in uplift, anyway. And the shop probably registered us as dead."

Gabriel lowered his eyelids and frowned. "You missed uplift? I wonder if you can still—"

Ailsa glared at him. "Have you been uplifted?"

Gabriel shook his head. "So, my brother brought you back to life? Is that what you're telling me, darling?"

Ailsa shrugged. "I was dead. I don't know. But he told us we were his property now, that our Republic rights were 'extinguished at death.'"

"He always was a greedy bastard," said Gabriel with a smirk, "But unquestionably brilliant. So, do you still want to die?"

Ailsa shot a glance at Texa. She brought a finger to her mouth and shook her head. She stood up. "Aren't you married or something?"

"All the women today want life easy. They won't fight for anything," he said.

Ailsa crossed her arms. "Oh, and what do you fight for?"

Gabriel laughed. "Ask me later." He patted the couch next to him.

"You must need some clothes washed or some food made or something?" Ailsa asked. She sat down and looked up at him with pleading eyes. "I can be a good housekeeper, at least until we find somewhere to go, and Texa won't be any—"

Texa stood up and walked away from the couch without taking her eyes off the screen. "Sh!" she whispered.

He put his arm up on the back of the couch. His fingers lay near her shoulder. "Relax," he said with a broad smile. "You guys need a few days of—"

The door burst open behind them. Gabriel and Ailsa were thrown through the coffee table and into the ground. The couch landed on top of them.

The darkly-clad soldiers entered the house. They scanned in all directions with their heads pegged tight to their rifles.

"This is a Republic safety inspection," yelled an artificially amplified voice. "Lay down on the—"

Texa whipped around. "Quiet! I'm watching my show!" A dark look crossed her face. She gritted her teeth and her head jerked to one side.

There was a sound of bones popping, like a thousand fingers cracking at the same time. The soldiers' writhing bodies collapsed to the ground with a gurgling sound.

Texa's head moved back to a normal position, her eyes rolled back and she fell to the floor.

* * *

Ailsa drew in a ragged breath through her mouth and choked on the thick dust. She coughed but lacked enough air to expel it. She struggled between breath and cough.

Gabriel stirred next to her. He got onto his hands and knees and pushed the sofa. It rolled off of him and landed on Ailsa's calves before standing upright again.

"Ow!" whispered Ailsa. She sat back on the floor against the edge of the couch and cleared her lungs. "Why is it so dark?"

Gabriel kicked something and it crashed to the floor. "What the hell...?"

A switch clicked and the room was flooded with light. "What happened?" Ailsa asked.

"Oh bloody hell!" yelled Gabriel. He ran backwards and fell onto an end table. It broke under his weight.

Ailsa stood up and screamed. "Are they dead? Texa? Texa! Where—"

Ailsa ran to Texa. "Wake up," she said. "Texa. Please." Tears streamed down her cheeks. "Gabriel..."

Gabriel climbed over the bodies of the soldiers and opened the door. His jaw dropped and he took a step back.

"What is it?" Ailsa ran to him. She looked outside and screamed.

Dead soldiers, collapsed like formless water bladders, littered the front yard and the street. Sirens sounded in the distance.

* * *

"We have to get out of here, darling," said Gabriel. "Is Texa okay?"

"She's breathing, but I can't wake her," said Ailsa.

"Grab her. Grab some food. I'll get the car ready," he said.

He grabbed a small toolbox from under the kitchen counter and ran outside. He opened the hood on his tiny black cab and ripped a small yellow box out with a pair of pliers.

Ailsa watched him for a moment. So big, so strong and he knows how to work with his hands. Her spine tingled. He'll get us out.

Gabriel put the hood down gently and returned inside, stepping carefully over the black bags of broken bones. He held up the yellow box. "They won't be able to track us now. Hurry up."

What about those injections? Maybe those are tracking chips? She limped to the kitchen. She grabbed bread, lunchmeat, cheese, mayonnaise and a banana from the fridge. She put them in a plastic bag and then stared into space.

"Let's go," Gabriel said. He turned to look at her. "What is it?"

"They injected us with something. Do you think it could be a tracking chip?"

"Goddamnit," said Gabriel. He massaged his forehead.

The sirens got louder and there were more of them.

Gabriel ran and grabbed Texa in his arms. "It doesn't matter. We have to go." He grabbed Ailsa's arm and pulled her.

Ailsa hopped into the front passenger seat. Gabriel eased Texa into the backseat. He squeezed his massive frame into the driver's seat.

"You have to get into the back," he said. "Cabbies aren't allowed to have passengers up front."

Ailsa gritted her teeth but she moved to the backseat. Gabriel gunned it and the car flew off into the murky evening sky.

Ailsa glanced out the back window just as the white-suited Gards arrived.

* * *

"I don't know where I'm going," said Gabriel. They rocketed through the evening sky outside of the airway lanes. He turned to Ailsa. "What do we do?"

"You should drop us off somewhere," she said. "You're a good man.

There's no reason for us to drag you down." She put her hand on his upper arm and squeezed.

He contracted the muscle and shot a tense smile at her.

She looked away from him, put her hand in her hair and breathed in through her mouth. Wow he is handsome! The current was back, and it was stronger.

"There are at least thirty Gards down there, inside and around my house. I'm screwed. I can never go back there. Even if they don't euthanize me, that's a lot of correction."

Ailsa closed her eyes. "I'm sorry, so— Wait. What happened to those guys? What did you do?"

"I didn't do anything, darling" said Gabriel. "They were like that when I woke up."

Ailsa turned to Texa. She sat back and thought. Do I tell him? But what if he wants to hurt her? I need his help. "It was Texa."

"What?" asked Gabriel.

"Her father could make you feel what he was feeling. I've suspected she had it, too."

"That's an interesting theory, darling, but where do we go? We're just hurtling through space and time right now. They'll catch—"

"Go to XLS1, where you found us," she said.

He turned around with one eyebrow raised. "Are you—?"

"Just do it. Trust me." She leaned forward and kissed him on the cheek. Their eyes met and she softened her face.

* * *

"Can you hover about a block away from the front door?" Ailsa asked.

"This is a bad idea," Gabriel said.

"Mommy?" Texa sat up and opened her eyes.

"Hey, baby girl." Ailsa turned and put her arm under Texa's head. "You were out for awhile. You okay?"

Texa squinted. Her voice was rough. "I'm really hungry. And thirsty, too."

"I'll get you something in just a minute, okay? Just hold on."

Gabriel hovered the car across the street from the main entrance to XLS1. "We're right out in the open here, you know. I'd like to understand what you're thinking."

"Mom, hungry," said Texa.

"I'm kind of hungry, too," said Gabriel.

"It's her… influence," said Ailsa. "I feel it, too. We have to be care—"

"Mom!" Texa yelled.

"Just hold on, baby girl. Look," she said to Gabriel, "there was a woman with us."

"Small blond in the white coat and glasses?" asked Gabriel.

"Zora's her name. She's a doctor. She works for your brother. She can get the chips out."

"Do we know where she lives, darling?" Gabriel asked.

Ailsa rolled her eyes. "How would I know that?"

"Why do you think she's still here? She could—"

"It's a feeling. I sometimes get feelings and they turn out right. Sometimes, it's Texa and she's sending me the feeling without even knowing."

Gabriel laughed. "So, we're sitting outside of the place where you guys face the greatest danger, where they could grab you and whisk you off back to a white room forever on the slight feeling that maybe some woman who didn't want to help you before might be here and might be willing to help you now. Did I get that right, little darling?"

Ailsa looked away from him and screwed up her face. I hate it when men mock me.

* * *

"Mom! Food, now!" Texa yelled.

Ailsa's face got hot. Her pulse accelerated and her stomach felt empty. Her head began to spin. "Put us down," she whispered. "I'll get her something to eat."

"And leave me here by myself? What good is that? I won't recognize this

192

woman! And if they're tracking us, they'll be here any minute!" Gabriel slammed his fist against the steering wheel. "I don't even know why—"

"Why you're with us? I don't know either!" yelled Ailsa. "Just set us down, Mr. Xemura. We'll take it from here."

"Mom," Texa groaned. "Mom. Please."

Ailsa's chest tightened. We're never going to be free of this. We'll never get out of here. They have people everywhere. Zora isn't here anymore.

Gabriel leaned forward. "Wait. Is that her?" He pointed towards a lone figure exiting XLS1.

"Oh, who cares—" started Ailsa.

"Mommy!"

Ailsa wanted to be angry but the desperation overtook her and she could only sit still with her mouth open. All hope and motivation drained from her.

Gabriel sighed. "You're right." He let his head slump forward.

The figure turned right and hailed a cab. It was a woman and she wore a wide pink hat and big sunglasses.

Get up, get up. Move! Ailsa pushed past the dread in her gut and grabbed the wheel. She turned to follow the figure. "Hit the gas," she whispered. "The gas."

"But—" started Gabriel. "Oh, okay." The taxi inched forward.

Ailsa grabbed his knee and pushed it down. The taxi zoomed up and then descended until it scraped the roof and hood of the other taxi.

"Oh, Jesus," whispered Gabriel. "They're going to correct me for this." His head hung forward and his shoulders hunched.

"Zora," yelled Ailsa.

The figure looked up. It was her.

"Get in this car," said Ailsa.

Zora exited the cab and ran back towards XLS1.

"Follow her!" yelled Ailsa.

"I don't know, darling," said Gabriel. "I feel... I feel so—"

"It's Texa! She's projecting her feelings onto us. Just work through it!"

Gabriel sighed. "I don't know."

"Then move and let me drive," said Ailsa. She pushed him but his bulk refused to budge.

Ailsa turned around. "Baby, I know you feel bad."

"So hungry..." said Texa. "My head hurts."

"But we're going to get food in a minute, as soon as we get Zora back."

Texa's eyebrows went up. "Zora? I like her! When can we see her again?"

Gabriel sat up straight. He ascended the taxi and turned to pursue Zora. "Wow, I don't know what came over—"

"I'm so thirsty," said Texa. She drew in a ragged breath through her mouth.

The taxi slowed down again.

Darkness enveloped Ailsa's mind once more. Her head hung forward and she breathed through her mouth.

No. She grabbed Gabriel's knee and pushed it down again. The taxi accelerated and passed Zora. "Look, baby girl, it's Zora!"

Texa looked at her with unfocused eyes. "She's kind of nice..."

Gabriel picked up his head. He whipped the car around one-hundred and eighty degrees. He advanced abruptly and the woman was on the hood.

"No!" the wide-hatted woman yelled. She scampered off the hood.

Ailsa opened her door, ran out and pulled her into the car. She closed the door behind her.

Ailsa ripped off the woman's hat and big glasses. "It is you!" She held Zora's neck between her thumb and forefinger. "What did you inject us with?"

"Hi Zora!" said Texa. "Mommy, be nice to her. And I want a cheeseburger, please. Real meat."

Zora rolled her eyes. "I'm in deep shit thanks to you. They interrogated me for I don't know how long and they didn't want to let me go."

"I don't give a—" started Ailsa.

"I helped you, you know," said Zora. She crossed her arms. "You owe me." She stole a sideways glance at Gabriel.

Gabriel turned and smiled at them. "I hate to interrupt this lovely reunion, ladies, but we can't just sit here. Where to?" He grinned at them and his perfectly straight and white teeth made Ailsa tingle.

Ailsa sighed. "We have to get outside the city but it has to be somewhere with medical facilities. Do you know a place?"

"Not a clue. And Princess Charming back there needs something to eat, ASAP," said Gabriel. "I know a good place for food, very discreet, then maybe we'll know where to go."

"You can't escape Xemura," said Zora. "He knows where you are, always. You can't get outside of this protectorate without papers and you don't have any." She laughed. "You're dead. You and your little girl are dead. You're stuck. You can't go anywhere. Xemura will catch up to you any second and then all of us are done."

Ailsa punched her hard in the nose.

* * *

"I need to know where we're going," said Gabriel. His beef and broccoli was getting cold on the front seat.

Ailsa fought to get spoonfuls of sweet and sour chicken into Texa's mouth.

"I don't like it! I want beef! Not chicken!" yelled Texa.

"Take mine," said Gabriel. "I like chicken just fine."

Ailsa grabbed it, flicked the iridescent aluminum box open and spooned some of it into Texa's mouth.

"Thank you Gabriel," said Texa in a sweet voice. "It's really good. I can leave you some, if you want."

This girl loves everybody but me. Ailsa shoved more food into Texa's mouth and handed her a bottle of water. She reached down and slapped Zora.

Zora stared up at her from the floor, eyes wide.

"We have food for you," Ailsa said.

"Do we know where we're going yet?" asked Gabriel. "It's miracle they haven't fallen on us already."

"They're nearby," said Zora. "They know exactly where you are. They'll show themselves—"

Ailsa slapped her. "Shut up!" She spilled soy-soaked broccoli on Texa's shirt.

"Mom!" Texa whined.

"Sorry, baby," Ailsa said. She turned back to Zora. "We need these chips out and you're going to remove them."

"I need specialized—" Zora started.

"All you really need is a knife, isn't it?" asked Ailsa. She shoveled another bite into Texa's mouth. She felt the weight lift from her chest as Texa was satiated.

"What's in it for me?" asked Zora.

"You're involved in this Xemura business up to your ears," said Ailsa. "I know you don't like it. This is your chance to do something about it. Help us. Help my girl. She's only seven. Her life hasn't even started yet."

Zora's eyes bulged and a sneer crossed her face. "You should have thought of that before killing yourselves!"

* * *

"Did you do something back there, Texa?" Ailsa asked her.

The tiny taxi rocketed towards a private clinic on the outskirts of the protectorate.

"They made me angry. They were interrupting my show. Finally, I get a nice viewscreen and the audio subscription and they were going to take it away from us," said Texa.

"Do you know how to control the power, use it when—" started Ailsa.

"I don't like it!" Texa's eyes sparkled with tears. "I don't want to talk about it."

"Can you leave her alone?" Gabriel said.

Ailsa's chest was empty. Every breath hurt. The current hummed. "Okay, little girl."

Texa yawned.

"Take a nap, baby. You need your rest." Ailsa turned to Zora. "So, you know these people?"

"Stop telling me what to do," Texa mumbled.

Gabriel straightened his back. "Thank God she's out. When she gets emotional, it's like I'm buried in here."

Zora cocked her head. "What do you mean?" She leaned forward from the back seat and touched Gabriel's shoulder.

Gabriel looked in the rearview mirror and said nothing.

Why did he have to open his big mouth? Ailsa grimaced.

"What does he mean?" Zora asked Ailsa.

"Shut up," she said.

Zora crossed her arms. "I can't help you if—"

"Zora, just tell us," said Ailsa, "how to get past the Gards at this clinic."

"It's actually a Xemura clinic," said Zora with a sheepish smile.

Ailsa smacked her across the face. "You stupid bitch, do you think I'm screwing around with my daughter's future here?" She hit her again. "Stupid upworlder. You have no clue what life is like for the rest of us."

"I—" started Zora.

"You look down on us like farmers on their livestock. So arrogant," Ailsa said.

"I have a job to do," said Zora. "I advance the human race through science. I am—"

"You prey on downworld. You people keep all the wealth for yourselves."

"Why shouldn't we?" asked Zora. "We produce it."

"You corral us. You experiment on us without our permission, you treat us like things to be toyed with as you please."

Zora crossed her arms and looked away.

"But we're human beings, just like you, free, equal. We want the same—" started Ailsa.

"You're rabble! You're the reason this planet is dying! Now we have to find ways to survive — new ways," said Zora.

"Ladies," said Gabriel in a deep voice, "you're going to—"

Texa opened her eyes. "Can you guys shut up!"

* * *

"How are we getting in, Zora?" asked Ailsa.

Gabriel pulled into the parking lot of Xemura Clinic No. 23. The wide, flat building snaked through an expertly landscaped forest on a hillside. Villas and small farms dotted the landscape around it.

Just beyond and above the clinic was another high, cement wall. Green, flowing fields framed little homes on the other side. Floating blimp cameras and weapons platforms created a two-kilometer high barrier between them and the other protectorate.

"What's in that other protectorate?" asked Ailsa. "And how far are we from 13477?"

Gabriel shrugged.

Ailsa turned to Zora with a harsh stare. "How are we going to do this?"

Zora smirked. She straightened her back and put her hands on her hips. "So, all of this abuse and now the proud downworlder depends on the know-nothing upworlder."

"Well?" said Ailsa.

Texa looked up at Zora and smiled. "You're nice. You're just scared."

Zora's eyes darkened. She looked out the window at the clinic. "It isn't right, what Xemura is doing, what he did to you. You did kill yourselves though?" She turned around and fixed Ailsa in a quizzical stare. "How do I know I'm not risking my neck for someone who's going to turn around and suicide again when things get tough?"

Ailsa's face fell. "That's not—"

"You killed her!" Zora yelled. "And you talk to me about helping her? You're not fit to be her mother!"

* * *

Gabriel pulled a gun from under the front passenger seat. "Maybe this will come in handy, darling?"

"Enough talk." Ailsa grabbed the gun. She turned to Gabriel. "Does it work? Where did you get it?"

"The dead soldiers," he said.

She pointed it at the roof of the taxi.

"Not in here! You'll damage it!" yelled Gabriel. "And who knows what else. Those things go through a lot and keep going."

"What if it doesn't work?" asked Zora. "We'll go in there and be prisoners."

"Relax," said Ailsa. "You're an upworlder. You'll be fine." She opened the door and grabbed Texa's hand. "Come on, baby girl. Zora's going to help us."

The three of them made their way to the front door. Gabriel edged the taxi's rear bumper up to the front steps and killed the engine.

Ailsa passed through the front door of the clinic. Zora and Texa passed through ahead of her. A shiny young woman sat behind a bright white plastic desk. A great, gray and green tree grew from smooth stone floor to atrium ceiling above them.

The woman looked up. Ailsa brought the gun up and pointed it at her.

"Get out from behind there!" Ailsa yelled. She pointed the gun down and pulled the trigger. A crater opened in the smooth granite floor between them. Ailsa stared at the hole a moment. Oh my God.

The woman's eyes got big and she tilted her head.

Ailsa walked around and grabbed the back of her neck. "Come on."

"Go!" Ailsa yelled to Zora. They walked past empty operating rooms and offices.

"This place is abandoned," said Zora. "It's not a good sign."

"Zora, I'm scared," said Texa.

Zora put her arm around Texa's shoulders.

"Get your hands off my little girl," said Ailsa. She pushed the stiff-necked receptionist ahead of her.

Texa stopped and turned around. "I asked her to, Mom, okay? Is that okay with you?"

Ailsa brushed past them, then turned around. "Well," she said to Zora, "which one is it?"

"I'm heading for the last one on the right," Zora said as she brushed past

Ailsa. "The major operating theatre is usually back there."

A short, dark hallway opened into a two story atrium illuminated with direct sunlight filtered through opaque ceiling tiles. Three unblemished steel operating tables waited in the middle of the room. Next to each was a series of screens, tubes and wires.

"Texa, you go first," said Ailsa. She forced the stiff-necked woman into a seated position behind the tables, in the corner farthest from the door.

"You must all wear proper protective garb in the operating theater," the receptionist said. "You may find it in the closets out in the hallway."

Ailsa turned to her. "Why don't—"

"Leave it!" yelled Zora. "It's not even human. Help me get Texa up on the table."

Ailsa walked over and hoisted Texa by the armpits. "Really? Are they that—"

Zora rolled her eyes. "I'm going to put her under."

"Is that really necessary?" asked Ailsa.

"Does she have any known allergies?"

Ailsa frowned.

Zora applied a quick injection to Texa and she was unconscious. She selected a long, tubular metal device with a black, rubber suction cup on the end. She pulled up Texa's duck-and-egg-patterned shirt to reveal her swollen abdomen.

Zora shook her head.

"What is it?" Ailsa asked. The current ebbed. She took a deep breath and relaxed her shoulders.

"You are not physicians," said the android. "Sounding silent alarm."

Ailsa glared at Zora. "Is she kidding?"

"No," said Zora, "and he put the tracker in with the new method."

"I thought you put it in," said Ailsa.

"No, it was Erik. I… didn't…"

"Anyway," said Ailsa. "Just get it out."

"What if it leaves a scar?"

"Just get it out! Now!" yelled Ailsa.

Zora grimaced and tossed the tubular device to the floor. She grabbed a scalpel and made a small incision above Texa's belly button and below the reducing swelling. She stuck a finger in, hooked it and pulled.

"It doesn't want to come," Zora said. She poked a second finger in and the incision expanded.

Ailsa's stomach tensed up and she looked away.

"It might be attached to her uterus," said Zora. She looked up at Ailsa. "What do you want to do?"

Ailsa froze. Rip it out and no grandchildren. Wait and Xemura's goons get us.

"Ailsa." Zora glared at her.

"I don't know! What do you think?" Ailsa leaned on the other steel table. Her head swirled and her stomach turned.

Zora pursed her lips. "Let me jiggle it a bit." She jammed her two fingers hard into the open wound.

Something cracked. Ailsa bent over and took deep breaths. "I think… I'm going to be—"

"I got it!" yelled Zora. "I got it! I had to break it in two, then the clamp lost power." She fused the wound and taped gauze over it.

"Your turn," she said to Ailsa.

"No sedatives."

Zora moved to the next table over and tapped it. "Hurry up."

Ailsa limped over and laid down. "Mine's in my leg," she said.

Zora undid her pants and pulled them down to reveal the red swelling on her thigh.

Ailsa looked away and cleared her throat. "This is just a little weird."

Zora guffawed. "I don't swing that way. Tall, dark and handsome is my type."

Ailsa glared at her. I saw him first.

"You ready for this?" Zora asked. She held up a shiny steel scalpel. The ceiling lights reflected off of it and Ailsa blinked her eyes shut.

"Just do it, bitch."

Zora slashed her leg. Blood oozed out and pooled on the metal table.

Pain flooded through Ailsa. She gritted her teeth. Stop, stop. All I wanted was to end the pain so how did this happen?

"It's hooked into your sartorius. Hold on."

The crack vibrated her bone and a jagged piece ripped into her.

"Ow!" Ailsa whined. She sat up.

"Lay down! Almost done." Zora pulled the two sides of the wound together and fused them.

Ailsa's head swam and she gritted her teeth. Each prick of the needle caused her jaw to ache more. "Would you... just... finish... already!" she muttered.

"It's done. It's done!" said Zora. She ripped off her plastic gloves. "Pull your pants up. I'll grab some antibiotics, then Texa and—" Zora stopped. Her face froze.

Ailsa raised herself up. A soldier brought his rifle butt down on her forehead.

* * *

Ailsa sat up and hit her head on the bottom of a steel table. "Damnnit!" she whispered.

She crawled out and got to her feet. She put weight on the leg with the incision and collapsed on her side to the red granite floor. She struggled to take in air.

"I just can't do it. I can't." Ailsa sobbed.

She got up on two feet again and leaned on the steel table. The shiny white android still sat behind it. "What the hell happened?" Ailsa asked.

"Xemura Security arrived and removed the disallowed personnel, to include Dr. Zora Collins, the juvenile and... They did not take you. This was against policy. I am sounding the silent alarm once more," said the android.

Ailsa groaned. "Where did they take them?"

"You are unauthorized personnel."

Ailsa limped over to the android and slapped its face. "Where did they go?"

"Violent behavior against Xemura corporate property is considered a severe crime under the category of property destruction and is heard by arbitration panel 37240. This crime has been reported," the machine said.

Ailsa screamed. She headed for the door. "Texa," she called.

There was no answer.

"Texa!" There was a scrap of cloth up ahead. She bent down and picked it up. It was the duck and egg pattern from Texa's shirt. Blood stained it now.

"Texa!" She yelled it louder this time. "Zora!"

She made it to the entrance. The frosted doors whooshed open for her. She walked out. The parking lot was empty.

* * *

Ailsa sat down on the front stoop of the clinic and cried.

I've lost her. The one good thing in my life. She's gone. I'll never get her back now. Gabriel either abandoned me or is being corrected. It's all my fault.

But why did they leave me behind?

She let out a deep breath and sagged. She buried her head in her arms. I deserve to be like this. I don't deserve Texa or Gabriel or anything. I killed my baby girl. The tears poured down her cheeks.

A long time passed. Ailsa did not want to get up. She did not want to open her eyes. She did not want to be alive. A wrenching pain clawed at her gut.

A tiny red and black bird landed on her shoulder. It dug its pointy claws into her flesh. She shrugged and it flew off.

The bird came back. She looked up. There were a half-dozen of them standing around her. Some pecked at the decorative landscaping but others watched her. Their tiny little eyes flickered here and there.

"Don't look at me!" she whispered. "I'm death. I'm failure. I'll screw you up, get you killed, poor, precious little birds." She buried her head in her arms again.

I won't look up. I won't move. I won't open my eyes. Someone will come for me. Someone will tell me where to go or what to do. I'll take the correction or the uplift or whatever. I deserve to suffer.

* * *

Ailsa plodded down the empty road from the clinic against her better judgment. "I can't even give up right," she whispered. "I don't even have the willpower for—"

She stopped. It was Texa. Her influence made me strong. She was angry when the Gards killed those men. She was sad when I killed us. Without her, I have no strength left.

She collapsed to the ground. "I am such a failure!" she yelled.

Get up. Get up. You have to find her. Not just for her but for you, too.

She stood up again. There was a red spot on her pants where Zora made the incision.

A loud beeping noise sounded behind her. She turned. A black car approached. Ailsa looked up. Gabriel?

The car hit the ground unevenly and bounced around before coming to a complete stop. The driver rolled his window down.

"Hop in," he said. "I can give you a ride, Lizzy."

Ailsa scowled. Who is this guy? The inside of the vehicle was dark in the approaching twilight.

"It's me," he said.

"Gabriel?"

"Who's Gabriel?" he asked in an angry tone of voice.

This is a trick. They sent him. She took a step back.

He activated the cabin light. The face was familiar. He had greying teeth, stubble and a face that sagged slightly.

"It's me! Milton!"

"Milton? You look different."

"I'm just a little cleaned up is all."

"What are you— Did you go through uplift?" she asked.

"It gets ugly around here at night, Lizzy. You should come with me. I have a place. I can keep you safe," he said.

She walked around the car and got into the backseat.

"I'm going to take care of you, Lizzy. You're safe now. I promise."

* * *

"How did you get this car?" Ailsa asked Milton. She looked around the interior. The front panels were cracked and the upholstery was worn down.

"I don't have much," he said, "but things are way, way better for me now. The uplift changed everything for me. I know you missed it but... yes, yes, I know I shouldn't pick up a woman... but I know her. I know her. She's a... fugitive? Maybe! We don't know that for sure yet!"

Ailsa looked out the window. The car sped over dark hills. Things moved down there. She spied homes, but there was no light.

"Are we crossing protectorate borders?" she asked.

"I said, we don't yet— Oh shit." He turned to her. "Lizzy, are you a fugitive?"

Ailsa stared at him blankly. *I probably am.* "I don't know," she said. "Why do you ask?"

Milton turned the back of his head to her and tapped the nape of his neck. A tiny metal box protruded. "Protecty Central says someone matching your description is wanted. Do you know anything about this?"

Her eyes widened and she stared at the box. "No," she whispered. "What's Protecty Central and what's that box?"

Milton laughed. "Oh, it's nothing, just a thing they gave me in uplift. I sent them your picture so they can see if it's you."

"What do you mean, you 'sent them my picture'?" Ailsa asked. "Why don't you let me out in the central district?"

"I... no, Lizzy. I love you," he said. "I want to be a good citizen of Protectorate 13491. Yes, I agreed to the terms. No, I do not wish to be in breach. Goddamnit." Milton shook his head. He clawed at the metal box at the back of his neck.

The car careened to the right and descended rapidly.

"Milton!" she yelled. "Stop!" She grabbed the wheel and righted the car but the decent continued. "Pull up! Pull up!"

Milton groaned. He got two fingers on the box and pulled. "Why won't you… come out, goddamnit!"

The car dived left. The golden arches of a Taco McDonalds invaded her view through the windshield.

Milton twisted the box. It came out. He laughed. "I got it! I'm free!"

He passed out.

* * *

Ailsa dragged Milton's unconscious body out of the remains of the car. His foot was wedged under his door.

Hamburger buns flew over their heads and razor sharp chopping blades cut nonexistent tomatoes against the stained cement. Ketchup spewed out of a tube in spurts at high pressure like a severed artery.

She dislodged his foot. She dragged him through a puddle of ketchup and over the counter where an ordering kiosk repeated, "Can I take your order?"

Ailsa stopped and stared a moment. I remember this. I don't remember being here but I remember this place. A dollop of ketchup landed on her face from a pressurized tube. She licked it. Why does that taste so good?

She pulled Milton's ketchup-soaked body out of the remains of the restaurant and into the parking lot. Cars raced off around her at high speed. A crowd gathered to view the carnage.

A woman screamed. "He's dead, oh my God, all that blood!" She fainted and hit the ground head-first.

Ailsa looked up. "It's just ketchup," she whispered.

She stepped back in and found a cache of water bottles. She grabbed as many of the icy containers as she could. Outside, she dumped them one by one on Milton.

She kneeled down next to him. "Wake up, Milton!" She shook him. His head flopped from side to side.

A Guardian aircar hovered above them.

* * *

"Papers, please," said the Guardian. He was the same height as all of them, medium build and well-muscled. His white suit glimmered from the reflections of the fire. His partner paced the edges of the crowd.

Ailsa searched for the least dangerous way to reveal her complete lack of papers.

"How long has it been on fire, citizen?" asked the Guardian.

"It… just started," said Ailsa. She turned to go.

"Papers, please!" said the Guardian in a severe tone of voice. "Citizen, stop."

Ailsa kept walking.

"Citizen, stop," said both Guardians at once.

Ailsa broke into a run. There was a brown gate at the back of the Taco McDonalds. She made for it.

A sharp pop sounded and Ailsa hit the ground hard. Her left calf burned.

Milton opened his eyes. He stood up. "Lizzy? Lizzy!"

"Milton," she yelled. She looked back at him as he rose from the ground.

The Guardian bore down on Ailsa and Milton limped after him.

"Please don't kill me," Ailsa whispered to the Guardian.

The pearly figure stopped a meter from her. "You have missed your uplift appointment, citizen. I will now take you to Protecty Central for uplift. I will not hurt you. This is a voluntary procedure."

"I don't want to go!" Ailsa yelled.

"This is entirely voluntary," it said. "You agreed to these terms—"

Milton got behind the Guardian and ripped off its helmet. The head underneath was all wires, shiny metal and iridescent circles.

"Run!" Ailsa yelled.

The grotesque head rotated. The body followed. It grabbed Milton's head and twisted. Milton's dead body thudded to the ground.

The machine turned back to her.

Ailsa screamed.

* * *

The machine-Guardian fell on her. Ailsa kicked and screamed and scratched but it was too heavy.

It's going to kill me now. The weight of the machine bore down on her chest. Ailsa struggled to breathe.

I want to see it. I want to see the end. She gritted her teeth. She opened her eyes.

A weapon discharged. She trembled. The machine lay motionless next to her. A dark figure stood over her, blocking out the streetlight.

She squinted her eyes.

"Get up," he said.

She grabbed his outstretched hand and pulled herself to her feet.

He was tall, dark and with a creeping midsection. He looked familiar. Ailsa searched her memory.

He smiled. He was missing teeth. Others were black. Large, dark purple bags pulled at his eyes.

She took a step back. "Who are you?"

He was silent a moment. "It's me, Gabriel," he said.

* * *

"Where did you go?" Ailsa asked Gabriel. "You abandoned me!" She pounded his nearest shoulder with both fists.

Below, the city was alive with light and fire. They passed through a low, dark cloud.

She tired of hitting him. "Do you have one of those metal boxes in the back of your head, too?"

"What?" he asked.

"I saw someone, from my old protectorate. They put a box in his head during uplift." She grabbed the hair at the nape of his neck and pulled.

"Ow!" he yelled. The car jerked to the right.

She rubbed her hand all over the back of his head. It was greasy. A stale smell released into the air. But there was no box.

She wiped her hand on the seatback. "Okay, you're clear. Why—"

"I was scared." He turned to look at her. "I'm sorry. They sent a dozen big ships in for Texa."

The sound of her name made Ailsa go rubbery. She hunched forward. She wanted to cry but she just felt empty and exhausted.

"You look different." She turned to study him. "You look like you got beat up."

Gabriel shrugged.

"And the man with the box in his head, he looked better than I remember. Am I going insane?"

Gabriel reached a hand over to caress her face.

She slapped it away. "You abandoned me!" she screamed. "Set the car down! I can't trust you. Everything is screwed up!"

"Relax!" Gabriel descended the car. They passed through thicker and darker clouds. The smell of burning plastic entered the car.

"What's burning?" she asked.

"It's the city," he said. "Just look at it. It's on fire. The Republic has called an uplift. We're rising."

Gabriel leveled off the car. She looked out into the street below. People carried fire and they were burning buildings.

It's Texa. The thought flashed through her mind. "Texa's doing this," she said. "She made me see Milton as ugly because he is ugly inside. She made me see you as handsome because you are good. And now..."

Gabriel turned and smiled. "But I am handsome."

"Did you see that the Guardians are machines now?" she asked.

"What! That's not true. I have a friend—" he started.

She giggled and her shoulders relaxed. "I know what's happening. I know how to get Texa back and how we can be free. I know what to do."

He studied her face. "You've taken Jubitol."

She took a deep breath and closed her eyes. She focused on Texa's face. It came to her in a flash.

"I knew it. Of course!" she yelled. "We have to go to XLS1."

Gabriel turned to her, his eyes big. "XLS1? Not with me, you're not. Forget it!"

* * *

"Enter," said Dr. Vernor Xemura in a whisper. He sat behind a polished metal desk. On the other side of the floor-to-ceiling windows behind him, flames from multiple buildings licked the sky.

A rotund, stooped man in a bursting tuxedo waddled into Dr. Xemura's office. "What the hell is this, Vernor? Unrest, yes. A little terrorism, if we must. Clean out some protectorates, yes, dear God. But burn the city? Everyone is blaming me!"

Vernor grimaced. "Relax, Alexander. I've—"

"I have called an emergency meeting of the trustees for tonight. They're going to find out about all this." Alexander pulled a handkerchief from his front pocket and mopped his neck.

"Where are your guards?" Vernor asked with a sly grin. "We need to keep you safe, Mr. President."

Alexander glared at him. "Safe from what? The Rising? Please. You're the only threat that concerns me!"

Vernor stood up and looked out the window. His gaze fell on the fires and his heart warmed. The sickly artificial smell of burning plastic at once raced his heart and lightened his head. He turned around. "A little creative destruction will do us good. The rabble will burn up their own protectorates and we simply re-prioritize the cleaning list." The corners of his mouth and his eyes creased.

Alexander glared at him. "More cleaning? What about when it reaches our neighborhoods? Do we clean them, too?"

"If need be," said Vernor. He turned around and tensed his jaw muscles. "I tire," he said in a louder voice, "of your questions. We must order the Republic perfectly. You know what is coming."

"But, is this really—" started Alexander.

Vernor held up his hand. "The trustees dither and you question. But I do! I am the only one preparing us for the inevitable." He sat down at his desk and took a yellow pill from a glass bowl. "If not for me, for my efforts, my experiments... my resolution and strength, the Republic would be dead already."

* * *

Gabriel touched his ear. "Who is this?"

"Gabriel?" a woman asked. The voice was familiar but it raised a tension in his gut.

Gabriel scowled. "I'm not—"

"It's Zora."

Gabriel took a deep breath. He looked through the windshield. Ailsa waited for her order to come up at the food truck.

"What have you done with Texa?" he asked.

"This has a simple solution," she said. "I don't know why the Rising didn't think of this before. Didn't you tell them you're his brother?"

Gabriel pursed his lips.

"You marry me, I kill your brother and we take over his holdings, including his trusteeship. Ailsa and Texa go on their merry way. Well, at least Ailsa."

"What?"

"You heard me. I'm telling it to you straight," she said. "I checked with the Committee. You are in his will. You get everything. It's a matter of personal survival now, anyway."

"I don't know if you noticed, Zora, but I am interested in Ailsa. I'm not interested in you. And it looks like you helped kidnap Texa again," he said. "Where is she?"

"Look, I'm just as much a victim here as she is. I got the devices out of them. It's not my fault that soldiers showed up and took her. They took me, too!"

"I'm not—" Gabriel started.

"I'm a prisoner here, too!" she yelled.

"Then how come you get to make a phone call?"

Zora was silent a moment. "Look, how much do you know about her?"

"Enough. They need me."

"She whores herself out."

"Go smoke yourself," he said.

Zora sighed. "I'll nutshell it for you, Gabriel. Your brother engineered them to—"

"What are you saying? He created them? They're clones? What?" he asked.

Zora sighed. "You know, it's not that important right now. Here's the important part. Vernor is engaged in a power play. He is trying to take over the Republic. He is using Texa's mental powers to do this. If we can kill him—"

"You want to kill my brother. Do you hear yourself?"

Ailsa left the food truck with their food in hand.

"With us, she can have a normal childhood. But for Vernor she is a lab rat, a tool, a weapon." Zora paused. "Listen, Gabriel, I know about your—"

Gabriel hung up. Ailsa got into the back seat and handed him his half of the food.

"I got your favorite," she said. "Kung Pao Soy, right?" She smiled at him.

Gabriel stared out the windshield.

"What's happened?" she asked. "Did somebody call? What?"

"No. No, it's nothing. Just hungry," he said with a tired smile. *What the hell do I do now?*

* * *

"I just can't," said Ailsa. "I can't eat anything."

"Aren't you hungry?" asked Gabriel. They sat high above the city in the black taxi and watched the fires rage below. XLS1 was straight ahead and just below them.

"I am so hungry, Gabriel, but... my whole body hurts. It's Texa. They're hurting her. I just know it."

"We can't just go in there," he said. "All we have is this half-drained Gard rifle. We won't make it past the front door."

She dropped her Chinese food and hung her head forward. "Give me an idea. You must have one. What's going to happen? What should I do?"

"I just—" he started.

"How have you avoided the Gards all this time? You know how to use a gun. You're his brother. There has to be something you can do..." Ailsa frowned and looked away from him.

"I've got nothing," he said. "I'm sorry. Yeah, he's my brother but we haven't—"

"Just shut up," Ailsa said. "I'll take care of this. Give me the gun and drop me at the front door."

"You are insane," Gabriel said. He opened the glove compartment and pulled the gun out.

"No," she said. "I'm a mother."

* * *

"I don't want you to feel that I'm—" started Gabriel. He set the taxi down in the street in front of XLS1.

He turned to face her.

"How much is the fare?" Ailsa asked.

"Oh, go bloody smoke yourself," he said. "I have taken a lot—"

Ailsa got out and slammed the door on him. He rolled down his window.

"Now, just hold on a second..."

Ailsa didn't hear him anymore. She held the gun at the small of her back and strode towards the entrance.

I'm going in there, I'm going to kill anyone who gets in my way, I'm coming out with Texa and then we're getting out of here. I can do it. I have to.

A robotic arm zoomed in on her from above the front door. At the end of it was a translucent black ball. "What is your business here, citizen?" it asked.

Ailsa brought out the gun and fired at it. She missed.

A red light flashed above the arm. "Hostile intent detected. Stop and present identification, citizen," it said.

She fired and missed again. "Damned thing!"

A loud metallic sound came from the front doors. "Lockdown protocol enabled." The voice came from inside XLS1.

"Subject identified as research asset 1176892-CS32," said the arm. "Lockdown disabled manually."

She held the gun right under the black ball and fired it. A piece of it disappeared and the ball crashed to the ground next to her.

She stepped forward. The glass doors slid open.

* * *

The robotic sentries were still. Ailsa walked towards the elevator and got in. The frosted, pentagonal '83' button illuminated with a gentle melody and the doors closed.

This is creepy. He's letting me in without a fight. He plans to kill me up there, neat and clean, like a lab rat or an old dog. One of his goons will be waiting for me. And it will be completely legal.

She looked around the spacious elevator car. It burst out of the building interior and climbed the outside of the building. Smoke billowed from the city. They were putting out the fires.

Gabriel. His taxi rose with her, he outside, she inside. She raised her hand to him. He looked away.

The elevator doors opened on the 83rd floor. She whirled around. No one was there. She poked her head out.

Ailsa stepped out of the elevator and walked down a pristine, white hallway. Frosted glass surrounded her. Lights illuminated on the floor to guide her path.

This is incredibly weird. She fingered the trigger of the Gard rifle. She held it close against the back of her thigh.

"Lizzy, I'm right here," said a voice behind her.

She swiveled around. It was Milton.

"You're dead," she said.

Milton smiled. His skin was pink and smooth. His face was taut. He looked to be no more than twenty-five years old.

"You're— He revived you."

Milton nodded.

"Why?"

"Same reason he revived you, Lizzy. We belong to him."

"Bullshit!" she yelled.

"Texa belongs to him, too."

"No!"

"He created us. He is our god, you could say. He keeps us young, saves us from our—"

"That's ridiculous!" she screamed.

"I know what I'm supposed to do," he muttered. He twisted his body to look back.

"Who are you—" Ailsa started.

Milton whirled around and kneeled. "I'm doing the best... I... Okay! I can do more. But..."

Ailsa spotted the box. "Your neck..."

Milton looked over his shoulder at her, his eyes wide and gritting his teeth. "I know!" he yelled.

Ailsa took a step back. "Anyway, I—"

He stood up and ran towards her. "You can't go in there. It's my job. Yes, I know! It's my job!"

He kneeled in front of her and reached for her hand. She jerked it away.

"We're an experiment, you see," Milton said. "He... Shut up! She deserves to know! He made us, together, as his perfect Adam and Eve. Together, we made Texa."

"You're not her father!"

He cocked his head. "I'm sorry. I know. I'm a little... pathetic these days. Yes! He let me keep my memory but he always took yours, and Texa's." He nodded his head with a strained frown.

"You're insane!" She kicked him and pulled out the gun. "Don't get in my way. I'm getting Texa and we're—"

He lay on the floor and giggled like a baby.

She proceeded down the hall. At the end were two huge double doors. They were ajar.

She threw them open and screamed.

* * *

A cold, wet wind greeted Ailsa. It stank of smoldering plastic, gunpowder and rot.

Dr. Vernor Xemura lay dead at his desk. A thin, shiny piece of metal extended out of his forehead.

Ailsa cringed. She picked up his head and examined it. It was the same man who had threatened her in the white room. It seemed so long ago. The wind hit her again. She looked straight ahead, to the left of the desk. A pane of glass was blown out of the wall.

A black car hovered outside on the other side of the wall. Zora carried something wrapped in white. She placed it into the trunk and slammed it shut. The car rotated and a back door opened.

"Zora!" Ailsa yelled. She ran towards her. "What are you doing?"

Zora threw herself head first into the car and hit her head on the edge of the roof. "Go! Go, Gabriel! Go!"

Ailsa reached out the window. She looked down. It was pitch dark. The raindrops disappeared into the void. She grabbed Zora's foot and pulled. Zora grabbed hold inside the car.

Ailsa looked into the front seat. A dark figure turned around. It was Gabriel.

Gabriel? She yanked on the leg and Zora's shoe came off. Ailsa watched it disappear into the gloom.

"Let go!" yelled Zora.

"Tell me where Texa is!"

"Bugger off!"

The car inched away from the building. Ailsa held on tight. Only her feet remained inside the building.

Zora kicked her. "Let go, you stupid bitch!"

Ailsa wrapped her hand tight around the top of Zora's calf muscle and dug her nails in.

Zora screamed.

Ailsa steeled her hand. Her feet slipped off of the edge of the building but someone grabbed them.

She turned her head. It was Milton.

"I've got you, Lizzy. Let go!" he yelled.

The wind buffeted all of them and the cab slammed into the building. Milton, Ailsa and Zora landed back inside.

Ailsa got on top of Zora and punched her. "Where is she? What did you do with her?" Ailsa pulled a fist back and droplets of blood splattered to her face.

Milton grabbed Ailsa's legs and pulled her away from the window. "We don't need them, anymore, we're back together now," Milton said, "and we can make another one."

"Let go of me! Another what? What are you talking—" Ailsa started.

Zora ran and jumped out the window into the cab. Gabriel sped off.

"Another Texa, of course," said Milton.

* * *

"You need to tell me everything you know. Where did they go?" Ailsa asked Milton. They sat on the floor of Dr. Vernor Xemura's office. The rain blew in through the hole left by Zora and Gabriel. The dead man sat in his desk chair. Ailsa shivered.

Milton shrugged.

"Do they have her?" she asked.

Milton nodded.

"Where did they take her? What do they want— This has to do with her power…"

Milton shrugged. "Zora wants Dr. Xemura's company. She says Texa can enable her to control the Republic Trustees, and then she will put the world back to how it was."

"You helped her kill Dr. Xemura and you helped her get away with Texa," said Ailsa.

"I did it for you, Lizzy. I did it for us," he said. "Now that he's dead, the messages will stop. I'm okay now."

"I have to find my daughter," she said.

"I can help you," Milton said. "And I fixed your device." He pulled a device out of his pocket.

She recognized it immediately. "That's my computer. Where did you get it?" She ripped it from his hand.

"When you died, Lizzy."

"Why did you take me there to die? Why did you let us die?" she asked.

"I knew he would bring you back and then we could be together again, all fresh and new like before… you know what."

A tremor ran up her back. She walked over to Dr. Xemura's desk and pushed the chair with his body out of the way. "How does he use his computer?"

Milton ran over and swiped his hand across the front right corner of the desk. "Use his hand to do it, hurry before it gets too cold. Are you worried about money? Don't worry, I have some."

She brought the body back and swiped the hand. A screen rose out of the desk.

"Authentication, please, Dr. Xemura," a voice said.

"The password," she said to Milton. "Do you know it?"

Milton twisted his head to one side and grimaced. "I don't know if I should tell you."

"Milton!"

"Why don't we just revive him?"

"He's got a hole in his head, Milton, and he has lost a ton of blood. He's not coming back."

Milton screwed up his face. "Okay. I heard him say, 'That which is yours cannot be denied.'"

Ailsa repeated the words. The screen came to life. "Track Gabriel and Zora," she said.

"Input insufficient," the voice said.

"There was a black taxi," said Ailsa, "right outside this window, owned by Gabriel Xemura—"

"Gabriel Xemura," said the voice. "Brother of Dr. Vernor Xemura, CEO of Xemura Life Sciences. Deceased May 17 of the current year."

"What?" muttered Ailsa. "When? He's dead?"

* * *

A photo of Gabriel Xemura appeared on the screen. It was her Gabriel.

"He revived his brother, too?" whispered Ailsa. "Who hasn't he revived?"

A call came in. "Answer," she said. "Hello?" She felt oddly comfortable in this office.

There was a silence. A thick male voice spoke up. "Who is this?"

"Who is this?" Ailsa answered.

"This is Alexander Nelson, President of the Republic Trust for Dr. Vernor Xemura. The nature of the call is very urgent."

"Well," said Ailsa, "he's dead."

Alexander was silent for a moment. "Oh my God. What happened?" he asked.

"His resurrected brother and his assistant jammed a piece of metal into his forehead and blew his brains out."

"Are you Ailsa Santamaria?" Alexander asked.

"Why? How do you know that name?"

"Listen, Ailsa, time is short and the Republic Trust is in danger."

Ailsa laughed. "Go smoke yourself."

"There's too many of us," said Alexander. "Too much rabble. Too many hungry mouths. And—"

"Save your bullshit propaganda, Alex. I want my daughter and I want out of here."

"I can probably help you with that."

"I don't believe you. You're all liars."

"Just listen, Ms. Santamaria! You and your girl are responsible for the chaos that's happening outside right now."

Ailsa turned around. The fires were bigger now and there were more of them.

"It's getting worse, too," said Alexander. "We must stop it before more people die."

"You kill people, so I should just hang up on you now," she said.

"I can help you get your daughter back!" Alexander yelled.

* * *

"What's in it for you?" Ailsa asked. She pushed Dr. Xemura's body out of the chair and took a seat. She crossed her legs and leaned back.

Alexander cleared his throat. "We restore stability to the protectorates. You get your daughter and safe passage to wherever your like."

"What if I want to kill you bastards?"

"Listen, Ms. Santamaria," started Alexander, "you're legally dead. You and your daughter. You legally have no rights. And right now, rogue elements in the Xemura family with sympathies for the Rising have your daughter. They plan to manipulate her and her power to destroy the Republic so that they can gain control of it for their own ends."

"Okay, good."

"When they're done," he continued, "they will either kill Texa or lock her away indefinitely under sedation as a lab rat."

"Gabriel wouldn't do that!" she said.

"The late Dr. Xemura's brother has already betrayed you, hasn't he? Do you trust Dr. Collins?"

Ailsa was silent.

"Collins and Xemura are outside the Republic central office. I am dispatching soldiers to accompany you there, right now, to safely get your daughter back and then you have my promise that we will send you wherever you like with enough funds to sustain you for many years to come."

"Don't trust them!" Milton whispered.

Ailsa took a deep breath. "Bring a gun for me," she said. "This one's charge is almost dead."

* * *

The air was thick with the smell of blood and sweaty men. Ailsa stepped out of the troop carrier. The early morning air outside was only marginally more breathable. Dark-helmeted soldiers poured out behind her and surrounded her. Two approached her from the front.

"What? Let's go," she said to the men.

"Proper protective gear is required, ma'am," said the one on her left.

She scowled at him. "Robots?"

The soldier took off his helmet. His jawline was sharp and covered in black stubble. His dark blue eyes pierced her. "Do I look like a bot to you?"

She smiled. Why does the Republic get the hottest men? Probably genetic engineering. "Okay, go ahead."

He wrapped her in dark blue body armor from head to toe. He offered her a helmet.

"No," she said. "No helmet. Now give me a gun."

She walked up the gray, cement steps of the Republic Trust Central Office. It was a simple red brick and cement edifice. The first rays of the morning sun glinted off of the sliding doors. They refused to open.

Ailsa brought her gun up and fired. It blew a hole in the door. She fired twice more, than stepped through.

"Ailsa! Stop right there." It was Gabriel.

She brought the gun up and pointed it at him. "Where's Texa?" she yelled.

"Now, Ailsa, just—" he started.

"Shut up! Just give me my daughter!" She ran up to him and put the gun to his neck.

Gabriel swallowed hard. "Just relax. Ailsa. You know I wouldn't—"

She swung the gun up and whipped him across the back with it. He fell to the floor and gasped for breath.

"Where is she!" she yelled.

A door opened behind Ailsa. She whirled around.

Texa carried her arms like a ballerina. She turned around and gently closed the door behind her.

"Texa?" Ailsa asked. "What did they do to you, baby?"

Texa walked right past her. She did not look at her mother. She put her hands on Gabriel's head. He awoke, stood up and dusted himself off.

Ailsa stared at them, her eyes wide and her mouth agape.

Gabriel sighed. "I wanted to spare you this. Texa is not your daughter. She's mine and Zora's. We ran the test. It's confirmed."

Ailsa laughed. "That's ridiculous. I gave—" Ailsa thought back to the moment of Texa's birth. The memory did not come.

Gabriel cocked an eyebrow. "You don't actually remember her birth, do you?"

"I... It's the stress. I'm really stressed right now." She cleared her throat. "Texa," she said in a firm, loud voice, "we're leaving. Let's—"

Texa turned to her and screamed. "You killed me! You're not my mother! Get out!" She pushed a hand forward and Ailsa was thrown down the hallway. She crashed through the unbroken glass door and continued until she hit the troop carrier she came in.

* * *

The soldier with the sharp jawline snapped his fingers in her face. His chest said, "Hanshin." He slapped her with an icy hand.

It came back to her. "They did something to her," Ailsa said. "She doesn't—"

"We heard," said Hanshin. "Your armor is wired up. What I need to know is what you plan to do about it."

"She doesn't want me anymore."

"They brainwashed her, ma'am," said Hanshin.

"Her powers have—" she started.

"We know, Ailsa!" said Hanshin. "But the situation is active. What is your plan of action?"

"Well, tell me what else you know!" she yelled. "How did they do that? How do I undo it?"

Hanshin shrugged.

"Well, can you ask somebody?"

Hanshin just stared at her with dead eyes.

Ailsa rolled her eyes and stood up. Her back ached and her steps slowed.

She stepped through the now larger hole in the entryway.

"Texa," she yelled down the now-empty hallway, "I love you and I'm sorry. I'm sorry I killed us. We were both so sad all the time and they were uplifting our protectorate. I didn't want you to feel that pain. It wasn't fair to you."

A dozen soldiers came in behind her.

"It's about time you guys made yourselves useful," she said to them. "Follow me in. I'm going to do whatever—"

"Put the gun down and lay down on the floor," said Hanshin.

Ailsa turned around to glare at them. "What the—"

They aimed their guns at her. She looked down at her chest. A dozen red dots orbited her heart.

* * *

Zora appeared next to Ailsa. "They answer to us now." She took Ailsa's gun and pulled her towards the wall.

Ailsa sat down against the wall. I've been the best mom I could. I've done what I can. Everyone is against me.

"Well?" asked Zora. She tapped her foot. "You have a couple options. We can kill you right here or you can take a flight out of the Republic right now. We'll give you some coin. Head to Jamaica or Barbados for a while."

"And do what?" Ailsa whispered.

Zora shrugged. "Find a man again, a real man. Enjoy the beach. Just stay away from the Republic and our truce will remain in effect. Texa will be safe."

"So," asked Ailsa, "you control the Republic now? And the Gards?"

"Gabriel and I have inherited his late brother's corporate holdings and his Republic trusteeship."

Ailsa glared at her. "Then why do you need my daughter?"

Zora looked down at her with amusement. "You know why we need Texa. She's my daughter, by the way. I switched the egg when we genned her. It's her power. She's the experiment that succeeded."

Ailsa looked at her quizzically. "I don't believe a word you say."

Zora's eyes darted to and fro.

"That's why you have personal control of the Gards now," said Ailsa. "It's my girl."

Zora smiled. "Influence is what you call it, right?"

"She's my daughter," said Ailsa. She stood up and grabbed Zora's throat. "She doesn't look like you. She doesn't love you! She's my girl!"

Zora scratched at Ailsa's arm. Blood welled up from the deep gouges in her skin. Zora fell to her knees. She waved her arms wildly for the Gards to take action. Ailsa tightened her grip and locked her other hand on the back of Zora's neck. Zora gasped for breath.

Gabriel ran out of an office and separated them.

"Just go, Ailsa!" Gabriel said. "There's nothing you can do here. I will make sure they don't hurt her. Just get out, while you can. You have no idea of what's coming now."

* * *

Hanshin grabbed Ailsa's upper arm. "Let's go, ma'am." He marched her out.

Ailsa jerked her arm away from him. "I can walk on my own, thank you!"

A memory sparked in her mind. Dr. Xemura was outside the cage and she was in it. 'She depends on you. You are the foundation.' That's what he said.

Hanshin handcuffed her and pushed her into the troop carrier. "Where will you go?" he asked.

"Did you forget that we were working together?" she asked.

"No. I remember."

"Then what has changed? Ask yourself, what has changed? Why are you—" she started.

He waved his hand to silence her. "My orders changed."

"Your orders are wrong! They're going to separate me from my child." She squinted at him and her voice broke.

"It's not my responsibility." He slammed the doors behind her.

Ailsa took a deep breath and focused on Texa. She focused on the current between them. No. No. No. She turned it off.

Ailsa listened. She pushed on the door and it clanged open. She looked out. The soldiers sat on the ground. Some reclined in the street.

She stepped out onto the street. A hot, dry wind blew dust into her face. Above her, aircars streamed in four lanes each way. She nudged one of the soldiers with a foot. He did not react.

She walked into the Central Office and opened the door to the room where Gabriel had been.

Zora jumped out at her and landed on Ailsa's neck. "What did you do!"

Ailsa hit the floor and Zora got on top of her. She landed punch after punch to Ailsa's nose. Blood spattered over Zora's face.

"I had them," Zora yelled. "I had the Republic. I was going to stop it all, the cleanings, the oppression, I was going to force sharing and provide education for all. What did you do?"

Ailsa smiled through the blood and a swollen left eye. "I almost believe you."

Gabriel ran into the room holding a dark screen. "Zora, I lost control! I'm locked out!"

"Damnit!" Zora rolled off of Ailsa. She kneeled and massaged her forehead.

Ailsa got up and ran into the room Gabriel had just exited. "Texa! Texa!"

Texa stood up from behind a table. She stared at Ailsa. Her eyes were unfocused and her face slack.

Ailsa ran to her. She fell to her knees and hugged Texa tight. "What did they do to you, baby?"

Ailsa ran her hands over Texa's body and through her hair. She stopped at the nape of her neck.

Her hand caressed a smooth, metal ball that protruded from Texa's neck. She grabbed it and pulled.

Texa screamed.

Ailsa grabbed Texa's hand and pulled her into the other room. "I want it out now!"

"It's a more advanced version of Vernor's control chip," said Gabriel. "It won't cause any permanent damage."

Ailsa squinted at him. Tears streamed down her face. "I don't care! I want it out now!"

Gabriel shrugged and turned.

"Can't you please just get it out of her. She won't help you anymore. We will—"

Zora stood up. "Why doesn't she work anymore? What did you do?"

"We have to get out of here," whispered Gabriel. "He's going to make his move and then it will be too late. We'll take them both. We'll figure it out."

Zora nodded. "Texa, come," she said.

Texa followed her.

"Come with us," said Gabriel to Ailsa. "Help us keep her safe."

* * *

"You drive," Zora said to Gabriel. "Texa and Ailsa, in the back seat." They exited the Republic Trust Central office and climbed into a Guardian aircar.

Gabriel hit the start button but the engine did not respond.

A shadow fell over them. Gards descended on ropes outside the car and trained their guns on Gabriel. Dr. Xemura appeared behind them.

"Out of the car," he said.

Gards opened the four doors and they all piled out.

"You have gravely disappointed me, Zora," said Dr. Xemura. He approached her and jammed his finger into her chest. "I offered you a position of trust."

"Which you used to further intimidate me," Zora said. "You involved me in coercive human testing. You used my work to initiate this program of mass population control. So save your sanctimonious violation of trust bullshit! You violated mine first."

Dr. Xemura felt the back of Texa's head. "Yet I see you did some coercive human testing and control of your own." He cocked an eyebrow.

Zora crossed her arms.

"And you, Gabriel? Have you forgotten that we are brothers?"

"Hello, Vernor," said Gabriel. "I'm glad you're alive. I just want you to stop hurting people."

"And you, Ailsa, my dear," said Dr. Xemura, "we are reunited." He turned to a Gard. "Take them to the Celtic Sea lab. "We'll soon have our lives back on track," he said to Ailsa.

"You will not!" Ailsa said. A Gard grabbed her. She ripped her arm away from him.

"Don't worry, my dear," Dr. Xemura said. "I will restore your memory and we will be together again. You have suffered for this crazy experiment long enough. There is enough data now, I think."

Ailsa turned to Zora and nodded. She closed her eyes and felt for the current. Yes. She forced herself to relax and become open to it again.

"Knock them out, Texa! Knock them out, now!" yelled Zora.

Dr. Xemura laughed. "Did you not think, my dear Zora, that I would disable the chip in her? You did not secure the interface in any fashion." He laughed with his mouth closed. "Very careless of you."

Zora looked down.

Ailsa kneeled down. "Texa, it's mommy. Texa?"

Dr. Xemura continued laughing. "I can assure you—" he started.

"Baby, I need you to use your power."

"—that her will is subverted right now by the technology. There is nothing—"

"I love you, baby girl. I promise to always take care of you, my little princess," said Ailsa. She hugged Texa's limp body.

"—absolutely nothing," continued Dr. Xemura, "that you—"

Texa took a deep breath. "Do you promise not to kill us again, mommy?"

A tear rolled down Ailsa's cheek. "I promise. I'm so sorry."

"—can do." Dr. Xemura's face hardened. "Take them now!"

Gards grabbed their arms behind their backs and started to handcuff them.

"Texa, I just need you—" started Ailsa.

"I heard your thought, mommy," said Texa. She twisted her head to the side.

The Gards collapsed to the ground.

Ailsa stood up and smiled. She covered her mouth. She picked up Texa and hugged her tight. "You did it, baby girl. Good job."

"Please stop that, dear." Dr. Xemura picked up a gun and pointed it at the ground in front of Ailsa and Texa.

Gabriel leaped at him and his brother opened a hole in his chest. Gabriel fell dead to the ground.

Zora ran at him. "You bastard!" She raised her hand to smack him.

Ailsa put Texa down. "Just hold on a minute, honey." She got behind Dr. Xemura.

Ailsa grabbed one arm, Zora the other. Zora bit his gun hand and he released it. Ailsa flipped him over and put a knee in his back.

"What do we do with him now?" asked Ailsa.

Zora reached for the gun.

"No!" yelled Ailsa. She grabbed Zora's arm and held the gun up. A shot fired off into the sky.

"We have to kill him," Zora yelled.

"People need to know what happened," said Ailsa. He has to be put on trial, exposed, the Republic ended. Otherwise, nothing will change."

"No," said Zora. She ripped the gun away from Ailsa and it hit the ground.

Ailsa picked it up and fired at Zora.

Zora gulped for air but her lungs were gone. She fell dead to the sidewalk.

Vernor sat up and laughed. "Very good, my dear. Excellent work. We are quite the team, as always." He looked behind Ailsa and a tremor crossed his face.

Ailsa turned around. Texa lay still, flat on her back on top of a Gard. A spurt of blood erupted from her chest. Her left arm and a piece of her chest were missing.

* * *

Ailsa sat at the kitchen table and sighed. She wanted to remember something. It tugged at her memory. She knew it was there but the details escaped her.

She remembered the last few years with Vernor. The surprise romance, the lavish marriage and now, the life of fame and luxury he provided her as President of the Republic Trust.

She walked to the kitchen window and looked out. Republic Guardians kept watch at the end of their drive. She admired the green fields around their home and thought of children playing in them. Her children. Lots of them.

A sound came over the radio. She smiled and softly traipsed up the padded stairs. She turned right at the top and opened the nursery.

The baby stood up in its crib. The pacifier fell out of her mouth and she gurgled at her mother.

She cradled the baby in her arms. "Oh, Alexa, you're such a beautiful—" started Ailsa.

A spark jumped into her mind. Protectorate 13477. Uplift. The Death Shop. Zora. Gabriel. Vernor. Her Vernor. Texa.

She touched the back of her head. There was something round and hard under her skin.

Her eyes went wide. She felt the current. Alexa looked up at her with curious yet knowing eyes.

The front door opened downstairs. "I'm home, dear! Where are my girls?" It was Vernor.

Connect

I would love to hear your questions and comments via email at me@georgedonnelly.com.

Be the First

Sign up at GeorgeDonnelly.com/updates to find out when I publish something new.

Be an Inspiration

Review this anthology at Amazon.com. Send me the link and I will send you one free novel or novella.

About the Editor

Rebel. Troublemaker. Accused terrorist. Idealist. When not dreaming up new rebel heroes, George Donnelly hikes and bikes Colombian mountains and unschools his 8-year-old son Clark.

On the Web

Visit us at GeorgeDonnelly.com/Defiant.

What to Read Now

by J.P. Medved

Things are changing.

For decades the libertarian fiction canon has been relegated to the same few works, including Robert Heinlein's *The Moon is a Harsh Mistress*, Ayn Rand's *Atlas Shrugged*, the works of "the Neils" — L. Neil Smith and J. Neil Schulman — such as *The Probability Broach* and *Alongside Night* — Vernor Vinge's anarcho-capitalist *The Ungoverned*, and Michael Z. Williamson's *Freehold* series. All great reads, but too few.

Luckily, a new generation of libertarian fiction authors is emerging, seeking to portray their ideas and values in rich, fully-imagined worlds and stories. We understand the importance of advancing liberty on the cultural, rather than just the political front. We know that dramatizing our beliefs in story form makes them more inspiring, more convincing, and more 'sticky' than dry position papers or polemical op-eds.

We're not, for the most part, backed by huge media and publishing companies. We're taking advantage of the democratizing nature of technology and self-publishing to bring our work directly to you. We're building followings, careers and lasting cultural institutions like the Libertarian Fiction Authors Association. We're spreading liberty.

And you should read us.

Here are some of our best works that you should be reading right now:

- *Withur We*, an anarcho-capitalist science fiction epic by Matthew Alexander;
- *House of Refuge*, a seasteading novella by Mike DiBaggio;
- *Lando Cruz and the Coup Conspiracy*, a dystopian look at a future agorist rebellion by George Donnelly;
- *High Desert Barbecue*, a fun clash of libertarians and radical environmentalists by Reason Magazine's J.D.Tuccille;
- *Darkship Thieves*, a traditionally published libertarian space opera by Sarah Hoyt;
- And, lastly, my own *Granite Republic*, a novella about a future New Hampshire trying to secede from the U.S.

These stories will inspire, inform and, hopefully, spread the message of liberty and defiance quite a bit farther than the traditional libertarian mainstays of arguing on the internet and writing policy reports.

Enjoy the thrill of liberty!

For even more libertarian science fiction recommendations, visit LibertarianScienceFiction.com.

Acknowledgments

I'd like to thank my fellow authors. It is a tremendous pleasure to work with you. I'm especially grateful for the support of J.P. Medved who was the first to jump on board and has been a steady and enthusiastic supporter during the arduous journey to a finished product.

Thank you to our twenty-two first readers, to our reviewers and Indiegogo campaign contributors. You have added immeasurably to this anthology.

John Joseph Adams's impressive string of anthologies inspired me as have the published works of L. Neil Smith, J. Neal Schulman, Phillip K. Dick, Ayn Rand and others.

Thanks to Indiegogo for enabling us to crowdfund the publishing of this book.

Thanks to Geoffrey Allan Plauché of the Libertarian Fiction Authors Association.

Indiegogo Contributors

Thanks to those who contributed to the anthology via our Indiegogo campaign. You have buoyed all of us quite handily with your support. We are deeply grateful to you!

Michael Glazier
Vivek Bhatia
Starr O'Hara
Vicen Morales
tylerluyben
pilar.sanroman
dbrlevy
Anonymous
Anonymous
Susan Savon
Christopher Greenstein
Jared Pilosio
Anonymous
Alex R. Knight III

www.ingramcontent.com/pod-product-compliance
Lightning Source LLC
Chambersburg PA
CBHW071856220626
47052CB00002B/137